THE

OCTOPUS AGENDA

SPIDER-MAN: THE VENOM FACTOR by Diane Duane

THE ULTIMATE SPIDER-MAN Stan Lee, Editor

IRON MAN: THE ARMOR TRAP by Greg Cox

SPIDER-MAN: CARNAGE IN NEW YORK
by David Michelinie & Dean Wesley Smith

THE INCREDIBLE HULK: WHAT SAVAGE BEAST by Peter David

SPIDER-MAN: THE LIZARD SANCTION by Diane Duane

THE ULTIMATE SILVER SURFER Stan Lee, Editor

FANTASTIC FOUR: TO FREE ATLANTIS by Nancy A. Collins

DAREDEVIL: PREDATOR'S SMILE by Christopher Golden

X-MEN: MUTANT EMPIRE Book 1: SIEGE by Christopher Golden

THE ULTIMATE SUPER-VILLAINS Stan Lee, Editor

SPIDER-MAN & THE INCREDIBLE HULK: RAMPAGE
by Danny Fingeroth & Eric Fein (Doom's Day Book 1)

SPIDER-MAN: GOBLIN'S REVENGE by Dean Wesley Smith

THE ULTIMATE X-MEN, Stan Lee, Editor

SPIDER-MAN: THE OCTOPUS AGENDA by Diane Duane

X-MEN: MUTANT EMPIRE Book 2: SANCTUARY
by Christopher Golden

IRON MAN: OPERATION A.I.M. by Greg Cox

SPIDER-MAN & IRON MAN: SABOTAGE
by Pierce Askegren & Danny Fingeroth (Doom's Day Book 2)

X-MEN: MUTANT EMPIRE Book 3: SALVATION
by Christopher Golden

FANTASTIC FOUR: REDEMPTION OF THE SILVER SURFER
by Michael Jan Friedman

GENERATION X by Scott Lobdell & Elliot S! Maggin

THE INCREDIBLE HULK: ABOMINATIONS by Jason Henderson

COMING SOON:

X-MEN: SMOKE AND MIRRORS by eluki bes shahar

UNTOLD TALES OF SPIDER-MAN, Stan Lee & Kurt Busiek, Editors

SPIDER-MAN & FANTASTIC FOUR: WRECKAGE
by Eric Fein & Pierce Askegren (Doom's Day Book 3)

SPIDER-MAN®
THE OCTOPUS
AGENDA

Diane Duane

Illustrations by
Darick Robertson & Jeff Albrecht

MARVEL®
COMICS
M

BYRON PREISS MULTIMEDIA COMPANY, INC.
NEW YORK

BOULEVARD BOOKS, NEW YORK

Special thanks to Ginjer Buchanan, Lucia Raatma, Stacy Gittelman, Mike Thomas, Steve Behling, Steve Roman, and Carol D. Page.

SPIDER-MAN: THE OCTOPUS AGENDA

A Boulevard Book
A Byron Preiss Multimedia Company, Inc. Book

PRINTING HISTORY
Putnam hardcover edition/October 1996
Boulevard edition/August 1997

The Putnam Berkley World Wide Web site address is
http://www.berkley.com

The Byron Preiss Multimedia Company web site is at
http://www.byronpreiss.com

ISBN: 1-57297-279-3

BOULEVARD
Boulevard Books are published by The Berkley Publishing Group,
200 Madison Avenue, New York, New York 10016.
BOULEVARD and its logo
are trademarks belonging to Berkley Publishing Corporation.

PRINTED IN THE UNITED STATES OF AMERICA

10 9 8 7 6 5 4 3 2 1

ACKNOWLEDGMENTS

Thanks once more to Keith of the adamantium hide for taking the flak and staying with me down to the wire.

Thanks also, *in extremis*, to Peter. If *Guns & Ammo* ever needs a demon typist, I know where they can find him. . . .

But *I* found you first.

t was 2:30 in the morning near Dolgeville, New York—which meant it was the middle of the night in the back end of nowhere, and Jim Heffernan was deadly bored.

Jim Heffernan was forty-five years old, not a tall man, yet a fairly cheerful one given the kind of life he'd lived so far. Everyone told him he looked like a pudgy version of Sam Neill, the actor. That was all very nice to hear, except that he would have much preferred to hear that he had Sam Neill's bank balance, pudgy or otherwise. He didn't let the discrepancy in their earnings bother him too much, though; it wouldn't really have helped if he did.

Jim had once been a miner. Most of the people around here had once been miners, or the wives and children of miners. That was when Jim was in his twenties, at a time when there had actually been another small town near Dolgeville, called Welleston after some Welles or other who had actually started up the coal-mining industry.

That had been a long time ago, near the end of the last century. The town and the industry had been very successful, and for many years the town's people had come to depend on ''Welleston money'' for their livelihoods. But things shifted. Things always shifted.

And that was why Welleston spent thirty years as a crumbling ghost town, and another thirty as the memory of a ghost town. And why Jim was now sitting in a tacky little box of a portable guardroom at 2:30 in the morning. Once again he was blinking in the harsh, faintly flickering glare of fluorescent light, trying to do a crossword puzzle that didn't interest him, trying to stay awake. Trying to be a security guard for something which was no longer a coal mine.

The room was just slightly larger than a walk-in closet. It had walls the color of adhesive tape, and no floor except the plain, poured-concrete base that it had been plumped down on. It was damp; even on a hot summer's night it was damp, and the screens on the window, though they looked effective, weren't quite fine-meshed enough, or well enough fitted to the windows, to keep out the blackflies. The insects happily descended on Jim as a kind of movable feast, and left itching red welts on any part of him that wasn't covered (as well as some that were). So, for most of the night, Jim tended to sit with the light turned off, to avoid attracting them. Should one or another of his bosses turn up (one of the rarest of occurrences, particularly after *they* had met the blackflies) his excuse came easily: having that fluorescent tube turned off helped his night-vision, and made it easier for him to see what was going on outside. Not that anything much ever *did* go on outside here, except for the sound of the occasional crazed moose or deer crashing through the woodland surrounding the place.

The quiet was endemic in Dolgeville and its environs. The township was a remote place, buried well away from any really big town. Nestled deep in the foothills at the southern end of the Adirondacks, it sat in an undulating landscape of granite-boned hills clothed in conifer and hardwood forest. Even when the coal mining had been at its height, very few people had ever come there except on business. Since that business had mostly involved coal in one form or another, society had been limited to those who dug the coal and their families, those who maintained or replaced the machinery for those who dug the coal, and those who came to truck the coal away. There had been a constant grubbiness about everything and everybody, a fine black dust that got under your nails and into your pores and into the grooves of your fingerprints. In those days, the whole world had looked the same: gray and dingy, with the exception of a brief period in autumn when the trees flamed through the coal dust and then dropped their leaves to stand bare and clean against a clear blue sky.

Now, at least, you were free of the coal dust, and you got to see the occasional unfamiliar face, especially with the new industry coming in. Jim Heffernan sighed. It was always the way: some big company got you and everybody in the area all excited, got the local government to put up money to help them move in—and then when they *did* move in, they always managed to claw back as much of that money as they could for themselves. But at least he had this job; better than nothing, something to feed Flora and the kids, something to make him feel even a little bit useful. He was luckier than many who had been waiting for jobs and never got them.

Even if this job was, in essence, no more than watching a large hole in the ground to make sure nobody ran off with it in the night. *Yeah,* he thought, *and maybe someday I'll move up to watching the Brooklyn Bridge in case one of these super-criminals from the papers tries to steal it. Think big, fella.* He grunted with amusement at the thought, and turned his attention back to the crossword puzzle. Yet another desperate attempt to keep himself awake. He hated the night shift, but the night shift was what they had been hiring for, and there wasn't much he could do about it, not with the mortgage to take care of, and the kids needing new clothes for school in the fall. He stared at the much-corrected puzzle and tried to think.

Seven down, dockside security, six letters, ends with e-r.

"Hawser," he muttered, not exactly sure what a hawser was, but knowing it was something nautical. Except that, like most crossword answers, though the word fit seven down, it made nonsense of nine across. And, of course, he had left the crossword-puzzle dictionary that Flora had given him on the kitchen table at home.

Then he heard a soft, quick shuffling right outside. It was way too loud for blackflies.

5

Jim Heffernan froze for an instant. Then he quietly laid the puzzle book aside, reached out to snap off the light, and even more quietly undid the flap of his holster. He hadn't been issued an automatic pistol, but his big Ruger Security Six revolver held half a dozen very good arguments against any casual intruder doing something stupid. He sat very still for a few seconds, letting his eyes grow accustomed to the darkness and listening to a silence that wasn't so much a lack of sound as someone—or something—carefully making no noise.

"It's okay, Jim," came a voice from outside. "It's me."

Jim let out a breath he hadn't noticed he was holding, but didn't bother turning the light back on again. "You shouldn't sneak up on a guy like that, Harry!" he said. "What if I made a mistake one night?"

"You?" There was laughter like a rusty saw in a log as Jim stepped out through the door. In the light of a bright half-moon, he could see where Harry Pulaski, the other guard on this shift, was leaning against the wall of the guard hut. He was grinning. "We both know you'd sooner pick your nose with that cannon than fire it at anybody."

"Yeah, well." Jim hated guns. According to his supervisor, that made him one of the safest kinds of people to use them. He wasn't too sure about that. Being safe around yourself and your coworkers was one thing; being safe up against some young punk with state-of-the-art firepower and no scruples about using it was something else. "Quiet round?"

"What else?" Pulaski shrugged. "Still, it's an ill wind, ya know? I'm set to lose another two, three pounds this week walking around in this heat, if it keeps up."

The site lay spread out before them, monochrome in the moonlight. Not that there was much color about it even in full daylight. All but a few of the security lights had been turned out this late at night. Only the big floods

6

around the graveled area where the heavy machinery was parked were still on.

Forty years ago this had been the biggest of several strip mines in the area, a huge concentric ulcer burrowing into the countryside, surrounded by heaps of spoil. Over the years since the supply of coal ran out and the mining company went out of business, the local county government had made several sporadic, halfhearted attempts to re-landscape the place, but Nature had proven more effective. Weeds and scrub plants that didn't mind the local coal dust–laden soil had moved in and made a great green terraced garden of it, where at least the various wild grasses seemed to prosper.

Much of that green covering had been scraped away now as the digging started again. The site was easily half a mile from one rim of the hole to the other, with the guard hut perched high up on one side. Jim often wondered how quick their reaction was supposed to be, if something started happening clear across the crater. All around the edges of that crater were Detex watch clocks, and a rough, graveled road that would have served a better security purpose if the guards had some sort of vehicle. As it was, once every hour one or the other of them had to leave the relative comfort of the hut and walk around the site, swiping his electronic key card at each of the clocks—and, naturally, keeping an eye open for anything suspicious.

What they were watching most carefully was the wire fence around the facility, which had been cut months ago. Three heavy trucks and two wheeled diggers had been stolen from the vehicle park by the time the next guard made his round. Jim was grateful it had happened on his weekend off, because the guards on duty that night had been fired at once.

Pulaski yawned, stretched, then leaned back against the wall of the hut. "Almost makes you wish for the good old days, when there was nothing here but wilderness," he said.

"No jobs, either," said Jim sourly. "I like it just the way it is, thanks very much."

What had happened to the town was nearly miraculous. A company that specialized in manufacturing artificial composite "marble" and "granite" had come to survey the old mine site. They had been specifically looking for quartz. From what Jim could gather, they powdered it, mixed it with resins, then turned it out as slabs of high-quality fake Carrara marble for tiles and countertops. They had found a rich seam of the stuff running underneath the depleted coal veins, and it had looked like this would provide the town with at least some jobs. After years when up to eighty percent of the population had been out of work, it was better than nothing.

The company, Consolidated Quartzite, moved in, hired a couple of hundred local people as both full-time and part-time labor, and began clearing the site and sinking boreholes to find the best—and most economical—way of extracting the quartz. The process had gone on without much fanfare for several months, and the town began to take on a slight sparkle of life. People started to eat out more than they had for a long time, the bar began to fill up again in the evenings, they even began talking cautiously about a return of the good times. Or at least, as good as times were likely to get these days.

And then it happened. There was a morning when one of the Consolidated site engineers came running from the site up to the main office so fast that his helmet fell off halfway and he didn't even stop to pick it up and put it back on. And this was the man who chewed out at least three workers a day for similar infringements of the safety regulations. He shot into the site office like a rabbit down a burrow, dumped a pocketful of something indeterminate all over the table, grabbed the phone, and began babbling to someone at the head office in Nevada.

There were some abortive attempts to hush up what had happened, but in a small town on a worksite where everyone knew everyone else—and more or less trusted everyone else as well—the truth came out fast enough. They had struck gold.

All over the world, gold and quartz are often found together—but no one had ever expected to find it *here*. Consolidated's chief geologist flew in from Nevada to look over the site for herself, and walked away shaking her head and muttering, "Anomalous, very anomalous."

But she had been smiling. Everyone was smiling. There had been the usual talk of how much fallout from this find—nobody was calling it a strike, at least not yet—would fall out onto the workers and the local economy, and for a change the result was better than anyone expected. To their credit, Consolidated took on as many more local employees to run the extraction machinery as they could. It was mostly heavy boring and digging equipment for which people had to be trained, and since they were paid while they were being trained, no one particularly minded. It was a skill that would be useful later.

In any case, by the time the quartz dust had settled, about a month after the initial find, many more people were employed, and nearly everyone was pleased. Except for the ones who had to stay up until 3:30 in the morning, or five or six, walking around a great big hole in the ground and hoping that no more machinery would go missing. Especially on their shift.

"I suppose I shouldn't complain," Pulaski said. "There's a lot of worse things we could be doing."

Jim rubbed his eyes. The brief adrenaline rush of Pulaski's arrival had worn off, and the night shift was beginning to weigh heavily again. His eyes felt grainy. "Right now, I can't think what. I'm going crazy just trying to stay awake." He knuckled his eyes again.

" 'Dockside security,' six letters, ends in e-r," he muttered.

"Hawser," said Pulaski at once.

"Won't fit." Jim glanced at him. "What *is* a hawser, anyway?"

"Dunno. Some sort of small boat, I think."

"Lot of help *you* are. I'm falling asleep here."

"You want to stay awake? Just start your round early."

Jim shook his head. "It'd show on the time clocks. And you know how they hate that. I could use a snack, though. Want a Three Musketeers?"

"No. I'm trying to knock the sweet stuff. The wife says she likes how I'm losing weight."

Jim laughed, barely more than an intake of breath. He had been walking around this site just as long as Pulaski, and was beginning to doubt *he* would ever lose weight by any means short of industrial-level liposuction. He gazed thoughtfully down toward the center of the site and the deepest of the boreholes sunk so far. "I heard they got half a ton of 'reef' out of that last week," he said.

"I heard it too." Pulaski frowned slightly. "Thing is, the more of the gold-bearing ore they pull out of there, the less they're talking about how much it is, or how rich it is, or how much more might be left. Guys coming off the dig have to change their work clothes, get searched as they come out. It's getting to be like those big mines in South Africa."

"I thought those were diamond mines," said Jim.

"Gold too. I read all about them once. All the ways you can sneak gold out."

"I can guess—and no, I don't want to know. But I wonder what else they might turn up. What else they're not expecting. I mean, in all the years of digging coal, nobody knew there was gold underneath it."

"Not diamonds. It's the wrong sort of ground. You

need some sort of blue clay for diamonds."

"Maybe in South Africa you need blue clay. In up-state New York," Jim shrugged again, "who knows?"

They looked out across the silent site. It was sur-rounded by forest, pine, and mixed hardwoods, and somewhere off among the trees some nightbird was singing. "I hear that every night," said Pulaski. "What is it?"

"Nightingale."

"Here? I didn't know we had those here." They fell silent again, listening to the distant trickle of birdsong, sweet and faintly mournful.

As if in answer came another sound, a quick, sharp crack as though someone had stepped on a twig. But much louder, and somehow more metallic as well. The two security guards looked at each other; the most common source of that particular noise was a car en-gine cooling after the long haul from town back up to the mine. But neither of them had been down to the all-night doughnut place tonight.

The sound had come from off to their left, behind the guard hut, and Jim's right hand slipped inside the still-open flap of his holster. He didn't draw the heavy revolver, not yet, but even for a man who didn't like guns, the cold wood and metal of the Ruger's grip was sometimes very comforting. Times like now. Pulaski looked at him, then reached for his own gun.

"Come on," Jim said, and stepped softly around the corner.

Behind the guard hut, just at the edge of the site, was a little parking lot. During the day it was used by some of the site crews; at night, it was mostly empty. Jim's car was there; so was Pulaski's.

And a bunch of aliens were standing there as well.

All of them were dressed in close-fitting black, with heads too big for their bodies and huge-lensed eyes that Jim hoped were just some sort of goggles. They looked like the meaner, bigger brothers of those skinny

11

little aliens that turned up on TV specials about government-concealed UFO landings.

Pulaski brought up his gun at once, but before he could squeeze the trigger, a black-clad arm chopped down on his wrist and the pistol clattered onto the gravel. There was another flurry of movement and then a meaty thud as one of the aliens stepped forward and slammed a gun butt hard against his head. Pulaski grunted, slumped, and followed his revolver to the ground.

Other dark hands seized Jim Heffernan, peeled his fingers from the undrawn Ruger, and jerked it from the holster, then shoved him down onto his knees. Several weapons were already leveled at him, and he guessed that whoever—or whatever—had grabbed him was already off to one side to give a clear field of fire, if he gave them reason to shoot. Jim froze, and hoped that would be enough.

One of the creatures held something that might have been the source of the crackling sound. It looked vaguely like a rifle or a submachine gun, but there was a dully glowing strip down one side of its barrel, which made a faint humming noise. The noise was building. Then he heard the sharp metallic crack again, and a little line of fire flared and died among the weeds at the edge of the parking lot. It was plainly meant as a warning, and Jim took note.

Yet when he whispered, "Harry?" the next warning was both more direct and far less unearthly: a boot rammed hard into his ribs. More of the dark shapes gathered around him as he bent over, wheezed, and sucked for air.

Jim Heffernan had done his military service in Southeast Asia and West Germany; even though he didn't like guns, he could recognize, or at least guess at, most of them. But some of the weapons these fellows carried, like the one fired as a warning, were like nothing he had ever seen before.

A vehicle came rolling into the parking lot. There was no sound of an engine; Jim only knew of its arrival from the sound of gravel crunching beneath its tires. It showed no lights, and even the moonlight reflected only dimly from its black surface. Approximately the size and shape of a big three-axle truck, it had no windows, not even a windshield. The front was a smooth, unbroken surface, and there seemed to be no doors, either, until it stopped and an oval section swung up and away from the thing's dark hide.

Out of the darkness within the black truck stepped a shape that made Jim Heffernan's stomach twist within him, a shape from a childhood nightmare.

Years ago, when he was just a kid, he had been exploring through the woods near his home and had found a dead squirrel. He had known it was dead from the smell, if nothing else. But the squirrel had been moving. When he looked closer, he found that its body was alive with maggots, literally heaving with them. The sight had made him throw up his lunch, and ever afterward, something moving in a way that eyes and sense and reason said was *wrong* had always produced the same gut-clench reaction.

He felt that reaction now.

A man had climbed from the truck; a big man, broad across the shoulders and heavy through the waist, looking not fat but massive. But something else came out with him. At first it looked as though he was carrying two armfuls of wide-bore tubing, but then, as Jim watched with increasing horror, he realized that the tubes weren't tubes at all. They were arms.

No. They were tentacles, and they writhed and squirmed as if each one had a life all of its own, rearing into the air or coiling back down again, like snakes, huge pythons like the ones Jim had once seen in the zoo, unwilling to bite the person they were constricting. Unlike the dark metal of the truck and the black clothing of the alien figures, these shone in the moonlight with the unmistakable gleam of polished steel.

Jim stared, swallowing hard to prevent himself from throwing up again. He had a feeling that retching would be regarded as an insult, and that this weird, ominous creature was not one to take insults kindly. All he could find to say was, "Please, Mister—don't hurt him. He's got kids."

The aliens moved away, and it was extraordinary how perceptions could change in the space of a few seconds; now Jim saw that they were no more than people in funny costumes, not frightening at all. Not when compared to something *really* frightening, like the broad man-shape stalking toward him, framed by the writhing silhouettes of its tentacles.

"Ah, the human condition," it said in a deep, dark voice. "Easily remedied, fortunately." Jim gulped. He didn't know what that meant, just that he didn't like the sound of it. "Secure him," said the dark voice. "And his friend with the children."

It was done quickly and effectively, not with ropes, but with the plastic binders favored by many police departments instead of handcuffs.

"Now tell me," said the man with the arms, leaning a little closer, "that new borehole at the center of the site is recently dug, is it not?"

"Yessir," Jim said. "They sank it just two days ago."

"And what security arrangements are there for that hole?"

Jim blinked and licked dry lips. If he told what he knew, he would get fired. But if he didn't tell—he risked a glance at the slowly writhing tentacles—his employment would be terminated in a far more permanent way. Getting fired was preferable. He could always get another job.

"There's a team of two down there. They make their rounds every half hour."

14

"Correct," said the man with the arms, gazing down at Jim through a pair of spectacles that were halfway between sunglasses and goggles. "Very wise of you not to attempt some sort of foolish deception. Alert Team Two. Have them secure the area." One of the black-clad men turned and darted off into the truck.

"And as for you," he continued to Jim. "To ensure your continued cooperation, you and your friend the family man will accompany us. Bring them."

The black-clad men didn't use their truck to negotiate the network of access roads that coiled and switch-backed along the terraces of the old strip mine. Instead, the group standing around Jim—presumably Team One—grabbed him and went scrambling on foot straight down the walls of the crater.

If Jim had been scared of the unknown, in the shape of the stranger with the tentacles, he was even more scared of something he knew all too well. Those terraces, sixty and even seventy degrees from the horizontal, had been exposed and weathering for years. The rock was friable—crumbling like old, stale pound cake, likely to give underfoot without warning and send any careless climber down to the borehole at the bottom a good deal faster than intended.

He had no choice in the matter. He was grabbed by the arms and hustled down between two of the men like no more than a piece of awkward luggage. For themselves, they moved with a sureness that suggested the function of their bug-eyed goggles, able to see every stone and crevice even with only moonlight and sky glow to work by.

By the time they were halfway down, Jim was past caring about who could see what, and how well. He could see just enough to know he didn't want to see any more, and for the rest of the descent he kept his eyes shut tight, not opening them until an end to the jolting meant an end to the climb.

They had made it to the center borehole in a matter of minutes, but Team Two had been there before them. The other two security guards had been dealt with as efficiently as Heffernan and Pulaski. Even though Hank Sullivan was unconscious, a lump the size of an egg plainly visible above his left ear, both he and Tom Schultz were propped against the wall of the lowest terrace with binders tight around their wrists and ankles. From the lack of gunshots, alarms, or even extra lights, neither had been able to do anything about it.

One of the dark-clad men approached the bulky figure with the tentacles and ducked his head in a little gesture that was half bow and half salute. "We're secure."

"Phone lines?"

"Cut, sir. We took them out before moving in, and the Detex time clocks are receiving a dummy signal from one of the portable computers."

"Very well. Let's get on. I have no wish to be here all night."

Bound as he was, there was little Jim could do after that except sit where he had been dropped like so much garbage, and watch—without trying to *look* as if he was watching. He was the only one. Pulaski and Sullivan were still out cold, and Schultz had slumped forward, head leaning against his knees. He looked like a man trying to pretend all this wasn't happening, as if by ignoring what was going on around him, it would all somehow go away. Jim knew how he felt. But when all this was over, and assuming they survived it, then the police or even the FBI would want detailed explanations and accurate descriptions. He was going to do his best to provide whatever they required.

Several of the black-clad men busied themselves around the drilling machinery for the new borehole, with a speed and precision that spoke either of considerable prior experience or equally considerable recent training. Firing up the big gasoline engine that powered its winch, they began raising the drill up and out of the shaft until at last the carborundum-diamond drill bit itself rose from the hole. It was unlatched and swung clear, the engine shut down again; and after that, they waited.

A few minutes later another group came down the terraces, moving with the same ease as the team that had carried Heffernan and Pulaski. This new group was carrying something else: a long metal cylinder, and for all that it seemed both heavy and clumsy, the team moved in a perfect unison that was almost graceful. They too had evidently practiced before going into action, so that now what they were doing looked easy.

It couldn't have been as easy as all that. When they finally came level with the boring machinery, tilted the cylinder upright, and lowered one end to the ground not too far from where Jim was sitting, he could hear and feel the ponderous thud of something far more massive than it looked. The careful way they handled it suggested something else as well: that it was dangerous in a way far beyond mere weight.

The man with the tentacles strode over to it and raised one of his real arms to touch it in a strange gesture that was almost affectionate, the way one might stroke a pet or pat the trunk of a familiar tree. One or two of the metal arms curved around to touch the cylinder, as if recognizing some odd kinship. Then the man said, "Carry on."

The lifting gear that had withdrawn the bore and its bit was now attached to linkages recessed into the shell of the cylinder; then the engine coughed into life once more, taking up the slack, and the cylinder was raised, swung into place, and slowly lowered into the waiting borehole. Jim, still making sure that his watching wasn't obvious, couldn't help but be impressed at how exactly the cylinder fitted. Someone knew exactly what equipment was being used here, even down to the width of the bore sampler—and that could change from day to day.

But what *was* that thing . . . ?

As the cylinder dropped out of sight, he was reminded of a huge cartridge being loaded into a massive gun. For a long time after it vanished, the cables supporting it kept unrolling from their drums. He had known in a general way how deep this bore was. Two miles, someone had said once. But until you actually watched how much cable two miles really was, and how long it took to feed that huge length down into the ground, the words had no real meaning.

The bits and the samplers were always hot when they came back up, sometimes too hot to touch. That was what one of the engineers had told him. The heat wasn't just from the friction of drilling, but from the massive heat and pressure of the earth itself two-plus miles down.

One of the pieces of machinery made an odd gulping sound, and Jim looked up. There was no reading of expressions through their hoods and goggles, but there was suddenly an air of expectation in the group.

"Well?" said the man with the tentacles.

"She's hit bottom," replied the team member who had been operating the crane.

"Then check the transmitter."

Another one of the team took an object from his belt. It was oblong, with a short antenna at one end, and looked as much like a walkie-talkie or even a cell phone as anything else. He studied it, adjusted a couple of controls, then nodded. "We've got a good signal. Five by five. Heat's no problem."

"Then our work here is done. Drop as many cores as you can into the shaft, and let's be away."

The group of black-clad men, no longer separate teams but a single unit of about fifteen, swiftly set to work. They gathered the thirty or so drilled-out core samples that had been placed near the borehole and began feeding them back down the shaft, one after another. The first half-dozen were reassembled into their original carriers and lowered with almost as much care as the cylinder itself, but after that the cores were simply rolled or carried to the top of the shaft and dropped inside.

Even when every sample around the site had been disposed of, the shaft was nowhere near filled to the top. It would take a lot more than that to completely fill a hole two miles deep. But getting at the cylinder was no longer a simple matter of reversing the winch and pulling it out, not with the better part of two tons of rock plugging the exit.

The man with the tentacles clapped his real hands together, an expression both of satisfaction and completion. "Let's be away."

Most of his various teams faded at once into the shadows, but a couple of them remained with their leader as he came over to Jim and the others. "You gentlemen will forgive me if I don't give you a ride," he said. "But we have miles to go before we sleep."

Jim was cold, he ached, and this guy, though still horribly frightening, had proved himself human enough to get on his nerves. "Any promises to keep?" he asked.

The man with the tentacles smiled at him, a smile Jim Heffernan didn't want to see again for the rest of his life, but he refused to flinch or look away. If this character was going to kill him, or have him killed, then nothing he could say or do would prevent that.

"Some say humor is the greatest gift," the man said, mockery edging that dark voice. "I have little time for it myself, and even less interest in gifts. I am more concerned with what I can take. Nonetheless, gallows humor can be appreciated. If I were you, I would not linger here."

He and his remaining followers vanished into the dark.

Jim waited a long time before he dared to move, and then every movement was an agony of cramp, or cold, or cut-off circulation from the tightness of the binder on his wrists. A voice in his brain yelled at him: *Run from here, run as far and as fast as you can!* A feeling of dread rose from him like a fog—or like the wisp of smoke curling out of a gun barrel—from that dark and silent hole in the ground. But he wasn't about to leave his friends and watch mates behind. No, not even if Hank *had* Krazy-Glued his lunch box shut last week. . . .

But he still managed to function. He concentrated first on getting himself as loose as he could. The damn plastic binders were still very tight, but he managed— with some wriggling and a pain that made him think he'd possibly dislocated his wrist or one of the little bones in the hand—to get his crossed arms under his butt, and then, more slowly, to fold his legs tight enough to get them through the looped arms as well. This involved much squirming, pushing off one shoe so he could fit the foot through, and bracing the other foot against Hank, who was convenient and (at the moment) not terribly conscious. After that, when he could get to his feet again, it was just a matter of hopping around a little to get the other shoe back on, and then finding something sharp.

Fortunately, sharp things were not in short supply around this particular building site. The men in black had left the carborundum-tipped drill bit lying with its end accessible, shoved against a wall, but not flush against it. The disk-shaped digging end of the bit had two sets of blades: the outer set consisting of small plates of industrial diamond and carborundum set alternately in a herringbone pattern right around the face of the bit. Jim picked one blade of the herringbone and started sawing away at the plastic restrainer with it.

It took a long time. Jim hated the sight of his own blood, but he saw a fair amount of it before he was finished. Fortunately he knew well enough where the big veins and arteries were—the mandatory employees' first-aid course had been pretty specific about that—and he was careful to miss them. But the palm and heel of his right hand would probably bear the marks for a long time. At first, his hands were so numb from the constriction of the plastic restrainer that they couldn't feel what was happening to them. Unfortunately, a minute or three after he got the binders off, they began shrieking at him that they hadn't had enough blood or oxygen for a long time, and were now going to repay him for the favor by letting him acutely feel every injury that had ever happened to them, with special attention to the ones he had just incurred.

Jim swore, and ignored the pain the best he could, and clumsily used his hands to sit Harry up and shake him a little. "You okay? Say something!"

Harry said something, all right: words that would have made Flora mutter something about being a bad example to the kids. Then Harry added, "I was feeling better until you started shaking my head back and forth. Cut it out!"

"All right. Can you get up? We've gotta get out of here. I haven't got my Swiss army knife with me. Go on over to the bit and cut those off you. Tom?"

Tom was still unconscious. "We're gonna have to carry him out," Jim said, "and I don't like the look of that head. We're gonna have to be real careful with him. I wish we had a backboard or something."

"There's a piece of plywood over here," Harry said, sawing away at his binders with the herringbone blade. "I guess we could use that—"

"Okay. Get it. Hank—"

Hank sat there, shivering. When Jim came to him, he said, "They said they were gonna burn me. They said they were gonna burn me, I couldn't do anything else!"

"Of course you couldn't do anything else," Jim said, furious that "they" should so casually reduce a nice, kind man to this trembling shape. *Bastards! Let me catch you sometime without your fancy guns*... "Forget it, Hank. Except for the boss, no one's going to talk to you about this—we're gonna see to it. All right? Now get up and get over there and get loose so you can help us with Tom."

Harry got himself cut free and went over to get the "backboard" while Jim helped get Hank free. Then carefully, the way they had been trained, they lifted Tom onto the piece of plywood. "Pity we can't go up as fast as they came down," Jim muttered.

"No, thanks," Hank said. "I saw you guys come down, after the first batch jumped us. Damn near gave me a heart attack."

"Well, don't have one now, for God's sake," Jim said. "What time is it?"

Harry looked at the sky. "Near enough to dawn—" He glanced at his watch. "Damn thing's not going," he said. "Yours going?"

Jim and Hank looked at their watches. Both of them were stopped as well. "Like something out of a movie," Jim said morosely. "Guys dressed like aliens. . . . Never mind, let's get going. He needs a doctor."

They walked up the switchback road as fast as they dared. It was not fast enough for Jim. He couldn't get rid of the idea that, down in the crater, something very bad was going to happen. And about halfway up the road, halfway up the terraces, the feeling grew stronger than before. "C'mon," he said to the others, "we've gotta hurry, let's *hurry!*"

To his great relief, none of them asked, "Why?" Hank and Harry saw him look over his shoulder, and they looked too—and they hurried. Tom, lying on his back with their jackets wadded on either side of his head to hold it still, never moved, only moaned a little every now and then. Jim hoped he wouldn't wake up just now. He was likely to slow them down, and if there was one thing Jim was sure about right now, it was that it would be very bad if they slowed down.

He could barely believe it when they actually came out at the top of the switchback road onto the ring road that led around the site.

"They've killed the phones," said Jim, "but there's that cell phone in the office. I don't think they got that. Come on."

As quickly as they dared, and making better speed now that they weren't climbing, they made their way around the ring road to the little security hut near where the chain-link fence and the gate met the road. There was no point trying to bring Tom into the hut; he was just as well left outside. Carefully, in the slowly growing light, they put him down on the ground, and Jim ran in to get the cell phone.

As he came out again he hurriedly dialed the emergency day-or-night number for the district Consolidated office in New York. A somewhat bored voice said, "Consolidated security . . ."

"Jeff? It's Jim Heffernan. Listen, there's been a break-in at the site." He looked out across the diggings in dawn's early light, wondering at how peaceful it seemed now after all the madness of the night.

"Break-in? Who was it?"

"A bunch of guys dressed in black like commandos or ninjas or something—and one guy who was really strange. This is gonna need a major debrief, Jeff, and we need a doctor right now for Tom. One of these guys hit him hard with a gun, and he's been unconscious for half an hour at least. These guys were fooling around with the new bore, Jeff, the deep one."

"All right, all right, listen. Let me get Ralph Molinari on the line, he's the one you want to talk to about this kind of thing. You tell him everything that's happened, and—"

Fizz. And a dead phone.

Jim, looking out over the site, saw it happen: something he thought he had seen films of, and more recently, videotape of, in the South Pacific, when people who should have known better were playing with their toys. He felt it, too—the ground booming and jumping under his feet as if a giant had kicked it, the ground rippling like a liquid thing. He saw the top of the wave, where it touched the surface of the earth, radiate outward like the ripple from a stone chucked into a pool, watched the ripple travel, the dust puffing up behind it. And then as the shock wave passed them by, making the ground right under them jump again, he saw the whole site sag. The crater subsided into itself as if half the stone and gravel and dirt in it were suddenly pulverized finer than they had been before, settling deeper, sagging down, subsiding into a shallow, churned-up crater. Dust arose and blew gently off to one side. Jim found himself desperately grateful that the dust wasn't blowing toward them.

Jim shook the cell phone again, half hoping that it would come back to life, but it wouldn't. It was dead—and why wouldn't it be, this close to an electromagnetic pulse? He doubted it would ever work again.

"Not my hundred fifty bucks, anyway," he said softly and put it in his pocket. Then he went over to one of the logs that separated the parking lot from the site proper and sat down on it.

Hank and Harry joined him. They sat there quietly, the three of them, for what seemed like a long while, none of them saying out loud what they were thinking. Jim thought he knew what those thoughts were. *If that was what I think it was, were we far enough away? Are we going to be alive in five years, or ten? I don't feel any burns—but then early on, you wouldn't . . .*

It took about twenty minutes for the police and the ambulance to get there, called by the New York office. One of the cops was Rod Cummings, who Jim knew fairly well. They drank and played pool together down at Bob's Bar in town. Rod looked down at the hole and said, "Dear God on a moped."

"Yeah," said Jim.

The ambulance people got busy with Tom. As they carried him away, Rod said very softly, "CalTech called the station and the state emergency services. Asked whether there had been an earthquake."

"Nope," Jim said. "Nothing like that. A disaster, though. . . ." He couldn't get rid of the image of that stocky shape with the metallic arms, looking down at Harry as if from a great distance, and saying, *"Ah, the human condition. Easily remedied, fortunately."*

Jim shook all over as he watched the paramedics put Tom into the ambulance, on a real backboard this time. "He'll be okay, won't he?"

"I think so. The question is," and Rod looked down at the crater, from which vague plumes of dust still very gently rose, "will we?"

"**P**etey?"

"Hmmm?"

"Where's the hand cream?"

Peter Parker was in his apartment in New York. It was one of many things for which, at the moment, he gave thanks. He was in the tub, up to his nose in suds. He lay there staring at the ceiling, and considered briefly that it was going to need repainting again soon; the dampness was making the paint over the tub bubble.

"Which hand cream specifically?" Peter said after a moment.

Mary Jane Watson-Parker, resplendent in a calico cotton bathrobe with a torn pocket, put her head around the bathroom door, looking vaguely worried. "It's the apple one, with the cuticle stuff."

"What's the bottle look like?"

"It wasn't a bottle. It was a kind of little bucket."

Peter sighed. A week ago, he had been washing Everglades muck out of his Spider-Man costume, thinking that if he could just get back to New York, he'd never complain about anything again. *How quickly things can change,* he thought, and said aloud, "A little bucket . . ."

"It had a design on the top," MJ said. "A little apple."

Peter closed his eyes, thought for a moment. The house had been filling with peculiar cosmetics recently, but he really couldn't complain about that, as it meant that his wife was working, rather than merely making herself more attractive than she already was—a tough job, if you asked him. "Bucket," he said, and opened his eyes. "Kind of a little tub thing? Okay. In the kitchen, on the counter by the dishwasher, there are about six pots and tubs and so forth there. All the little short squat ones were there."

"I looked," MJ said fretfully. "It's not there."

Peter closed his eyes again, trying to see where he

had last seen the thing. "Not there, huh? Okay. Try on top of the refrigerator."

"The refrigerator? Why would I put anything there?"

Peter restrained himself from suggesting numerous possibilities. "Just go look."

A brief silence ensued. A moment later, MJ reappeared, smiling a little sheepishly, with a pot of hand cream in one hand. "It was behind the Rice Krispies," she said.

"Yeah, I thought I saw you use it the first thing this morning," said Peter.

He sank back into the bubbles, and MJ smiled at him, less sheepishly this time. "You're being awfully good about all this."

"It's money," he said, smiling back. "Why not?"

She went off, probably to do something about her cuticles. MJ's hands had become more than usually useful in the week since they had come home from Florida. In a way, Peter regretted it. He had half hoped they would have at least a week or so to themselves to sit quietly, not doing any more work than they had to, and trying to recover a little from the rather frenetic period of heat, humidity, and super heroing without skyscrapers. But it seemed that fate had intended otherwise.

It had been a lively time. Work had taken them down there initially. First MJ's intention to hunt for more modeling work in the Miami area with one of the new PR or modeling agencies relocating down that way, and then, on Peter's end, when he was sent down by the *Daily Bugle* to help investigate some strange goings-on at Cape Canaveral, things that wound up involving not only his old acquaintance the Lizard, but Venom as well. That business was now cleared up, or as much as it was going to be anytime soon. The Lizard had vanished again; Venom had taken himself away with what Peter knew he would consider "unfinished business"— namely the killing of Spider-Man—still incomplete. *But even Venom,* Peter thought, *must want a few days off every now and then. . . .*

While Peter, as Spider-Man, had been swinging all over the countryside—a matter not made simpler by the generally low-lying quality of Floridian flora, and the fact that only in Miami proper were there skyscrapers worthy of the name—MJ had been modeling away at her best speed. She had been working, among other things, on magazine shoots and some other light photographic work. She had also been indulging in her usual fairly frenetic networking—it would not have been MJ's style to ignore the possibility of future work, even though she was presently working her butt off. Between work sessions in a bar in South Beach, she had met, completely by chance, another model who knew someone who knew someone in New York who needed a hand model.

Peter had blinked at her when she told him about this the first time. "You mean to tell me," he'd said, "that there are actually people who just show their hands and nothing else?"

"Sure," MJ said. "You see them on TV. I bet you've just never thought about it before. Commercials for jewelry and softer-than-soft dishwashing liquid and hand creams and rubber gloves—things like that. It's all hand models."

They had been sitting in a restaurant at the time. MJ had been admiring her nails in a general sort of way. "Mikey—he's the underwear model I was telling you about—Mikey said that it's really hard to find a hand model without any wrinkles or spots at my age, the way the ozone layer's been changing the past ten years. It seems everyone suddenly has freckles and stuff. Whereas I"—and she glanced again at one hand in bemusement—"I just don't seem to have had that problem."

"That," Peter said, "is because you always keep your hands in your pockets. Most unladylike."

"Yeah." She giggled. "That's what they all said when I was growing up. If I'd known then that I could get a thousand bucks a day for it, I'd have ignored them even harder than I did."

"A *thousand*—! You're kidding, right?"

She shook her head. "If you can find the work," MJ said. "It's very specialized, and there just aren't that many people who can do it—whose hands still look perfect up close to the hot lights and the big sensitive camera lenses. Once you start doing it"—she smiled; it was a slightly feral look—"they tend to keep you on, and they tend to give you as much more of that kind of work as you can take."

"A thousand bucks a day. I think you can probably take a fair amount of it."

Peter sighed at the memory and blew out so big a breath that bubbles blew off the top layer of suds. From the next room came the sound of a cheerful woman la-laing to herself as she rubbed cream into her hands. Peter had to be amused by it. Normally MJ couldn't have cared less about her hands, at least in terms of doing anything to them in the course of a day. But the photographer on the shoot she was presently working had yelled at her that she needed to be "moister," and after some confusion on all sides, it was discovered that he meant he wanted her to use more moisturizer. So she had begun doing so, and had started meeting a couple of other hand models whom the director of the present project suggested she have a chat with. Suddenly, on their advice, the house had begun filling up with—Peter rolled his eyes a little, in amusement—tubs and pots and bottles and heaven only knew what else.

Still, the timing suited him. Peter had made a fair pile of money from the pictures he took of Spider-Man in the attack on the Space Shuttle at the Cape, and the resolution of that attack. The picture that had caught the bomb going off after it had been dropped into the flame-suppression tank at the bottom of the Shuttle launch facility had made the front page of the *Bugle*, much to his delight, and he had picked up a bonus for it. But that bonus and the money from the AP wire wouldn't last him forever. MJ had satisfied herself that the Miami modeling scene wasn't everything it was cracked up to be in terms of steady work, so, happily enough, they had come home again when both their assignments were done—only to find that instead of having a few days to call their own, MJ had to go straight out and spend ten to twelve hours a day with her hands artistically decked in what the ad described as "Ever-Lovin' Bubbles." It was just dishwashing detergent, which Peter found it beyond his ability to love even temporarily, let alone forever. But at a thousand bucks a day. . . .

He felt around under the water for the soap. Things could have been a lot worse. They *had* been a lot worse, but after this last stint of work, each of them had managed to contribute enough money to the household kitty to get the credit cards paid down—at least to the point where they could use them—and to put a small but reassuring lump into their joint savings account. It was a little bit weird, actually, to feel somewhat secure, to feel that for the next little while, they didn't have to scramble desperately just to keep groceries in the kitchen and the landlord happy.

Peter looked forward to spending the next few weeks doing assignment work at the *Bugle* again, and having the leisure, as Spider-Man, to web-swing normally again, among proper tall buildings placed close together, in a city where he knew his way around, and in a place where you could be fairly sure that if you hit the ground suddenly, you wouldn't be on top of an alligator. He had found Florida pleasant enough for a short visit, but it was a little too flat for his taste, and there were things living in the wet part of the flatness that considered human beings, Spider-Man and others, to be perfectly acceptable hors d'oeuvres.

He heard the front door *clunk* and glanced up at the

clock on the top shelf above the towels. Nine-thirty: MJ was going down to get the mail. Peter lay back in the tub again, gazed up at the ceiling, and thought, *We could try a new color in here next time. That beige is really beginning to look like masking tape.*

After a few minutes the door went *clunk* again, and he heard the jingle as MJ chucked her keys onto the telephone table. "Anything interesting?" he said.

"Mmnh," she said, going through whatever she was carrying as she came toward the bathroom. "Junk mail, junk mail, restaurant menu . . ."

"Which restaurant?"

"Uh." A pause; she appeared in the bathroom door in jeans and T-shirt. "The Blarney Rock."

"That's a restaurant? I thought it was a bar."

"The bar's opened a restaurant. Real Irish food."

Peter made a bemused expression. "Corned beef and cabbage?"

"Nope, it says specifically they don't do that. 'Boxty'—" She furrowed her brow. "What's that? For that matter, what's 'champ'? Or 'colcannon'?"

"You've got me. Maybe they're taking big old guns away from terrorists and cooking them?"

"Best use for them, maybe. Don't think I need that much fiber in my diet, though." She put the menu aside for later perusal. "Junk mail, junk mail, you may already have won . . ."

"Oh, sure," said Peter. "What's the prize in this one?"

"A trip to Miami, if you go see one of their condos."

"Too humid this time of year," Peter said. "Too many super-villains."

"Yeah." MJ continued going through the pile. "Junk mail, junk mail, I can't believe trees are dying for this. Oh—phone bill. Two of them."

"Two? I thought we paid the phone bill last week."

"No, these are for the cell phones." MJ smiled as she opened the first one. She had bought a matching set of cell phones for the pair of them in Florida. Each had approximately a hundred functions, only two or three of which Peter understood. He had found that his phone was one of those instruments of the technological age that was actively dangerous if you didn't know how to work it. And he was embarrassed to find that—while he could manipulate cameras and web shooters and spider-tracers with the greatest of ease—he could not for the life of him get the hang of the cell phone. Once he had tried to use the phone's "number scratch pad," and had wound up destroying its entire "address book," which had taken him hours to install. Since then, Peter had resolutely refused to touch any buttons on the thing except for the dial pad and the "accept" or "hang up" buttons.

MJ unfolded the first bill. "I've used mine about five times this month," she said, "and you've used yours maybe three times, if I'm any judge."

"I called the weather once," Peter said, "and once I called for a pizza. Everything else was incoming."

She smiled, then took a look at the bill. Her mouth actually fell open, assuming the position at which Aunt May used to warn Peter, "You'd better shut that or a fly will get in."

"What the heck—?" She said it in a tone of voice that suggested that "heck" was not the word she really wanted to use.

"What's the matter?"

"They've given us somebody else's bill," she said and walked over to the tub, holding the bill between thumb and forefinger as if it were a recently deceased rat. "Look for yourself."

He looked. The first thought Peter had about the bill was, *That's a bit long, isn't it?* There were several pages to it. The second thought he had was on looking at the total at the top of the first page. "BALANCE PAYABLE," it said. "$4,689.72."

Four thousand . . .

Peter looked at MJ in total bewilderment. "They've made a mistake," he said. "It can't be your bill. What's the other one say?"

"Hm—" She reached for the other envelope, which she had stuck up on the towel shelf with everything but the junk mail she hadn't yet thrown away. She ripped it open, unfolded it. "Twenty-three dollars and eighty cents. Twenty of that is just the rental for the number—"

They both looked at the other bill. "Four *thousand—!* It's just a mistake," MJ said, riffling through the six or seven attached pages, all covered with very small print. "CellTech's computer must have had a fit or something, that's all. They can't make me pay this. I didn't make any of these calls. There's not a single number I recognize."

Peter twitched a little, under the suds. "Some of these cell phone companies," he said carefully, "can be a little sticky about billing."

"They can stick all they like," MJ said, laughing, "but I'm not paying this. I didn't make *any* of these calls."

"Better call their helpline and tell them that the computer's barfed all over your bill," he said. "If you like, I'll—"

"No, I can handle it myself, no problem," MJ said and headed out into the kitchen. "By the way, what do you want for breakfast?"

"Oh, just some toast. I'll get some coffee later."

"Right."

Half an hour later, Peter was out of the tub, shaved, dried, and getting dressed in their bedroom—and becoming more and more determined to put off going into the kitchen for as long as he could.

MJ was still on the phone. He had heard one loud cry of *"What?"* and another of, "But, you can't—that's—

it's, it's not fair!'' and another of, ''But I didn't! I've only had it—''

A long silence had followed that. Then came a quieter tone of voice that Peter knew, and didn't hear often: the sound of MJ being very controlled, and probably politer than she needed to be. It was a tone of voice which suggested that the person on whom she was using it had better never run into her at a social occasion or things would turn quickly antisocial.

Finally, he heard her hang up, very softly. To Peter's educated ear, the quiet little click sounded like a bomb detonator going off. Not too quietly, and he hoped not too casually, he made his way into the kitchen.

The toast had come up about ten minutes ago; it sat cold and forlorn in the toaster. It wasn't so dark that redoing it would ruin it, so Peter pushed it down again and walked through to the little table between the kitchen and the dining area where MJ was sitting, the cell phone off to one side, and staring at the bill.

''So what did they say?'' he said.

She looked up at him bleakly. ''They say we have to pay it.''

''But they weren't your calls,'' Peter said.

''They weren't my calls,'' MJ said, ''but it looks like I'm responsible for them.''

''What do you mean?''

''According to the lady I talked to—she was really very nice, she was good to me, but she couldn't help it—my phone was probably cloned.''

''Cloned—someone stole the number, you mean.''

She nodded, looking morose, and sat back in the chair. ''There are people who wait near the ends of bridges and tunnels with scanners because when you come out of there, when you lose the shielding effect, the phone broadcasts its ID number to the system—its PIN number, more or less. Tells the cell phone network where it is. That's an easy time for them to steal your number. People wait with their scanners for cars to come out and record as many numbers as they can. Then they put them into 'blank' phones and start making free calls. Free to them, anyway.''

MJ scowled at the table. "I'm so angry, Peter. It's not like I don't know about this, like I haven't heard about it. When I'm in a cab and go into a bridge or a tunnel, I usually make sure the phone is off. I'm pretty careful about it. But just one time I must have been in a hurry, on the way to a job or something, and I must have forgotten—''

Peter shook his head. "Hon, you can't remember *everything*. We've had a fairly lively time of it these past few weeks. It's only natural, when you get home, you relax, you forget something—'' He sat down by her, took her hand. "Don't look so tragic!''

She looked at him sidelong and gave him a lopsided smile. "Whatever you say,'' she said, "just don't say 'It's only money.' Think about it, Tiger. What have we got in the bank?''

"I guess a little less than—''

"Five thousand dollars, yes. That was going to last us a month or two—maybe more if we stretched hard. It was going to buy us some time to get a little bit ahead. You know how it is when you start a new job—it takes a little while to get the accounting department straightened out, they take a little while to get the check cut.'' She shrugged. "Well—''

She looked at the bill. "The due date on this is two weeks from now.''

"You don't think you could make that much money in two weeks, do you?''

She looked at him. "Not after taxes, no. Probably not. Hand work tends to happen only a couple days at a time.''

Peter shook his head. "It's just wrong, though. They shouldn't be able to make you pay it. They're not your calls!''

"Apparently they can,'' MJ said. "The law in New

York at the moment is that there's a ten-day window during which you can inform them that your number's been cloned: if you do it within ten days of the first 'spurious' call, then they won't charge you." The grin she gave him now was much more lopsided. "The problem is, it's a catch-22—how do you know your phone's been cloned until you see the bill? If you're lucky, and it happens at the bottom of a billing cycle, you'll do better, but—" She shook her head.

"But there has to be some way that they can establish that these aren't your calls."

"Not yet," MJ said sadly. "Not for us. We haven't had these phones long enough to establish a billing pattern for either of us. The lady I was talking to said that the only way not to be liable for the cost of the bill was to produce concrete proof that the phone had been cloned. I don't know how we would do that. The lady said that you would have to have the phone's number turn up in an ongoing criminal investigation. If they've actually caught some crook using it, and found your number in his phone, then naturally they'd let you off."

"Oh, jeez," Peter said. The odds of this seemed poor.

In the kitchen, the toast popped up. He ignored it. MJ sniffed. "It's burned."

"It's burned? *I'm* burned! I'm not going to give them four thousand dollars of our money when we didn't use their service!"

"Tiger," MJ said, "unless we can find some way to prove the phone was cloned, we're going to have to. Otherwise this is going to trash our credit rating. We've got enough trouble keeping that straight as it is, and without it, we're sunk. We could take them to court, but who's got the money?"

"Yeah," Peter said.

MJ reached out across the table, sighed deeply, and smiled at Peter once more. This time it was a much more normal smile, but there was a sense of it being applied, like makeup. "I've got to start thinking about going," she said. "They're going to be ready to start shooting in about half an hour, and I can't take the chance of getting caught in traffic."

"What're we going to do?" Peter said.

MJ shook her hair back and looked noble and brave. "We're going to stall," she said, "until I can find out whether we really have to pay this thing. If we have to pay it—" She shrugged. "We've been worse off before."

"I was hoping we wouldn't have to be worse off again," Peter said. "There's nothing hot coming up at the *Bugle* that I know of—I'm not going to be able to be of much help to you."

"Just knowing that you're thinking of ways to be of help to me, to us," MJ said, "makes me feel just fine. Come on, Tiger. Fresh toast for you, and then I'm going to go."

She got up and made him fresh toast, and put on fresh coffee, and the more she was kind to him, and thoughtful, the more Peter began to stew and fret as well. By the time she was ready to go out, still just in her T-shirt and jeans, and (a new development) with her hands covered with the kind of white cotton gloves that commuters used to read the *New York Times* on the train, for his own part, Peter was so angry he could hardly speak. "You going to the *Bugle* later?" MJ said.

"That's right."

"Okay, give 'em my best. When'll you be back?"

"By evening, anyway," Peter said. "Today is just a mooching-around day, to see what's going on, which editors need a photographer. After that, I might do a little night work."

She nodded, recognizing their code for web-swinging. "Okay. I won't wait to eat dinner if you're not home when I get back." She picked up her cell phone, looked at it with an expression of tremendous annoyance, and dropped it into her purse. "You know the number," she said.

"Yeah," Peter said, for a moment allowing the same annoyance to show. "So does someone else. Let me know if your schedule changes. I'll call if mine does."

"Gimme a kiss," MJ said.

Peter drew her close, and for several long warm moments, even the thought of the phone company was drowned out. When she let him go at last, Peter said, "It's a waste, them only using your hands."

She waggled her eyebrows at him. "They have other uses," she said, "as you'll doubtless find out when we're both home again tonight. 'Bye, Tiger." And she was off down the hall.

He watched her for a moment, then shut the door quietly and began to pace a little bit, looking across the room at where his own cell phone sat. *It's not fair—not in the slightest. There has to be something we can do. Something I can do—or that Spider-Man can do. . . .*

Peter went over to the window that looked uptown and stood for a moment. Spider-Man certainly had various friendly police contacts here and there; it had often been his pleasure to do one cop or another a good turn, and they had done him some in the past as well. *Unfortunately, there is a basic flaw in the logic here,* he thought. Spider-Man's contacts weren't guaranteed to do Peter Parker that much good, especially since to get this particular problem solved would involve showing MJ's phone bills to the police. That would raise just too many questions leading, if he wasn't careful, to the question of his secret identity. *No,* Peter thought, *that's not going to do it—at least not directly.*

He looked out over the roofs of midtown. A brief taste of freedom, of something just a little like security, and now it was gone. *Ten million people out there—certainly there couldn't be more than a million of them who were crooks. Probably a lot less.* It just *seemed* like a lot more. Turn your back for a minute, and you found them in your soup. What still staggered him was the injustice of it all—that the phone company could recognize theft as coming from one specific direction, but hold *you* responsible for it in the next breath, even if you weren't. Though they would probably say that she was careless, she wasn't careless.

Peter stalked back and forth in front of the window, getting more furious—and then sighed. Standing here being angry did no good, but there were things that would. He'd go in to the *Bugle,* see what work was around. And then, later—well . . .

He couldn't do anything about the phone company, but the crooks—that was something else.

Peter went to get his keys and got ready to head out.

TWO

Night fell and turned the city golden.

Spider-Man knew that light pollution was a problem. He knew that the sodium-vapor lamps that lit New York City streets made astronomers crazy, blanking out the frequencies of light that they were most interested in. But when he stood in a high place, as he did right now, and smelled the cold sweet air—well, sweeter than it was in the daytime, when the sun baked the ozone stink into everything—and when he looked down at those luminous golden pathways between the buildings, all traced with ruby and diamond light, he loved the sight and he wished the people at Hayden Planetarium could find something else to complain about.

He stood at the corner of the roof of the Met Life building and looked northeast. It was a good vantage point, and a good place to jump off from suddenly if you needed to. Plenty of skyscrapers as tall or taller were just north of him: the heart of midtown, his favorite playground. Just west was the unique design of the Flatiron Building; to the north, the traffic lights of Park Avenue, all red and green down the central mall.

Spider-Man stood on the gravel, looking down. He had spent the early part of the evening web-swinging. It was amazing how much frustration you could work off that way. The wind in your face—well, against your mask, anyway—as you snagged the corner of a building with webbing, swung down, whipped around, got a grip on some wall of empty plate glass, scurried up it, then launched yourself out into the void again. Not even riding a line of webbing, just counting on the spider's leap to take you across the gap to the next building. It was exhilarating and a great way to keep an eye on things without being seen. Only rarely did New Yorkers look up, unless a helicopter crash or an alien invasion was happening over their heads. Mostly their attention was at their own level, or below. So was Spider-Man's, but for different reasons.

He was watching pickup trucks, and had been for some days just before he went off to Florida. It was a feature on the news that had started him on this particular avenue of study, a story that made it plain how hot "ram raiding" was becoming in New York.

It was uncertain where the art had originated. Some said it was first practiced in the densely packed, small shopping malls of midlands England. Others said it had been invented in the Midwest, or among corner minimalls of Los Angeles. Wherever it originated, it was entirely too attractive a method of crime for those who were properly equipped.

The proper equipment tended to stand out: you needed a four-wheel-drive vehicle, or a pickup, or a combination of both, some chains, and several willing accomplices. The idea was that you rammed the back or front of your truck, whichever was more convenient, into a store, and then you jumped in and robbed the place, tossed your loot into the truck, and drove away. Other forms of ram raiding were slightly more opportunistic. Those with a tow point on the back of their truck and enough chain would back their truck up to a store's security shutters, or the post that anchored the shutters, fasten the chain to the shank that secured the post, and drive away at top speed, usually taking the post out. The crooks would then quickly return, loot the store, and flee.

Spider-Man stood there a moment more, breathing the mild summer night's air, and then sprang over to the other side of the roof; there he looked down toward Twenty-third Street, shot a line of web across toward the Park Avenue South corner, and swung out into the night, heading downtown. Ram raiding, he reflected, did have its dangers. You might chain something to your fender and drive away and have your fender come off. This could be embarrassing, especially if your license plate was still attached. An NYPD detective of his acquaintance had told him about how one group of ram raiders decided to steal the cash machine from a bank. They wrapped their chains around the machine and pulled it out of the bank's wall, but the bad guys had failed to notice that the back entrance to the Fourteenth Precinct was directly across from that particular branch of Chase Manhattan. While the crooks got busy securing the cash machine to the back of their pickup, some of the bemused cops who had been watching the raid from inside their offices came strolling outside, crossed the street, and arrested the guys—only to have one of the crooks explain to them, absolutely straight-faced, that the object chained to the back of their truck was in fact a washing machine. One cop laughed so hard that he tore a newly repaired hernia and had to go back three days later for keyhole surgery. Other cops, unchaining the machine, made god-awful jokes about ''money laundering'' as they took the crooks and the cash machine across the street. Spidey considered this yet another example of how absolutely anything can happen in New York, no matter how absurd you think it is.

The nice thing about ram raiding, though, was that it was fairly detectable. The sound of such a large amount of glass breaking at once, or of the clatter of metal shutters in the street, was much louder than mere vandalism usually produced. For a costumed hero with sharp ears, a built-in ESP-like warning system that he called his spider-sense, and an eye for trouble, it was a happy sound.

Spidey had an eye for trouble tonight. It was difficult, if not impossible, for even a super hero to punch out an entire phone company. But as surrogates for them, he would be more than glad to punch out any crooks he ran across tonight. It would be a small consolation, but better than nothing. Additionally, he had his little motion-controlled camera with him; should any action occur, he would get pictures of it, and tomorrow Peter Parker would take them in to the *Bugle* and see who might be interested in them.

He swung on down Park Avenue South a ways, humming absently to himself as he watched the traffic flow. Ahead of him, under the sodium lights, he could see several pickups of the kind favored for ram raiding, but they seemed to be going about their business peaceably enough. Nonetheless, he followed them for a while, watching the cross streets as he passed them by. It was pleasant to be doing a simple night's work for a change. The previous weeks' run-ins with Venom and the repeated revelations of the underhanded dealings of the Russian-backed import-export company CCRC had made life more complicated than he liked. Having Manhattan almost destroyed in a nuclear explosion a few weeks prior to that hadn't done much for his composure, either. "Super-villains," he muttered. "Fooey. Give me punks. I'm ready for punks."

He swung right down Park, practically to the Village, hung a right at Fourteenth, and headed west, past dozens of little stores that sold discount clothes, electrical equipment, and other odds and ends. But everything was surprisingly quiet; the city was well-behaved tonight.

Typical, he thought. *When you want a crook, you can never find them, but when you don't want them, they're everywhere.*

At Thirteenth and Sixth Avenue Spidey paused thoughtfully, looking down at the Burger King there from the skyscraper where he clung. One of the problems with web-swinging in this town was that cooking smoke and steam from restaurants and snack bars rose upward in a great cloud, and he could always smell them on his rounds. If he hadn't eaten before he left, he soon wished he had, and he almost always ate before he got home. MJ's comment was that the only creature in the city to which Spider-Man was *not* a hero was his refrigerator, because he robbed it himself every night.

MJ. . . . He swung along up Sixth a ways, thinking of her patient look as she sat at the kitchen table after that phone call. *How does she stay so calm?* It seemed to be a natural gift. Her bubbly personality didn't usually extend to noisy complaint, but she had confessed to him what serious fun she had had pitching a major fit one evening on this Miami trip in the direction of a misbehaving director—and the astonishment it provoked from the others in the area, especially those who had known MJ for a little while and had never heard her make a loud noise before. *There may be something to that approach,* he thought. *Save it for later, and people pay more attention—*

CRASH! Glass shattered not too far from him. Spidey paused in mid-swing, swung himself around to the plate-glass front of a building at Twenty-fourth and Sixth, and there held very still, listening above the soft roar of the city for the rest of the crash-and-tinkle. It always took a little while to settle down.

North, he thought, *and west. A block up.*

He spider-scuttled around the face of the building from the Sixth Avenue side to the side facing north, and there made a huge leap onto the roof of a convenient warehouse that stood directly across the street. He came down fairly in the middle of the roof without too much difficulty. Streets were pretty easy to jump: avenues were trouble, and he hadn't jumped one without webbing in a while.

He bounced across the building's roof to where it abutted with another, slightly taller; leapt up to that one's roof, scuttled straight across it to the Twenty-fifth Street side, paused, and peered over the square-cut, fake-castellated brick rampart that topped it out.

About halfway down the block between Sixth and Seventh on Twenty-fifth, a metallic brown Dodge four-by-four pickup had rammed the front of what looked to be a small jewelry store, whose alarm was ringing forlornly. The truck was sitting up on the sidewalk, nose well in through the dark window, while dark figures danced about the truck's hood, grabbing things out of the store, and stowing them away in their coats. Two other figures held long objects—assault rifles, Spidey guessed.

"New York, New York," Spider-Man muttered under his breath, smiling under the mask as he got out the camera and set it on the "rampart" on its little tripod, switching it on. The camera went *zzzt*, turning its "head" toward the action down in the street.

Spidey swung down.

He hit the first of the robbers with no warning whatsoever—his favorite way. He simply took him feet first in the back, knocking the gun the punk carried clear across the sidewalk and under a parked car. It skittered along the concrete, spitting sparks as it went, and Spidey had just enough time to recognize the shape. *Kalashnikov,* he thought. *Very stylish—not!*

The two crooks who had clambered in through the window and loaded themselves with stuff from the counters inside now noticed him. One of them stuffed a last glittering necklace inside his jacket, pulled out a pistol, and started emptying it at Spidey.

This, the crook shortly found, was a futile tactic. Spider-Man bounced around on the sidewalk, rather like a drop of water on a hot griddle, keeping the truck between him and the other two crooks, and waiting for the sound he wanted to hear: *bangbangbangbangbangbangbangbangclick.*

"Aha," Spidey said cheerfully. "That's a Glock, and you've had your seventeen." He jumped at the man, a big heavy guy with a five o'clock shadow several time zones ahead of itself. The crook was still fumbling for the replacement cartridge when Spidey's fist caught him just under the jaw, and sent him and the gun flying, it one way, he another. As the man flopped out of the way, his coat fell open and rained jewelry on the sidewalk.

From beyond the Dodge came more gunfire: some machine-gun, some pistol. Spidey ducked as the slugs whined and ricocheted around him on the pavement. "Impatient people," he muttered. "You'd think they'd wait and take better aim. But never mind.'' It was half a second's work to web his first crook up against the lightpost against which he had conveniently come to rest. After that, Spidey crouched down again and bounced toward the truck, ducking down behind it.

The guy with the Kalashnikov ran around one side, and the guy with the pistol around the other. It was as much as Spider-Man could have hoped for. ''Now, who says New Yorkers aren't considerate?'' Spidey said, shooting out a line of webbing and neatly tripping the guy with the pistol as he came around the corner of the Dodge. The crook slammed down onto the sidewalk; the pistol flew off to one side and embedded itself in a big lump of a substance for which there was a $50 fine for leaving it on the street.

''There's a message there somewhere,'' said Spidey— and then his spider-sense stung him, and he jumped right over the truck. Not a moment too soon: a spray of bullets dug a little crater on the spot of sidewalk where he had been crouching.

The crook ran for the driver's-side door of the Dodge and yanked it open. He had just gotten himself in behind the wheel when Spidey did the same with the passenger-side door, climbed up onto the cab step, and shot webbing all over the would-be driver, his gun, his legs, his arms, and anything else that showed. Then Spider-Man leaned in and pulled the keys out of the ignition, smiling at the furious, struggling man. ''You should have gotten out of Dodge while you could,'' he said and jumped out again.

Bullets rattled and whined off the truck's body. Spidey looked toward the jewelry store and saw the one remaining crook, whom he'd briefly forgotten. ''Can't have you feeling left out,'' he said as he rolled and bounced off the sidewalk, bounced again, and wound up clinging to one of the second-floor windows of the building that had been rammed.

The last crook stared wildly around him, spraying the

area with bullets. Spidey hugged the wall, only having to move a couple of times—the big jutting brownstone windowsill protected him somewhat. Then he heard the sound he wanted to hear—not so much a click, but a sort of *mmf,* as the Kalashnikov ran out of things to fire.

He jumped from the window and came right down on the fourth man. The gun spun away. The two of them rolled together briefly. The gunman struggled. Spidey reared a fist back. "Night night," he said, and struck.

A couple of moments later he stood up, breathing hard and looking around at the mess, then walked over to the truck, while hearing, in the distance, the sound of sirens approaching.

The inside of the truck's cab was surprisingly clean. *It's either brand new,* Spidey thought, *or I've come across a bunch of neat thugs.* The back of the flatbed was empty of everything but the boxes and jewelry that the crooks had tossed into it. But inside the cab, on the little parcel shelf under the back window, he found a cardboard box. On the outside it said A&P 12 O'CLOCK COFFEE. On the inside were four cell phones.

He reached in and looked at one. Considering his current mood, Spidey was tempted to chuck the thing across the road—but it was evidence. And who knew what numbers might be inside it?

He carefully took the box out of the truck and put it on the hood. Up and down the block, as Spidey looked up at the windows, he could see a venetian blind bend down, or a curtain twitch aside, as people looked curiously out and decided that what they saw was nothing to do with them. Inside the mask, Spidey smiled gently.

The sirens got closer. Spider-Man watched with some caution as the cop cars came around the corner, into Twenty-fifth. He was not universally loved by the police. Now two squad cars pulled up, and a third "unmarked" car: five uniformed officers got out, and a sixth, in shirt-sleeves and dark pants and a tie thrown over his shoulder, a face he knew. He last saw it months ago at an

NYPD safe house in the Bronx one time when Venom was in town.

"Sergeant Drew," Spider-Man said as the cops came up.

Stephen Drew nodded to him cordially enough; and said to one of his people, "See if you can't shut that thing off—it's enough to wake the dead." And for a moment he said nothing more as he walked around the scene and looked things over.

"Okay," he finally said to the others. "Get the web off these guys' hands, anyway, so we can cuff them and take them downtown. You caught them in the act, I take it," he said to Spider-Man.

"I did. Burglary anyway. Maybe grand-theft auto as well."

"Could be. Run the truck," he said over his shoulder, to one of his officers. "Now, what have we here?"

"Four cell phones, at least. There may be more hidden in the truck—"

"Not that," Drew said. "This." He took out a handkerchief, wrapped it around one hand, then bent over to pick up what was half sticking out from one of the parked cars nearby: the Kalashnikov machine gun.

"AK-47," said Spidey.

"Nope," said Drew, with odd relish.

Spider-Man blinked. "Nope? I thought I knew these guns pretty well."

"Take another look at this one." Drew held it out for Spidey to examine. "Check the muzzle."

Spidey looked at it, shook his head. "I'm not sure what I should be seeing."

"Bigger caliber," said Drew. "This isn't just Russian, it's Russian military. And—" He turned the gun over, looked at the stock for a moment, then raised his eyebrows. "Interesting. This doesn't even have the Russian Army brands or reg numbers on it."

"Is that good or bad?"

"I'd stick to 'interesting' for the moment," Drew

said. "But I doubt this was bought on the street here—
or, if it was, that it's been here for long."

"Russian . . ." Spidey said.

Drew turned the gun over again, looking at it. "Very
shiny . . ." he said. "Oh, Russian, yeah. And not just in
origin. I expect one or two of these guys are Russian
themselves."

Spidey nodded. It was no news to him, or anyone else
in New York, what new influence had become something to be reckoned with in the New York crime world.
When *perestroika* took hold and the old USSR fell,
many people who were not oppressed in the usual sense
of the word suddenly found themselves free to seek out
the Land of the Free. It wasn't finding work they had in
mind, though—again, not in the usual sense of the word.
The USSR had always had an active network of criminal
organizations. At the end of the Eighties, those organizations, as individuals and groups, had actively begun
colonizing the United States, in force, either to exploit
what they considered a profitable new market for crime,
or else to mine the U.S. for technology and new scams,
which they would then export to the growing consumer
economies in Russia and the former Eastern Bloc.

Drew took another look at the machine gun, unloaded
it, cleared it, and then peered down the barrel, squinting
a little in the golden light. "If I'm any judge of these
things," he said, "this hasn't seen a whole lot of use.
It's very new. Must just have come in. Possibly via Long
Island. There have been reports of some odd movements
among the fishing fleet, last week."

"Drew," Spider-Man said, amused, "is there any
gossip about shady stuff in this town that you don't
know about?"

Drew chuckled, glanced up. "If there were, I'd hardly
mention it. I have my rep to think of, after all. Let's see
those phones."

Spider-Man handed him the small box. Drew had a
look at them. "Top of the line, these," he said. "Ex-

pensive. They may be from a legit supplier—or they may have been traded as part of some money-laundering scheme. Either way, they'll have been cloning existing numbers into these. That way these guys can keep in touch with their bosses, while they're doing their dirty little jobs, and no one can trace them. They just ditch the phones when they're done, and steal new ones.''

''It's a subject,'' Spidey said, ''which has been interesting me lately.''

''You onto something?'' said Drew, catching the intensity in his voice.

''I don't know yet,'' Spider-Man said. ''I don't really know which questions to ask.''

''Well—'' Drew looked briefly embarrassed. ''You did me a mighty favor, once upon a time. Vance Hawkins wouldn't be alive if it weren't for you. Anybody does my partner that kind of favor, I tend to remember it. Look—''

The sound of more sirens was beginning to echo in the background. ''I've got to clean this scene up and get these guys out of here,'' Drew said. ''And the town is hopping tonight—at least the West Side is. Got a lot of stuff that's going to keep me busy. But if you'll give me a day, and then call me here—'' He reached into his pocket, pulled out his business card. ''If you've got some questions about 'cell crime,' I've got somebody who might be able to give you some info that'd be useful to you. Would that suit?''

''It'd suit very well. Thanks, Drew.''

''Hey, listen,'' Sergeant Drew said, as yet another squad car pulled up, ''like I said, favors are no good if you don't pass 'em back. And now I suggest you make yourself diplomatically scarce. I'll talk to you later in the week.''

''Right,'' Spidey said.

''Get outta here, bug,'' Drew growled, more (Spidey guessed) for the benefit of his men than anything else.

In a much better humor than he had been, Spider-Man

went straight up the wall and headed for Twenty-sixth Street, and taller buildings that would let him web quickly home.

Peter got up early the next morning, and spent a happy couple of hours in the darkroom, developing the pictures from the previous night. He had been experimenting with a new low-light 1200 ASA film, which got surprisingly good results under sodium-vapor lamps—even though, if you were too close to the light source, the shots tended to get a bit washed out. Luckily, these weren't washed out at all: the contrast was crisp and the color good, though flushed with the inevitable golden tint of sodium lighting.

There was the front of the jewelry store, there were the spilled jewels on the floor and the sidewalk, and there were the bad guys, also on the floor though a lot less pretty to look at, webbed into tidy or untidy packages as speed of capture had dictated. It was all very picturesque, and Peter went to his meeting with city editor Kathryn Cushing with a high heart.

Kate went through the prints one after another, picked one—a glittering strew of gemstones and jewelry catching the light, and for contrast, the dull, oiled-metal gleam of the machine gun lying alongside—and looked at it thoughtfully. "Are these guys anybody in particular?" she asked Peter.

"The cops thought they may have been Russian."

"Really?" She picked up a slick-surface pen and began making crop marks on the paper. "I like the color on this. Almost sepia tone. You do that on purpose, or is it just what the film produces under street light?"

"A little of both."

"Do I hear the sound of a man protecting his secrets? Well, never mind. It looks good. That's what matters. Russian, huh? Mel Ahrens would like this . . ." She pushed the picture away and leaned back in her office chair, steepling her fingers and staring at them for a moment. "Never mind that right now. You did a super job on the Miami end of things, Peter. A difficult assignment, but very good results. I wasn't entirely sure you had it in you." She grinned. "I don't mind admitting to being wrong. So now I want to start putting you on more high-profile work—and I think I have just the thing." She started rummaging around in her file drawer.

Peter had long since learned that the safest kind of response to this kind of rather mixed compliment was to smile and say nothing. But something was niggling at the back of his mind. "Forgive me for being nosy," he said, "but why would Mel Ahrens be interested in these?"

"Huh?" Kate looked up from the drawer for a moment. "Oh. He's been working on a series of stories on the Russian infiltration of the New York crime scene. Well, that's not quite right. He's been working on a book, and the paper's been printing extracts. Very interesting stuff—maybe a little too interesting." She went back to rummaging in her drawer. "Now where did I put that Belgian stuff? Now listen, Peter. Vreni Byrne spoke very highly of you in terms of—"

"Sorry," Peter said, "wait a minute. This is the guy that the mobsters keep trying to kill?"

Kate looked up, nodded. "The names change from week to week, but yes. Mel's been lucky so far, and he's such an alert guy that I could see why anyone who wanted him dead would need to move pretty fast."

"Does he need a photographer?"

She paused a moment then, and blinked. "Now that you mention it, over the past few weeks he *has* dropped some hints that he might need a photog to work with him occasionally. You were busy then, so I tried a couple of other people on him. It didn't take. He can be a hard man to get along with." Kate gave him a cockeyed look. "Are you saying *you* want to try? Wouldn't you rather go to Belgium and the South of France for a couple of weeks? I was thinking of sending you along with the stringer who's going to the European Film Festival in Brussels.''

''Uhhh . . .'' Peter stared at her. Then he said, ''Kate, I really like the sound of this.''

''Of what? Being shot at by men with heavy accents?''

''Not that, specifically. It's just that the Russian thing has been—interesting me for a while.'' *A very little while,* he thought.

Kate looked at him thoughtfully. ''You haven't actually met Mel, then.''

''No. I've heard the usual newsroom stuff, though. Isn't he one of the guys who made such a stink when we went over to computers?''

Kate laughed quietly. ''That was diplomatically put. You mean, the only guy who made even more of a stink than I did.'' She gave her own desktop terminal a sidelong look. ''Yeah, that's Mel. Well, I guess you might as well meet him. Be warned, though—I said he's kind of a hard man to work with. That's not just where his partners or assistants are concerned. He's got this tendency to jump in with both feet where—''

''Where angels fear to tread?'' Peter suggested.

''I was going to say, where walking softly would produce a better effect. Like not letting certain people know you're there at all. If this assignment works, then remember that he'll take you with him when he jumps. That could lead to trouble.''

''I think I can cope.''

''Good. Come on; I'll perform the introductions.''

Kate led Peter out to the City Room, right into the interdenominational desert of desks called, appropriately enough, No Man's Land. Most of these desks were for temporary use by journalists on short-term assignments, or by staffers in transition between one section of the paper and another. Robbie Robertson, the editor in chief, often referred to them as the ''Flying Dutchmen.''

Kate and Peter made their way across to one desk in

particular. There was a computer on it, and a great drift of papers, and—set pointedly in front of the computer monitor—the hunchbacked bulk of a splendid old 1940s-period Smith-Corona commercial typewriter. Black, with gold lettering and hair-fine gold lining along what Peter could only think of as its coach work, the typewriter gleamed with that deep patina that could only have come from much polishing throughout its working life.

"Wow," he said admiringly. "Just look at this thing. It *shines.*"

"He's gonna like you," Kate said with a certain air of amused resignation. "But then, he likes anybody who doesn't call it a piece of outdated junk."

"This isn't junk. It's an antique. No, it's more than an antique, it's—"

"It's a work of art," said a sharp voice from behind them.

Peter turned. From the stories he had heard about Mel Ahrens, and from the look of the desk, he had been expecting an older man. But the guy with the shock of blond hair who was advancing on him, one hand already extended to shake, couldn't have been more than in his late twenties.

"Mel," Katherine said, "this is Peter Parker. He's the photographer I mentioned to you a couple of weeks ago."

"So you're the one who keeps pulling in those action shots of Spider-Man," said Ahrens. "Good. Very good. Not like those other losers." He shot Kate a look. "Here, pull up a chair."

As they appropriated the chairs from a nearby empty desk, Peter looked around him at the other temporary desks. "Why have they stuck you over here?" he asked. "I mean, you've been working with the paper for a while now."

"A year or so, yeah." Ahrens laughed. "But I like the buzz here, the feeling of uncertainty. God knows, it's everywhere else in my work. At least this office gives me a background I'm familiar with. Sit, sit, sit.''

They did.

"That's a beautiful typewriter," said Peter.

"It's a noble instrument," said Ahrens, favoring Kate with another dirty look, "and if there were any justice in an unjust world, I'd be able to submit my stories typed on good heavy paper stock rather than using that travesty." He waved an accusing, dismissive hand toward the terminal that squatted dark and silent at the corner of his desk.

"Why don't you at least leave it running?" Kate said. "We've got perfectly good screen savers in the system."

"I have no desire to sit here and be irradiated by the thing," said Ahrens, "just for what someone else perceives to be my convenience. Which it's not, particularly, but never mind. I don't want to get into that all over again."

He turned to Peter and, as he did so, gave the gleaming black bulk of the typewriter an affectionate pat. "I typed the first story I ever sold on this machine," he said. "It was my dad's. And it will have to be pried from my cold, dead fingers before I give it up."

Peter smiled inwardly. If this was the notorious Ahrens eccentricity, at least it seemed amiable enough, and the other things he had heard about the man suggested that Mel could be granted the right to a little bit of eccentric behavior. He had heard a lot of people around the *Bugle* refer to Ahrens as an old-fashioned newshound in a young body. Very sharp, they said; a good writer who never missed a deadline, a man with an eye for detail in both story and pictures, and a real gift for helping his photographer to find just the right picture for a given story.

"Has Kathryn told you what I'm working on?" he asked Peter.

"In general."

"I just brought him over so you could fill him in,"

said Kate. "You mentioned something about a photo opportunity coming up."

Ahrens laughed. "Yeah, and I just bet the people involved in it think that as well. It's the night after next."

Kate raised one eyebrow. "So soon? Then I presume you've already put all your affairs in order."

"If you mean, am I leaving you my porcelain collection, then the answer is no. You're greedy, you know that?"

"Where Meissen is concerned, I've known it for a long time," said Kate, standing up. "I'll leave you to your briefing." She nodded to Peter, then headed back to the elevator.

The two of them sat back in their chairs and looked at each other. Peter was very aware that Ahrens was studying him, sizing him up, almost filing him away in a mental card file. He smiled thinly and returned the favor with a long, hard stare.

Mel Ahrens nodded at last, after a few seconds of intense scrutiny that had seemed more like minutes. "I saw the Kennedy Space Center pictures," he said. "Those were pretty impressive. You've got something of a head for heights."

Peter grinned. "A little. They've never really bothered me."

"Well, it's the depths we're heading for this time," said Ahrens, reaching into his desk drawer and coming up with a Tootsie Roll. "Want one?"

"No, thanks."

Ahrens chuckled and unwrapped the candy slowly, then swung his feet up onto the desk, narrowly missing Peter as he did so. "The Russians," he said. "This is going to sound funny, but they really have a gift for organized crime. And they're independent. The American version of the Mafia has always had associations, however distant, with the old *Cosa Nostra* from Sicily and Southern Italy. Tradition and old habits, maybe. But the Russians, no. When the reforms began, when *glas-*

nost and *perestroika* set in for real and the Wall came down, they realized that the West was the place to be.

"Whole families have been relocating in the U.S. for some years now, including *crime* families. One of the favorite cover stories," he chuckled a little ruefully, "was religious persecution. A very sensitive subject, that, and a very powerful argument. It would be a very determined U.S. administration that would refuse. A lot of them claimed to be Jews, and some of them even are—but nothing like as many carrying papers that say so. That way they were able to gain direct asylum in the States, or favored immigration status through Israel. Or Germany. The Germans had very liberal asylum laws."

"And again," said Peter, "that claim of religious persecution was one that Germany would be reluctant to ignore."

"Exactly," said Ahrens. "But either way, the big gangs severed their ties with the Mother Country and started moving here. Needless to say," he coughed, delicately, "certain, ah, concerns already well entrenched here didn't take too kindly to the intrusion. You get the occasional turf war. Well, more than occasional. That sort of free and frank exchange of views has been getting very active lately. Last night, apparently."

"These pictures," said Peter, pulling another sheaf of prints from their envelope and handing them over.

"Yes, indeed," said Ahrens with great satisfaction. He studied each picture in turn, then looked intently at the close-up of the assault rifle. "Well, well. This is a Kalashnikov AK-74. You can tell by the shape of the muzzle brake. Among other things."

"The policeman I spoke to at the scene said that this was an army-issue weapon."

"A *current* army-issue weapon," Ahrens corrected. "Everybody who thinks they know about military weapons in the hands of criminals goes on at length about the AK-47." Peter stifled a smile. Ahrens might well have said just that to Spider-Man last night. "After all, the old regime handed them out to satellite states and, ah, freedom fighters, rather like a jolly uncle with a box of candies.

"However," Ahrens tapped the photo, "this is another matter. It's frontline equipment, and something the Soviets *never* did was to give away or export anything they were still using themselves. Tanks were stripped to the basics, aircraft had inferior weapons and radar, that sort of thing. They called them 'monkey models.'

"The AK-74 rifle isn't quite state of the art, of course—at least, not so far as the West is concerned. *Guns & Ammo* wouldn't be terribly excited about it. No caseless ammunition, no flechette projectiles, not even an impressive rate of fire. It does its job quite adequately, however, and that's all the Soviet military ever worried about. Funny thing, though—"

"No issue numbers."

"Exactly. This was never in service. It came straight from the factory into the hands of whoever was using it last night—and I notice they weren't wearing Russian uniforms. Like every other manufacturer in the former Soviet Union, the armaments industry is desperate for hard currency now that its major customer has almost stopped buying. My guess is that this gun, and the rest of whatever consignment it came from, was acquired by barter. That method avoids leaving a trail, either paper or electronic."

"What about the end-user certificate scam?" asked Peter. "A legal arms sale to a second party, who's already arranged to pass the goods on down the line to a third. After all, counterfeit end-user certificates are supposed to be the third most popular forgery on the planet, after money and passports." Ahrens raised his eyebrows, and Peter shrugged innocently. "Hey, I'm a photojournalist," he said, then grinned broadly. "And I've been reading Frederick Forsyth for years."

Ahrens's own smile was a good deal thinner. He nodded, just once, and continued to leaf through the photographs.

"Anyway," Peter continued more soberly, "I've been hearing about a lot of Russian activity over the past few months. That CCRC thing."

"Yes. A nasty business. The whole affair was a bucket of dirty water so deep that I don't think the authorities have reached the bottom yet. There were more scams and scandals being run out of that place than—well, never mind. And I have a feeling that what wasn't discovered in time has already been hived off to other holding companies."

"They would have to be, I guess. The parent organization was supposed to be shut down. There's going to be some huge audit of it."

"The only way to audit a company like that is with a battering ram at three in the morning," said Ahrens firmly. "Anything that needed to be shredded has been confetti for a long time now. The government, the authorities, even the IRS, are never going to find all the evidence they need. It's hopeless. A waste of time and resources. You can't give people like CCRC time to cover their tracks. And they're just one aspect of what's been going on."

"So? What else?"

Mel took a moment to munch on another Tootsie Roll. "The mobs in New York," he said, "Coney Island and Brooklyn, have really stepped up their activities in the past few months. By something over a hundred percent, according to one of my better-informed sources." Peter whistled through his teeth. "They've been getting into new rackets. Oriental, some of them. Franchised from the Triads, for all I know. But it all eventually turns into money laundering, and there's been a lot of laundry done. Massive amounts. Do you know where the biggest supply of U.S. bank notes is, outside of the continental United States?"

Peter shook his head.

"Russia. It's partly because they trust our currency more than they trust their own. The government there still isn't completely stable, at least not enough to be relied on when you're dealing with sums of money the size of small national debts. They tried to cut in on money laundering at a national level a few years ago by just abruptly withdrawing all the currency and issuing a new print—but it didn't work, because nearly all the laundering was already in dollars rather than rubles anyway."

"Laundering how, specifically?"

"Mr. Forsyth hasn't gotten into this yet, eh?" said Ahrens, with a little flicker of dry amusement. "All right, here's how the laundry works. First thing is to conceal who really owns the money, and where it came from. There's no point in laundering at all if the origin is still known at the end of the process. Next, you've got to change its shape, preferably by increasing the value of each bill. If you're starting out with ten million dollars in twenties, you don't want to finish up with the same thing."

"Even if all the bills now have different serial numbers?"

"Not good enough. You want *no* leads. Also, think logistics. If you change to higher-denomination bank notes, your ten mil at once becomes a much smaller package. That's why the Treasury took the thousand-dollar bill out of circulation—"

"I never saw enough of them to notice," said Peter sourly, but Ahrens didn't even notice the interruption.

"—so that now it takes ten times as much paper, ten times as much bulk, to shift the same amount of cash from one place to another. It makes a transfer less convenient and more noticeable. Useful for surveillance.

"So." Ahrens held up one hand and started counting points off on his fingers. "You want the origin of the money hidden, and you want the size of the bundle to shrink without reducing its value. Then the actual laundry trail itself has to be hidden. Why go to all that trouble if each step can be followed backwards?''

"I see your point." Peter was beginning to understand why there had been attempts on Ahrens's life. He was hearing a lecture on theory, but that theory was based on practical knowledge. The quickest way to get rid of what someone knew had always been to get rid of the someone.

"But the last and I suppose the most important thing is that you, or people you can trust implicitly, have to retain control of the money at every step of the laundering process. If the whole purpose of what you're doing is to make sure that nobody can prove this money was yours in the first place, then if it's stolen, you're in trouble. If it's dirty money, you can't exactly go to the police, and even if it's *clean* money, the tax folks are going to take an unhealthy interest in why you were laundering it in the first place.

"Let's try the double-invoice method. One end of the laundry is, let's say, a grocery store. The other is a wholesaler who sells stuff to the grocery store. And you're both friendly. The same nationality, the same Family, whatever." He pronounced the capital letter without difficulty. "One day you order fifty barrels of borscht from your wholesaler."

"Does borscht come in barrels?"

"Who knows? I'm not a beet fan. Anyway, it might look like your wholesaler isn't a fan, either, because he only sends you forty barrels—but then the person 'doing the laundry' hands you cash to make up the shortfall. That money, dirty for whatever reason, gets into the system disguised as clean. It looks fine to the bookkeepers, fine to the tax people, and pretty soon, if that's doing well, you open another grocery store and start ordering more borscht. The more legal outlets you have, the better it gets.

"Well," Ahrens leaned back in his chair and looked at Peter, "Brooklyn and the Bronx, parts of Staten Island

and Nassau County, are all awash in that sort of legal outlet, all busily invoicing for less than they've delivered, and all laundering money like it's going out of style. But that's just one of the things the Russian mobs are getting involved with. They do the usual organized crime stuff: protection, numbers, gambling, all the rest. But in the past few months, for some reason the volume of money laundering has skyrocketed. At least, so my sources tell me, and I've no reason to doubt the accuracy of their information. But nobody knows why—or if they do know, they're not telling.''

Ahrens reached into the drawer again for more Tootsie Rolls. ''Sure you don't want one? Fine. Anyway, something else has been happening. A lot of the big bosses made themselves very comfortable in New York. They bought themselves big apartments, they brought their families over, they settled right into the city. Like it or not, Russian organized crime was becoming just one more community—very clubby. But now all of a sudden several of them are getting ready to leave town. One of them bought himself a little private island down in the Caymans. Another bought some place in the Bahamas that Tony Stark didn't need anymore. A third now owns a chunk of rock in the British Virgin Islands, and he's having it covered with a beautiful—and heavily fortified—holiday mansion.''

''Why all this sudden interest in the Caribbean?'' said Peter. ''More money laundering? I remember hearing that the Cayman Islands are almost as good as Switzerland for private banking.''

''Could be,'' said Ahrens. ''Certainly the BVI is a tax haven, and the status of several other islands is still under negotiation. They might be owned by the Dutch, or they might be owned by the French, or they might be completely independent—or they might be open for sale to the right buyer. One with enough money. But the coincidence struck me as odd. It can't just be conspicuous consumption for its own sake. That's not these people's style, or they'd have been doing it a long time ago.''

''Are they afraid that things might be getting too legally hot for them in the States?''

''I don't think so. They've been flouting various tax laws here, almost like they're testing to see how far they can push. And so far, they've been getting away with it thanks to expert legal help. Locally sourced, of course. As for the money laundering, their trails have been professionally concealed. So far there's no evidence stronger than suspicion.''

Ahrens shifted his legs, touched the gleaming typewriter slightly with the edge of one shoe, and leaned forward at once to polish away a mark Peter couldn't even see.

''Something is going on. I don't know what it is, and that's what's making me crazy. Call it just basic nosiness, but there's a connection somewhere, and I can't find out what.''

That *would* drive him crazy, thought Peter. And as for this man being just ''basically nosy,'' then water was just ''basically wet.'' ''Even if trying to find out might get you killed?'' he said.

''I don't think it'll do that. I've got a fairly good rapport with some of these people, and enough college Russian to get by—though they seem to prefer practicing English on me. It's the usual thing.'' Ahrens chuckled dryly. ''They want to become experts in the local language, since it'll make exploiting the locals so much easier. And as for the others, the real hard men, I've been able to stay out of their way.''

Peter looked thoughtfully at the casual jacket Ahrens was wearing. The cut was loose enough that a fairly big handgun could be concealed beneath it. Ahrens caught the look and nodded.

''Yes,'' he said. ''Heckler and Koch VP-70Z, if you're interested. The civilian version, not the full-auto. With a full concealed-carry permit, of course. I've done

the police department a few good turns in the past—
strictly on the Q.T.—and they've been more than happy
to return the favor. But that's not the point at the moment. Would you be willing to work with me on this
for the next couple or few weeks? As I said, things are
heating up for some reason, and I—we—need to know
why. I can't call it any more than a gut feeling, but that
feeling tells me that something profoundly threatening
to this entire city is getting ready to happen. If there's
something I can find out, then maybe it won't come as
a complete surprise."

"Maybe it can even be stopped dead," said Peter.

"Maybe." Then Ahrens grinned at him. "But like I
said before, I'm just nosy. I want to know what these
people are doing."

Peter smiled back. That kind of nosiness he was entirely familiar with. It was probably what prompted his
next question. "How good a shot are you?"

"I'm okay. I shoot twice a week at the range, and I
can usually hit what I'm aiming at. The rest of the time,
I try not to think about it. The whole point of a Veep-
70 is that it's got lots of bullets; that helps keep heads
down while you vacate the premises. But don't forget
that among these people, guns are a badge of rank as
much as a weapon. So I wear the badge. Without it, you
might not even get past the front door of some places.
That's not to say they aren't something to be used. At
least it doesn't happen as often as with—other import
organizations."

"That sounds good enough for me," Peter said.
"When do you think you'll need me?"

"Tomorrow night. I've got an interview under slightly
unusual circumstances. One of the local, I guess mafiosi
is the best word for them—"

"Or mafioski, maybe?"

"Very nice," said Ahrens, grinning again as he scrib-
bled the word onto a pad. "I like it. Anyway, this character seems to have an ax to grind regarding some of

the competition. If I'm reading him properly, he might be willing to shed some light on the sudden increase in local 'business'; and what's going on with these king-pins who've suddenly all decided to go ex-pat together. So far as I can make out, they're all rivals rather than allies; in a couple of cases it goes as far as hatred. So it's not a linkup or a business deal. That could be done as easily on-site. Something else is going on."

"And you think this could have links to CCRC as well?"

"It might. I'm putting out feelers in that direction, but it'll take a couple of weeks before I get any feedback."

"Okay. But in the meanwhile, you've got a photographer." He stood up. "Thanks for the background detail."

"The free lecture, you mean," said Ahrens, also rising. "I charge for the college-level one." He put out his hand again, and they shook. "Where shall we meet?"

"Here's good enough."

"Five o'clock Thursday, then."

"Five it is."

Peter flicked one hand to his brow in a casual hail-and-farewell and turned away. As he did, the phone rang, and an expression of loathing crossed Ahrens's face as various of its lights began to flash. "This thing has too many buttons," he said, jabbing one at random as he picked up the handset. "Hello?" There was no reply from the evidently wrong line, so there was a quick sequence of more buttons being punched and a steadily more irritable repetition of "Hello"'s before he finally got it right.

Peter walked away, smiling at the performance. Then his smile went a little sour. If that display of techno-phobia was anything to go by, then Ahrens would never have a cell phone—or a four-thousand-dollar bill generated by someone else.

He shot a final glance over his shoulder as he made for the stairwell rather than the elevator. Ahrens had reluctantly moved his beloved Smith-Corona aside and switched on his monitor, but as the screen came up he could see a saver program that was plainly one of Ahrens's own devising. The words crawled slowly across the screen, black on white, as close to type on paper as the phosphors could create.

I Will Be Obsolete Some Day.

Peter went downstairs. "CCRC," he muttered to himself. That corporation had been involved in so much recently that he half expected to find them under every stone. First they had stored toxic waste in New York City. Then they had transported it covertly both cross-country and overseas for illegal reprocessing, theft and money laundering of their own, counterfeiting . . .

It was a big, tangled web, and now here was another strand of it, while he remained the same small spider in the middle, trying to make sense of the weave, trying to unravel it, and at the same time doing his best not to be strangled by it in the process.

He almost wished he could get in touch with Venom, to ask him some very pointed questions about his own research into CCRC. That research had brought Venom clear across the country, from—Peter assumed—somewhere near San Francisco straight to the center of the CCRC-financed and -managed smuggling operation in the Florida Everglades. Toxic waste again, for reprocessing.

But even if he knew where Venom had gone after suddenly removing himself from the scene in Florida, Peter couldn't really bring himself to make the first move. After all, Venom and Spider-Man still had some unfinished business.

Spider-Man was still alive.

No, he told himself. *Even if you knew his phone number, calling for advice would not be a good idea. And anyway, you might be finding out a few things all by yourself in the next few days. Wait and see.*

Peter headed home.

THREE

A bout 9:30 the next morning, Peter was sitting at the kitchen table with the phone more or less glued to his ear. That ear was beginning to hurt, less from the pressure of the phone than from the sound of a slightly deranged computer at the other end playing "Für Elise" in a horrible electronic harpsichord-tinkle. And playing it, moreover, for the eighteenth time.

A voice said, "Are you holding for someone?"

Peter looked at the sketch pad on the table in front of him. It was covered with curly lines and little arrows, scrawled in a helpless sort of way while listening to the hold music ritually slaughtering Ludwig van Beethoven. In amongst the squiggles were several names, each one crossed out by increasingly heavy layers of scribble. "I'm waiting for, uh, Mr. Jaeger."

"He's on another line. Will you hold?"

The temptation to shriek, *Do I have a choice, since it took me the best part of an hour to get past your voice-mail system?* was very strong, but he restrained himself with a massive effort. "Yes, I'll hold. Thank you." The hold music, as remorseless as a Chinese water torture, started playing "Für Elise" again.

Peter tuned out its tinkly mutilation of melody—he'd had plenty of practice so far this morning—and stared out of the window, into the bright day and the smog. A butterfly went by. It was a big monarch, and it wasn't moving with the usual aimless flutter. This particular butterfly not only had places to go and people, or at least other butterflies, to see, it was flying with the sort of purpose that suggested a flight plan logged with La Guardia Control.

Peter desperately wished he could be out there with it instead of trapped in the Seventh Circle of Hold Hell. *I brought this on myself,* he thought. Earlier that morning, when MJ had gotten up still thoroughly depressed about the phone bill, he had foolishly offered to give them a call.

She had looked at him wistfully, then after a moment

75

said, "I guess it couldn't hurt, really. The world isn't entirely liberated yet. Maybe the sound of a guy's voice. . . ."

"All right," he had said. "You go and get your hands ready for work, and I'll give them a try."

With a sunny dawn ahead, and a satisfying night behind him in which he had not only pounded some bad guys, but possibly also gained a lead that might help with the phone bill, there had seemed no harm in trying. After all, if it could be resolved this way, then he wouldn't have to bother Sergeant Drew's contact. And so he had innocently called CellTech, and asked to speak to someone in customer service.

Or rather, he had *tried* to ask. CellTech prided itself on the sound quality of its system, and several times Peter had started talking to what he had thought was a genuine human being, only to find that the voice was human only at one remove: a recorded voice linked to a voicemail computer possessed of all the literalness of the species.

Its courteous little voice kept telling him that "if you have a question about routine billing, please press one. If you are interested in new services, please press two. For all other inquiries, please press three."

He had pressed three and had continued to press three, early and often, as each time the system made a polite electronic hiccup and said, "Please enter your account number, followed by the number sign."

When he did so, there had been another hiccup. "Please spell your name using the alphabet keys on your phone and ending with the number sign. Please enter your last name first. For Q or Z, please use the number one."

If they already have my account number, why do they need my name as well? Peter had wondered as he started tapping at the keys. And that was when the problems began. The phone's keypad was quite small, and his fingers were quite large, and every time he hit the wrong key that dulcet voice would say, "I'm sorry, the name you have entered does not match any in our records. Please try again."

By the fourth or fifth time, he simply wanted to punch the voice in whatever passed for its face. So he hung up, took a few deep breaths, then dialed again and this time tried for a routine billing inquiry.

"If you want to verify your account balance, please press one. If you wish to add another user to your account, please press two. If you want . . ." It then went on at some length, detailing a number of options which he most definitely did *not* want, then finally said, "For all other account inquiries, please press six."

Peter had mashed his index finger down on six with all the pent-up fury of an exasperated world leader starting World War III. The phone hiccuped, and the voice told him what he should have been expecting all along.

"I'm sorry, all our accounts personnel are busy. Your call will be answered by the next available operator. Please hold." And that was when they began playing "Fúr Elise" at him.

The first real person he had spoken to had sounded seriously hungover, and a veneer of businesslike briskness hadn't done much to conceal that fact. "CellTech-Customer-Services-Brian-here-how-may-I-help-you?" was all run together like the health warning at the end of a pharmaceutical commercial and uttered in a hoarse growl.

"I have a question about a very large bill," Peter began.

There was a pause at the other end that suggested more clearly than any words that the very large bill was Peter's problem, and nobody else's. "Your account number, please?"

Peter rattled off the number, deciding that he preferred speaking it to typing it out on the keypad.

Another pause. "I'm sorry, but I'm not authorized to give you any information on that account."

"What? Oh, because it's in a girl's name and I'm a boy. That's all right. I'm her husband. Peter Parker. She's Mary Jane Watson-Parker."

"I'm sorry, but I'm not authorized to give you any information on that account." The repetition was so exact that for a second Peter thought he was back with the voicemail system again. This guy, he had thought, has been spending too much time around his firm's computers. "Ms. Watson-Parker will have to call us herself and ask for an authorization number. If she gives that to you and you give it to us, then we can give you the account information you require."

Peter raised his eyebrows a little, but the intention behind the request was honest enough: protecting the customer. "Okay, will do. Thanks."

He called MJ on her cell phone, and the first sound he heard was a yawn. At that point it was only about 8:30, and what with fretting about the bill, MJ hadn't slept well.

"Hello?"

"Hi, hon, it's me. Listen, the CellTech people won't talk to me until you talk to them and tell them that it's all right for them to talk to me."

"Uh, yeah. I got that. I think. A pity they wouldn't let anyone else use my phone number without asking me if it was all right."

"I know. Look, can you call them? Otherwise I'm not going to be able to get anywhere with them." He read her the number quickly. "Just beware of the demon voicemail. Hit one for routine billing, then go for other options; that's, uh, six."

"Okay, Tiger. I'm on it."

About ten minutes later the phone rang again, and he picked it up. "Wow," said MJ's voice, "bureaucracy is *not* dead, is it?"

"Yeah, I get that sense. But did they give you a number?"

"Eventually. Here, write it down." She rattled off a

number that had no obvious connection to the account number. "Got that?"

"Yeah." He read it back, twice, to be sure.

"Great. See what you can do with them."

"And how are *you* doing?"

"Oh, fine."

"Still doing the suds?"

"Yeah." There was a snicker at the other end of the line. "Petey, I am *never* going to use this stuff."

"Why? Do they give you tons of freebies after the commercial? Does it bother you?"

"No—and if they did give me any, I'd chuck it out. They've put a sort of tea-rose scent in it, and, well . . ." She chuckled again, very softly, and the sound of her voice on the phone changed slightly as if she had cupped her hand around her mouth to muffle what she was about to say. "Remember the roach powder we had to get one time? It's exactly like that . . ."

Peter made a face. It had taken weeks to get the smell of the stuff out of the kitchen; the stalest, most oversweet rose perfume that anyone could ever have conceived. It had smelled, well, pink. "As bad as that, huh?"

"Worse. This is their new 'flower-fresh' fragrance"— she smothered a nasty laugh—"and if this is what they think flowers smell like. . . . Anyway, look, they're about to start. I'll call you back. Bye."

"Bye."

Peter dialed again, fought his way through the gauntlet of the voicemail system to where the live people had been hiding, and waited until finally a familiar, still-hungover voice said, "CellTech-Customer-Services-Brian-here-how-may-I-help-you?"

"Hi, this is Peter Parker. I spoke to you a few minutes ago about getting an authorization code so that I can discuss my wife's account. I have that number now."

"Thank you, sir. What is it, please?" Peter read it out, then waited through the inevitable pause.

"I'm sorry, sir; that number isn't showing on our system."

All the phone calls my wife didn't make are sure as hell showing on your system, Peter wanted to say, but he didn't. "Maybe that's because she just got the number?" he suggested. "The authorization number, I mean."

"That wouldn't normally be the case, sir—uh-oh." This time the pause was far longer than usual.

"Uh-oh?" Peter echoed mildly. That was not a noise he liked hearing from anybody who was so plainly dominated by the technology surrounding him.

"I'm sorry, sir. The system's gone down. Can I get you to call us back in, say, ten or fifteen minutes?"

"Certainly," said Peter and hung up as gently as he could.

That exchange set the tone for the next hour. He called back three times to find the system still down. The fourth time, it was refreshing itself and wouldn't be back online for another ten minutes. That response was the first sensible thing he had heard all morning. Refreshment.

Peter got up and made himself a cup of coffee, very strong, with a lot of sugar. Then he sat at the table again, and stared at the phone, and drank his coffee very slowly, thinking that maybe Mel Ahrens's attitude to modern technology wasn't quite so eccentric after all. He also couldn't help hoping, at least a little, for some kind of emergency to crop up that required Spider-Man's presence. Web-swinging—not to mention hitting something very hard—carried a certain amount of appeal just now.

Gamely, he dialed again, battled his way through the voice mail, and this time, to his relief, failed to find Hello-this-is-Brian-nursing-his-hangover.

"CellTech-Customer-Services-this-is-Alan-how-may-I-help-you?" Well, this one sounded bright and eager to please. It made a pleasant change. He greeted this-is-

Alan courteously enough, gave him the authorization code, and this time not only was it in the computer, but the computer stayed up and running.

"So, how can I help you, Mr. Parker?"

"I'm trying to work out what can be done about this particular phone bill. . . ."

Slowly and patiently, Peter told the whole story, while Alan listened and made encouraging noises. But finally he said, "I'm sorry, there's not a great deal I can do to help you. Under the present regulations, your wife remains responsible for the calls, and when the bill comes due, she's going to have to pay it."

"That's going to be a real problem."

"I understand it's going to be a problem for you, Mr. Parker. But please bear in mind, this kind of thing is a problem for us as well. We still have to pay the government a tariff on every minute of telecommunications used by our service on the frequencies which they lease to us, and this year already CellTech has paid over two million dollars to cover what have been fraudulent calls. We have to recoup those funds somehow, and I'm afraid that until the regulatory structure changes, it has to come from our clients."

"But isn't there anything that can be done to establish where the calls came from, or who did this, or even just to prove that they weren't made by my wife or with her permission?"

They went back and forth over it, and Alan was understanding, very understanding indeed. Professionally so, Peter thought. But it always came back to the same response: there was nothing that could be done. Finally he fell silent, and in that silence thought he sensed Alan twitch just a little bit.

"Mr. Parker," he said, "I'm sorry for your trouble. I really am." There was another silence. "I can do this. I can add—we'll call it an adjustment period—two weeks onto the due date of your bill. That way you won't have to pay until the fifteenth. Would that help you a little?''

''It's certainly better than nothing,'' Peter said. ''And it might even give us a chance to establish where those calls really came from.''

''If you can get the police to help with that, it would be your best bet,'' said Alan. ''I'm sorry I can't be more helpful, but that's about all I can do.''

''Listen, I guess it's as much as we could have hoped for. Do you have an ID number or something, so that we can call you back?''

''No, sir. Just ask for Alan. Alan Soames.''

''Thanks again for your help, Alan. I really appreciate it.''

''Anytime, Mr. Parker. Thank you for calling Cell-Tech. Good-bye.''

Peter hung up, feeling both disgusted and at the same time guilty about his disgust. The guy had really been trying to help, and had sounded genuinely sorry that he hadn't been able to do more. Now he was left with the same problem as before, except that the date of execution had been postponed a little.

If we still have to pay this, he thought, *then there goes our safety net.*

But if those extra couple of weeks gave either him or MJ or both of them the chance to make some extra money, then it might not be so bad. He stared at the coffee cup, still a quarter full of now-cold, sweet coffee, then got up, went to the sink and emptied it out, then poured himself another cupful and over-sugared that, too.

No solution for this problem, not yet. But boy, if I ever catch the guy who cloned MJ's phone. . . . He shook his head at himself, and sat down. Murder was of course out of the question, but when the guy or guys were turned in, and if Spider-Man was responsible for their capture, then he intended to make sure they got a little wasted first. For MJ's sake, as well as for his own.

The sound of keys in the lock brought his head up suddenly. At least, it sounded like keys. Was someone trying to pick the lock? The first deadbolt was thrown, then the second; and the chance of anyone doing that with a lock pick was pretty minuscule.

The door opened and MJ stalked in. She looked around, saw him sitting at the table, and threw him an expression of such fury and sadness and upset that he stood up and went straight to her. "MJ, what's the matter?"

"I cut my hand," she said and waved her bandaged left hand at him as if it were something offensive. "I cut my *hand!*" This time it was more of a wail.

Having received his share and then some of bruises and cuts during his career as a super hero, Peter assumed the worst. "Let me see. Is it bad? Do you have to go to the hospital? Will it need stitches?"

He took her hand gently between both of his, turned it over, and eased off the bandage. Then he let out a long sigh of relief. There was a gash running across the first and second knuckles, but it was thin and shallow, already dry and clotted. He hadn't known what to expect, but at least this was no worse than any kid might pick up after a fall in the schoolyard.

"Want me to kiss it and make it better?" he said.

She glared at him. "Better not. If you start it bleeding again, then I might really lose my temper." She flumped down into the chair, looking flushed and angry beyond all reason.

"You're back early," said Peter.

MJ snorted. "You're damn right I'm back early. I can't work anymore today. God knows if I'm going to work anymore, ever!" She reached for his coffee cup and eyed the contents. "Sugar?"

"A lot."

"Good." She took a long swig. "We were shooting, and things were fine, until about half an hour in. Just after we talked. Then somebody tripped over a lighting tripod behind me. You know, the tall ones with the spots on top? They fell, the tripod went over, and I tried to catch it. I should never have done that, never. Always trying to be helpful.'' She took another gulp of coffee. ''One of those big knurled locking nuts had a rough place on it. It caught the back of my hand as it went over. So now I'm out of work.''

''What? Did they fire you just because you cut your finger?''

''Well, what else could they do? Anyway, they didn't fire me. They just—let me go until this thing heals. But they're on a tight schedule. They're not going to be able to hold the shoot for me, and no one's going to use me for anything anyway until this is better. And what if it scars?''

Her frustration was palpable. Peter sat down with her, and took that hand again, and held it. ''Have you ever scarred before? I mean, you must have cut your hands. Lots of people do.''

''I don't, usually. At least, I don't think so.'' She looked at both hands. ''I can't even remember the last time I got a good cut. But it doesn't matter. Scar or not, it's going to be weeks before this heals so you can't see it anymore, and at least a week before they can even think of covering it with makeup. Anyway, even if they could use makeup, it would have to be waterproof because of the suds and things, and waterproof makeup's far too thick for the sort of close-up shooting that they need. . . . Oh, Tiger.''

She put her head down on her folded hands and let out a long breath. ''So much for a thousand bucks a day.''

''Aren't they even going to pay you for what you did today?''

''I don't know. When I left, they were still discussing whether they could use the footage they had, or scrap it and bring in another model. I assume that union rules mean I'll get paid for the couple of hours' work this

morning; but I doubt I'll get the whole day's worth."
She sighed. "This is so *infuriating*. Never mind. How
did you do with the phone company?"

"Better than I expected, but nothing like as well as I
had hoped." As he explained, her face fell further.
"They were pretty good about it, but I've a feeling
there's only so much slack they'll cut us. We'll have to
cope. But I did get one scrap of information last night
that might be of use."

"Yeah, last night. I was too dozy to pay much attention when you came in."

"And I was too tired to tell you much, so you didn't
miss a thing." He told her briefly about his meeting with
Mel Ahrens. When he got the bit about the Russian Mafia, MJ started to shake her head.

"Those are not nice people," she said.

"Well, I would have thought that came as part of the
job description."

"No, I mean . . . There's been so much about them in
the news lately. And they're not like the Italian gangsters—they always seem to be more careful about involving innocent bystanders. But these guys—if they
even think you're any sort of threat at all, they'll shoot
you."

"You've been watching too many movies. They're all
crooks, they're all dangerous, and they'll all involve as
many bystanders as they need to get the job done. Besides, I'm not that easy to shoot. Some of them found
that out last night."

He told her about the Kalashnikov-toting ram raiders.
She tsked at him—then looked slyly at him from the
corner of one eye. "All that jewelry, and you didn't
bring me any."

"Now, now. Some of the police are uncertain enough
about Spider-Man as it is. All it would take would be
me seen lifting one little stone, or one pretty necklace,
and that would be it. Open season on web-slingers."

"I guess so."

"Hey, you've got a girl's best friend already. You don't need any more diamonds than the one you've got on your finger right now."

"I don't know about *that!* You know what they say: you can never be too thin, too rich—or have too many sparklies."

"I don't think I've heard that last bit before."

"Maybe not. But all the same, I like this diamond a lot. And I like you a lot." Then she grinned. "But what was this other lead you were talking about?"

Peter tapped Sergeant Drew's card, lying on the table among the other paperwork left over from last night. "It seems he has somebody coaching him where cell phone fraud is concerned. I'm supposed to give him a call today or tomorrow, then go talk to his technical adviser. Whoever he is."

"Or she," MJ put in.

"Okay. Or they. Drew was walking a company line; the police are always pretty closemouthed about 'private contractors.' "

"Do you think he-she-they can help us?"

"I don't know. But it's worth investigating, anyway. Even just for the sake of general information."

MJ got up and went over to the coffeepot. "So, what's the plan?"

"I'm going out with Ahrens tonight, to cover an interview with some disgruntled Russian crook who might spill a few cans of beans on his ex-comrades."

She looked over her shoulder at him, the sunlight from the kitchen window catching in her hair and setting it ablaze. "I really don't like this, Peter," she said. "It's bad enough that Spider-Man has to deal with crooks and gangsters, but if you're going as Peter Parker—"

"Spider-Man comes too. Even if he doesn't show. You know that. If I have to move fast to get out of harm's way, then I'll move first and look for explanations afterwards. An adrenaline rush or something like that. Look, Ahrens was being cautious, but I didn't get any feeling that he was worried about his safety.''

"That's fine for him," said MJ. "But it's *your* safety that *I'm* worried about."

"He wasn't concerned. Not for his life, or mine either."

MJ poured her cup of coffee, went to the fridge for milk, then stirred fiercely. "So he's always right about things like that, is he?"

He shrugged. "Well, he's still alive."

MJ came back to the table. "Did you say that he thought the Russians were connected with this CCRC organization?"

"There may be a connection. We'll know better after the interview. The guy Ahrens is talking to didn't want to say a lot up front."

"It couldn't be a trap, could it?"

"I don't think so. If they wanted to shoot him, they'd just shoot him. They wouldn't invite him to their hideout and *then* shoot him."

"Why not? If you wanted to keep it private . . ."

"No. At least, not if you ever wanted to use that place again. Killing people in it would count as fouling the nest. He says that they're trusting him not to have a tail—whatever 'trusting' means in the circumstances. Still, he's never let his contacts down before, so I suppose he's got a reputation to maintain."

MJ stirred her coffee again, then looked up. "Did you catch the news this morning after I left?"

"No. I was either in the shower or holding in cell phone hell."

"Then you didn't hear about the nuclear test?"

"What nuclear test?"

"In upstate New York."

"What?"

MJ nodded, looking somber. "It seems that somebody detonated a small nuke in a little town upstate."

"Dear God. Was anybody hurt?"

"No. It seems they did it underground, in some mining facility like the French did last year in the South Pacific. Mururoa Atoll, wasn't it? And the authorities are 'refusing to comment' on who they think might have been responsible.''

"Meaning they haven't a clue."

"Or don't want to start a panic. Either way, the AEC won't even say how big the 'device' was." She made quotes in the air with her fingers. "But Cal-Tech said that the shock wave they detected was equivalent to a yield of about one kiloton."

"Sheesh," muttered Peter.

"That wouldn't have anything to do with your Russians, would it?" said MJ.

Peter shook his head and got up to see if there was enough coffee for a refill. "No way to tell at the moment. Not until the authorities are more inclined to talk about what they've found. And they may not do that for a while."

He leaned against the kitchen counter, remembering what Ahrens had said about the Russian hunger for hard currency, about how an armaments industry that had once been supported by one of the largest armies in the world was feeling the pinch along with everyone else— and was very reluctant to make that final connection even in the privacy of his own head.

"Whoever exploded the bomb," said MJ, "was not very considerate."

That struck Peter as one of the great masterpieces of understatement. "In what specific way was a nuclear explosion, ah, inconsiderate?"

"Well, the local community had just started some new commercial venture up there. Mining quartz or something like that. And now all the rock is radioactive. Literally too hot to handle. And it's going to be that way for fifty, a hundred years. So everyone's out of a job again. A whole little town with a new lease on life, destroyed just like that. Whoever could do something like that is a bad person."

Of course, thought Peter grimly, *there's destroyed and then there's* destroyed. *Whoever fired off the device could as easily have done so above ground.* But he nodded in agreement. "There's no telling who it could have been," he said. "But at least the last person we caught messing with nukes is still locked up safe in the Vault."

Hobgoblin had made a determined attempt to blow up New York City, or at least most of Manhattan, and Spidey had been lucky enough—though with Venom's often-reluctant help—to stop him. But just because one super-villain had been locked up, it didn't necessarily mean that there weren't others with equally grandiose schemes.

MJ stared at her coffee cup. "If I drink much more of this stuff," she said, "I'm going to get so wired that I won't sleep for a week. And it's just too early for me to be home." She held up the injured hand and wiggled her fingers, looking at the cut with much milder annoyance than when she had first come storming through the door. "I think, given the state of this, that I might as well just go down to a couple of the restaurants where the 'resting' models hang out, and pick up some gossip about other work."

Peter looked at her affectionately. "You are just so persistent," he said. "How do you do it?"

"Right now? Probably to keep from crying." She wiggled the finger again. "The last time I ever came to another human being and bawled 'I cut my finger!' like that, I can't have been much more than six. It's just too funny."

"I still think I should kiss it and make it better," said Peter. "Or at least, kiss *something* and make it better."

MJ reached out and touched his cheek, smiling. "Your kisses always make it better," she said. "Why do you think I married you?"

"I thought it was all my other sterling qualities; my wit, my savoir faire—"

MJ just laughed, then got up and stretched. "I'll go

down to the Baja,'' she said, ''and hang out there until after lunchtime, then pick up a few things to bring home. I take it you don't know what time you'll be in tonight?''

''I have no idea what sort of business hours Russian gangsters keep, but I think you can take it that I'll be late.''

''The burden of the hardworking super hero's wife; or in this case, the investigative photographer's wife.''

''Something you can actually talk about, for a change.''

''Well, listen, if you're not here when I get back, and if you're not going to be back before you go to this interview with Ahrens and his Russian friend,'' she said as she took his head between her hands, ''you be careful. Be nice to these people. They have weird cultural differences.''

''Ours are probably pretty weird to them, but yeah, I'll be nice.''

She pulled his face close and kissed him, then picked up her keys and headed out the door.

Peter listened to the sound of her footsteps going down the hall, then slid down into a chair and stretched his legs out in front of him. His mind turned back to the Consolidated Chemical Research Corporation. CCRC, he thought, had seemed quite innocent to start with. Just one more merchant bank and its associated business concerns among the horde of them in New York. But a series of accidents—including a most unusual one involving an alien creature that actually ate fissionable material—had revealed that CCRC and the companies connected to it had been storing barrels filled with toxic waste in and around their buildings in the city.

More investigation, including an early evening Spider-Man had spent going through the files in their CEO's office, had shown that the company appeared to be involved in the transfer of transuranic elements from the Eastern Bloc. In earlier years, East Germany had been the usual doorway through the Iron Curtain, but later on, as walls came down and frontiers opened, the access routes moved slowly back into what had once been Soviet-controlled Eastern Europe. It was material that had originated in Russia; and the reason why so much of it was being channeled into the States hadn't been immediately obvious, even from files far more detailed than they should have been.

What was really disturbing was the casual way that storage areas had been established in the center of one of the world's most densely populated cities, and the equally casual means of transport from one point to another. The drums were simply relabeled as something innocuous with no apparent concern for the consequences of an accident or leak.

And there was another person—or persons, really, if you counted his symbiotic ''other''—who was also very interested in this transit of lethal radioactives across the oceans of the world and up and down the roads of America and Europe as if it were no more hazardous than sugar.

He—they—knew that no precautions were taken, and why: because it would have attracted too much attention. And knew, too, that if anything had happened, it would have been the innocents who suffered most.

The innocents. They had always been Venom's great concern, or so he constantly claimed. But interference from that quarter was one factor this equation didn't need right now. Peter tore off the topmost sheet of the pad he had been scribbling on while dealing with CellTech, and started scribbling again.

CCRC had come under investigation fairly quickly after the revelation of toxic waste stored in its properties all over New York City. After a while, the DEA had become involved as well, though entering the investigation from another angle entirely. Questions were asked about large amounts of money being channeled through CCRC's Miami branch. At first the suspicion had been that this was plain old garden-variety drug money; but then a connection to some German banks was established. A lot of Deutschmark transfers had been linked to the movement of radioactive material inside and across Europe, and the investigation had widened at an exponential rate.

Shortly afterward, the German banking consortium sold all their shares in CCRC—or were told to sell them. No one was clear on the details. Spider-Man had been following up on the case during his Florida trip and had been bemused to learn that, despite this massive vote of no-confidence by their European stockholders, CCRC was still very much a going concern.

He had thought that Hobgoblin had been mostly behind its operation, but Hobby was now snug in the Vault after his failed attempt to blow New York into the Atlantic. Of course, it wouldn't be the first time that a company kept going very-nicely-thank-you while its boss cooled his heels in prison, but it hadn't been Hobby behind it after all. The true mastermind remained obscure.

More investigation had suggested that CCRC was behind the biggest shipment of nuclear waste that anyone had ever seen. The stuff was being shipped in under fake invoices from Eastern Europe to Brazil, then north across the Caribbean—past some of the most delicately balanced island ecosystems in the world—and into Florida. There it was stored in great quantities, secretly refined, again mislabeled as who-knew-what, and finally returned to Europe, where someone was recovering significant amounts of unmarked and untraceable weapons-grade plutonium without the knowledge of half a dozen national Atomic Energy Commissions. After that, who knew where it went?

CCRC had been making vast amounts of money—and the possibilities as to where they then channeled it were fairly horrific. Countries a little east, a little south, who would be only too glad to get their hands on already-refined plutonium, for example. Peter was sure that the bottom of this particular barrel hadn't been plumbed yet. Perhaps this evening's conversation with Mel Ahrens's Russian contact might throw a little more light on it.

And maybe the man could illuminate an even worse possibility, one that even now Peter was reluctant to consider: that for all the shipping of nuclear waste one way, and refined material the other, a lot of that refined plutonium was staying right here, in the continental U.S., waiting to be used for God alone knew what purpose.

Peter got up, switched on the TV, and turned to WNN, the news channel. After about ten minutes the headline news came around again, and he found himself looking at a video shot—taken from what he hoped was a safe distance—of a flat, shallow crater maybe half a mile across. It was smooth-sided, looking as if it had collapsed from the bottom instead of being dug out from the top. Peter had seen that shape of crater before, in footage of underground tests from the American West, and more recently mainland China.

Government agencies had been queuing up to take CCRC apart; he knew that much. The corporation was under too close scrutiny right now to even risk playing with cherry bombs, never mind nukes. So who was doing this? Was there somebody, somewhere, watching him tie himself in knots of wrong theory and mistaken supposition while they quietly got on with their own agenda?

Peter didn't know; and like Mel Ahrens, knowing that he didn't know was starting to drive him crazy. He got up and set about getting ready to go out to do a couple of errands.

Elsewhere in the city, someone else was busy with an errand of his own.

The Corporate Registry Office of the New York State Bureau of Records is a granite-fronted building. One might call it plain, especially when compared with the more classical architecture of the oldest parts of New York. Professional people, mostly lawyers and accountants, are in and out of its doors all day, so nobody paid any attention to the tall, harsh-faced man with the blond brush-cut hair and immaculate suit and tie, carrying a briefcase so thin that he appeared to deal with only the most important paperwork, summarized and refined for his convenience by a legion of subordinates.

He paused for a second to study the front of the building, then walked up the flight of ten steps into the bureau's front lobby. If he looked a bit more brutal than the normal run of professionals, well, the more rarefied levels of corporate affairs had always been something of a cutthroat business.

It was just that this man looked all too ready to take that part of it quite literally.

He stepped up to the counter and handed a letter to one of the clerks. They conversed pleasantly for a few minutes, then the clerk excused himself and went off, returning shortly with a small printed map, a set of file envelopes, and a card with a magnetic strip to allow the man to operate the Xerox machines. The man in the dark suit thanked him, then walked up the broad stairs to the right of the reception area, heading for the stacks.

These were not stacks such as might be found in a library. Instead, they contained row upon row of filing cabinets, some tall enough to need the ladders that ran on rails across the face of the stacked files. The visitor made his way to one of the polished wooden tables set in a double line between the cabinets, opened one of the file envelopes, and fanned its contents across the surface of the table like a cardsharper playing with a new deck.

He opened the briefcase, removed several freshly sharpened pencils, set them on top of the papers, and then went across to the files and began systematically going through them. Every movement was quick, economical, and without wasted effort. He carried himself like someone who knew exactly where he was going, exactly what he was looking for, and exactly where he stood in his personal scheme of things: right at the center.

He was there for several hours, reading some files on the spot, carrying others to the table for closer scrutiny, taking still others to the Xerox machine and putting the copies carefully into his briefcase. None of the other accountants or attorneys who were using the place paid him any heed, except in a general sort of way, admiring the expensive cut of his suit, wondering why they hadn't seen him before, since he was so evidently a highflier—or, more straightforwardly, trying to guess which legal firm had started insisting that its partners spend so much time in the gym.

None of them saw him go, because he was the last one—apart from the staff—to leave the building. He packed his briefcase, closed it, then strode down to the reception desk and returned the map, the file folders, and the Xerox card. When his copy charges were totaled, he paid in cash, thanked the clerk, and left.

The Wall Street area gets fairly quiet after business hours, but there are still some good restaurants an easy walk away. The dark-suited man made his way to one of these on Duane Place and ate a leisurely supper of veal saltimbocca with peppers, washed down with half a bottle of Montepulciano d'Abruzzo. He considered the tiramisu, then declined in favor of a double espresso-corto, paid again with cash, and finally stepped out into the cool of the evening and the yellow glow of the streetlights.

He looked up and down the street, then headed east and north. Again, his path was very direct and he seemed to know exactly where he was going, even if that was right into one of the less savory parts of town. The streets where he walked now didn't have boutiques and shops and restaurants in them, or even the heavier frontages of banks and accountancy firms. Instead they had shutters rolled down over warehouse garage doors, boarded-up windows, garbage in the streets, cracked curbstones, and broken streetlights.

A voice spoke to him from the shadows. "Hey, Suit," it said.

The man paused, half-turned, and stared into the darkness. "Were you speaking to me," he said softly, "or to my clothing?"

Three men materialized in the alleyway, emerging from the shadows or stepping in from either end to block the exits. One was short and dark, wearing leather and an incongruous knitted hat with a bobble on top. It might have been funny, except that his face was not one that would take kindly to jokes.

Another was tall, fair, and shaggy, in hole-riddled jeans; a younger man than the others, with a face that looked oddly young and innocent on someone carrying such a large knife.

The third was of medium height, very pallid, his hairstyle a Medusa nightmare of dreadlocks so tangled that it was hard to tell where his hair started and his head left off. He was wearing denims and a pair of the trendy sneakers that lit up with each step.

The man with the knitted hat wasn't wearing shoes that lit up, but as he stepped forward, he produced a large, shiny semi-automatic pistol with the same self-satisfied air of a cheap conjuror performing a cheaper trick.

"Desert Eagle," said the man in the dark suit. He sounded amused instead of frightened. "My, what a great big expensive gun for such a little punk. You know, if you had bought a cheaper gun, you could afford some better clothes—and even get rid of that stupid hat."

"You got a smart mouth, Suit," snarled Hat. "Maybe you like another mouth." He gestured vaguely with the gun barrel. "Jus' 'bout behind your belt buckle."

"Maybe I like the mouth I've got."

" 'Nough talk," said Dreadlocks. "Briefcase is worth about five hundred. Just take the bag and waste him."

The blond youngster with the knife swallowed hard, his Adam's apple bouncing in his throat, and the man with the suit watched it move up and down with the same sort of savoring expression he had earlier given to the saltimbocca as it arrived on his table in the restaurant.

"If you want some advice," he said gently, "I don't think you should do that."

"Don't remember askin' for any," said Dreadlocks. "C'mon—let's see if his fancy suit'll stop a Teflon tip. I said waste him, man!"

Even though Hat was standing no more than eight feet away, he went through an elaborate performance of taking careful aim before he squeezed the trigger. The boom of his gun's heavy Magnum load was deafening in the confined space of the alley, its muzzle blast a stab of yellow-white flame almost a yard long. In the clanging silence that followed the shot, all of them heard the tiny tinkle of the spent cartridge-case hitting the street. But none of them really noticed.

Because this suit, at least, *did* stop Teflon tips.

Hat and Dreadlocks stood with their mouths hanging open, but the blond man with the knife took a step backward, and then another to where his companions couldn't see.

"Yes," said the man in the dark suit, watching him. "You were beginning to suspect as much, weren't you? And so only you alone shall come away alive to tell the tale. Watch, now."

The suit stopped being a suit. It boiled away from its wearer's powerful body in a whirlwind of strand and threads and ribbons that flashed and hissed as they cut through the air. Then they contracted again, snuggling close, weaving and knitting until the harsh face and the cropped hair and any semblance of a well-dressed corporate lawyer had completely disappeared, and nothing showed but the jagged, angular design of a stylized white spider across his massive chest.

Two huge pallid eyes studied them, while an impossibly wide mouth crammed with jagged fangs gaped wide, and a tongue the size of a boa constrictor came drooling and coiling out at them from between the picket fence of teeth.

"Mouth . . ." said Hat.

"Mouth," said the dark shape, taking a step forward. "Yes, indeed. And as you can see, we don't need another. We already have one." It grinned, and the fangs dripped slime as the grin went right around, and no matter how broad the grin became, there were always more teeth behind it.

Ribbons of ferocious darkness came swirling like tentacles from the black costume that the man was wearing, and grabbed Hat around the chest and neck, lifting him up without the slightest trace of effort until his feet dangled clear of the ground. One more tentacle reached out playfully to pull off the knitted hat, then flicked it away. Under it, on Hat's shaven skull, was an impossibly elaborate tattoo, all Celtic knotwork and tangled animals.

Dreadlocks tried to run, but another half-dozen tentacles lashed out at his legs, wrenching them from under his body so that he came splatting down full-length on the filthy pavement. The tentacles wrapped around Dreadlocks's legs tightened, dragging him closer, and then lifted him clear of the ground to dangle beside Hat. "You didn't ask for any advice before," said Venom, "but we'll give you a little more. No charge. Just remember, next time, not to attack an attorney going about his legal occasions. Everybody *knows* how nasty lawyers can be. And there's always the chance they might be someone even nastier. Like us."

The blond man with the knife knew that he could run now, *should* run, but he didn't dare to move. Instead he just stood and stared, too frightened to even drop the knife in case its clatter on the ground attracted Venom's attention.

"My word," said Venom, lifting Hat even higher and then tilting him upside-down to look at the tattoo, "that must have hurt. Not, however, as much as this."

The next few minutes were noisy and unpleasant for almost all concerned, a nightmare blur of tentacles and pseudopods that was far worse for being mostly lost in shadow. Finally Venom raised the two limp, barely breathing bodies even higher, and dropped them like so much garbage into the gutter at the side of the alley.

"These streets haven't been kept too clean recently, but that will change," he said. "Don't forget what we told you." Then he turned to the blond youngster. "They roped you into this, didn't they?"

The blond nodded his head, a tiny movement that looked more like a tremor, and let the knife slide at last from between his fingers.

"So we thought. Well, we have other business this evening, so you just run along and tell your other friends that we're back in town. Tell them that we're after one of our own this time. There's a super-villain busy in town and we want him. If someone helps us, then we'll help them. And in the meantime, those of you who prey on others should stop. Take our advice. No charge."

That terrible grin spread right around Venom's face again. "Because until we find the one we're looking for, we'll keep ourselves busy with you. And after we find that one, then there are other pleasures, long deferred. There'll be time to take care of it now. So go on now— and spread the news."

The young man didn't run. Instead his eyes rolled back in his head and he slithered down the wall in a dead faint. A pseudopod reached out and delicately pulled one of the fluttering eyelids back. "Well, we suppose you've had a busy night," he said. "Rest awhile."

Darkness shimmered around Venom, and a moment

later he was dressed once more in his dark suit, with the briefcase in his hand. "No rest for the wicked," he said. "At least, not while we're around."

Then he walked off into the night.

FOUR

Mary Jane Watson-Parker walked down the street in a foul mood. She had been walking for about an hour, trying to ditch the mood, so far to no success.

She glanced at her watch. It was pushing eleven-thirty, and she had walked all the way down to Seventieth Street and all the way across to First Avenue. Now she paused at the corner of First and Seventieth, looking down toward the newly constructed towers of Cornell and New York Hospital Medical Center. Over on York Avenue, a couple of blocks down, was Baja, the restaurant that was a haven for models and the occasional confused nurse who stumbled in.

She had been putting off actually going into Baja, partly because it was still fairly early, and also because she knew that the sight of other people in there with work would annoy her. *All the same,* she thought, *it'll be a poor state of affairs when you can't face down your own kind—even when they're working and you're not. The tables turn fast enough in this town.*

She walked on up to York, turned the corner, and headed back up to Seventy-third. Baja stood on the corner there, yet another pseudo-Southwestern-chic restaurant with cloth cactuses in brass pots, too much white stucco, and too much bleached oak, but fairly passable Tex-Mex food, and a bar the size of the launch deck of an aircraft carrier. There the models perched on the stools, leaned their sometimes fairly ample cleavages on the bar, and complained to each other, male and female together. MJ smiled slightly. She was in the right mood for the complaining.

The outside sidewalk terrace was empty as yet—too much sun. It would start filling when the shadows swung around to cover it. MJ stepped in through the front door into the relative dark and looked around.

Sitting back there at the long polished bar were two models she knew, one male, one female. The man was Ted Huron, one of the tall-dark-and-handsome school, with cheekbones that could have been used to chop trees down, and stunning green eyes. The other was a female model called Hendra, with trademark six-inch-long nails, and hair that was never the same color twice. It was blue today, fading to white at the punked-out tips.

"Hi, Hen, hi, Tom," she said, strolling up and sitting down by Tom. They muttered at her cordially enough. Their nonvolubility was no surprise: it was early yet, and when they weren't working, they were club people. MJ was surprised even to be seeing them up and about before noon.

Bob the bartender came up. "Hi, MJ. Whatcha having?"

"Double kiwi," she said, "heavy on the lemon."

He went off to get her the juice. She glanced at the others. "How're you two doing?"

It was a noncommittal enough question. If they were here this time of day, it *might* mean they weren't working; but then again, *she* was here this time of day.

"Resting," Tom said glumly.

Hendra rolled her eyes. "I just finished a gig," she said. "A week in Bavaria."

"Oh? How was it?"

"Rained constantly." Hendra pushed her orange-juice glass back toward Bob as he approached with MJ's kiwi juice in a tall glass with a transparent umbrella sticking out of it. "You off today?"

"I just blew a job off," MJ said.

"Oh? What?"

She held out her injured hand. Tom gazed at it for a moment, not comprehending immediately. "You need a thorn pulled out of your paw or something?"

"No, dummy. I was doing hand work."

"You won't be doing any for a couple of weeks," Hendra said regretfully. "You want to put some vitamin E on that, make sure it heals right."

"Sure, why not?"

They gabbed for a little while, talking sports (the present hopelessness of the Mets), art (Christo's intention to wrap the Statue of Liberty), the utter uselessness of TV in the summer ("They're showing reruns of *Gilligan's Island* again," Tom muttered), politics (the recent coup d'état in Atlantis and Reed Richards's dramatic, and failed, plea to the UN for assistance). All these things were generally agreed by the three of them as signs of the imminent downfall of civilization as they knew it. After that, the subject turned rapidly to the bashing of producers, directors, and shoot administrators that they had known. No more than ten or fifteen minutes into the character assassination, the door swung open, and they all looked over to see if it was someone they had been assassinating.

Lalande Joel came in. Six feet three, weighing possibly a hundred and sixty pounds, Lalande had long, raven-black hair that had caused her to be cast in a couple of commercials as a Morticia Addams clone, and beautiful cerulean-blue eyes, blue as a Siamese cat's. Lalande had a reputation as a friendly if slightly loopy sort, and they all greeted her cordially enough as she swung up to sit by MJ.

"And how are you this fine day?" Tom said.

"Very retrograde," Lalande said wearily. "Hi, Bob. Gimme a Coke?"

"Retrograde?" MJ said.

"Well, not me. Neptune."

"Oh." MJ thought for a moment. "Neptune's a long way out. Isn't it going to be retrograde for a long time?"

"Yes," Lalande said sadly. "Forty-five years, I think."

"By the time that changes, you'll be doing senior citizens' insurance ads," said Hendra. "If I were you, I'd stop worrying about it."

"Oh, I'm not worrying, it's just—I'm conscious of it, that's all." Her Coke came and she took a sip. "And I just blew off a job."

"Oh? What?"

She presented her perfect face to them, and pointed at it with an expression of profound annoyance and regret. "Look at that," she said.

They all looked. "I can't see anything," MJ said.

"That's because I've covered it up so that I can walk the streets without someone walking in front of me ringing a little bell and saying 'Unclean, unclean,' " Lalande said. "It's a *zit.*"

"It's a very *flat* zit," said Tom.

"It's not flat enough to be covered up by the amount of makeup they'll let you use in a lipstick ad," said Lalande. "And see that?" She pointed at the corner of her mouth. "There's a cold sore coming up right there. It'll be the size of my head."

MJ raised her eyebrows. It was nowhere near the size of Lalande's beautiful head yet, but she understood the problem. "Yeah," she said, "welcome to the 'I am scarred' club." She held up the offending finger for examination.

Lalande looked at it, then looked at her face. "But you're fine."

"Not for hand work, I'm not."

But Lalande was still examining her face. "Have you ever done lipstick?" she said.

"Well, I did something for Max Factor a while ago. Why?"

"Look," Lalande said, "your face is in good shape. And our lips are kind of the same shape. And you still have a SAG card. Why don't you beat it over to the job I just blew off? Maybe they'll hire you."

MJ stared at her. "Lalande," she said, "that's very kind, but what makes you think they'd take me?"

"It's like I said. They're desperate, they're on a timetable, and they have to get this thing finished by, what did they say, Wednesday, Thursday? Anyway, they've got to get it moving. And they're all just standing around there right now, howling that they can't find another model. But our mouths are really kind of close—you ought to try."

"My teeth aren't as good as yours, though," MJ said.

"I don't think it's going to matter. They were doing mostly closed-mouthed stuff with me, except for one smile—but—I don't know. MJ, go try!"

"Lalande, that's really nice of you."

"I might as well be nice," Lalande said, rolling her eyes expansively, "since I'm going to have to go into a leper colony pretty soon, at this rate. I look like the poster child for Dr. Jenner's Smallpox Cure."

"*Lalaaaaaaande,*" said MJ and Hendra and Tom, more or less in exasperated unison. And MJ added, "It's not quite that bad, yet. Where is this job, anyway?"

"Here." She pulled out a business card, handed it to MJ. She turned it over; the address was just up Third Avenue, near Seventy-eighth.

"Go, just go," Lalande said. "They were ready to start about an hour ago, when I had to walk in and show myself to them like this."

MJ finished her juice and stood up. "Well, I'll give it a try."

"One thing," Lalande said as MJ slung her purse over her shoulder. "The director."

MJ raised her eyebrows again. "What about him? Her? It?"

"It," Lalande said. "No question. Scuttlebutt has it that this guy has dumped a bunch of models over the past few weeks. Having worked with him for a whole day, I suspect it may be the other way around. He may hire you, but make sure you get his name and yours on the dotted line, and the pay amounts inked in and dry before you actually do any work. He is"—she glanced up and around as if looking desperately for a cue card— "indescribable."

"Okay," MJ said. "Lalande—do I really want this job?"

"I don't know," Lalande said. "*I* really wanted it,

until I turned into Pockmarked Grandmother Ma. But the pay's not bad. They were going to give me fifteen hundred.''

"What did they wind up giving you?"

"Seven. But then they shot with me yesterday, and they couldn't use me today."

"Small world," MJ said. "Okay."

"Let me know how it comes out," Lalande said, taking another drink of her Coke. "And I hope you bite the bastard for me."

MJ heard that, though she wondered whether she'd been meant to. *Yet another interesting director. Well, we'll see . . .*

She headed out and looked around for a cab so as not to get sweaty on the way over. She had had her share of "indescribable" directors in her time, including the unforgettable Maurice, on this last shoot in Miami: a master of the crazed waffle, a man who didn't know what he wanted whether he saw it or not. If he did see it, he usually danced around it for an hour or so before getting down to it. Now, as MJ climbed into her cab, she wondered whether she was about to be saddled with something similar. *At least,* she thought, *I probably won't find* this *guy standing on the beach, signaling to drug runners with a flashlight.*

When she got to the address on Third Avenue, she was surprised to see that it was a side building of Auve, one of the new European cosmetic houses that had established itself in New York over the past year, and was busy making inroads into Elizabeth Arden's and Helena Rubenstein's business. It was all plate glass on the outside, and trees and green marble on the inside. She walked in the front door, paused at the front door, and mentioned—she consulted the card—Delano Rodriguez's shoot.

"Oh yes," said the young blond receptionist, with a look that suggested that MJ had asked to do a commercial shoot with Jeffrey Dahmer. "Second floor, photo studio B."

MJ nodded and headed for the elevator. She spent the next few seconds admiring the spotless white carpet on its floor, and the shining stainless-steel walls. *How do they keep this clean?* she wondered as the bell dinged and the doors opened for her to step out. *If we had any carpet like this in my house, Peter would drop a pizza on it, facedown, within the first week.*

She headed for the studio to which she'd been directed. Down yet another white-carpeted hall with brushed-aluminum walls and a softly glowing ceiling. A pair of brushed-aluminum doors finally said STUDIO B. She pushed one of them open and went in.

The soundproofing was very good here. She actually had to get the door right open before she heard the voice screaming, "How the *hell* am I supposed to make this commercial without a warm body to put the lipstick on?"

The place was chaos, the usual large number of bright lights trained on a very small space, the usual small and very uncomfortable stool on which the working cosmetic model got to perch while thousand-watt lights were positioned three inches from her perfect skin. Three of the tremendous wide-aperture movie cameras used for this kind of work sat idle around the chair. People rushed around in all directions. And storming back and forth across the room, like a beast in a cage, was the director.

ADs, assistants, script people, sound people, who knew what else, ran all over, and Delano the director was banging around in the midst of them, aimless and screaming. A few quiet people stood around on the sidelines looking like they weren't going insane, but also looking like they didn't work for this director. The room, taken as a whole, looked like a commercial for Brownian motion.

MJ had seen shoots like this before, and they had long since ceased to faze her. She strolled slowly into the maelstrom, and eventually the director's eye lit on her as he careened back and forth. He more or less screamed, "Who let you in here?"

"Lalande Joel suggested that I come over," she said coolly and held out the business card she had been given. "I understand you need some lips."

There might have been a better way to put this, since the director was the thinnest-lipped, thinnest-faced, palest, narrowest little man she had ever seen; he looked like a two-dimensional life-form trying out the third dimension, and not sure whether he shouldn't just take it back to the shop. But he seemed not to notice the verbal misstep, came over to MJ, and stared at her mouth as if it were the first one he'd ever seen.

He'll ask to see my teeth next, MJ thought. "Open, please," Delano Rodriguez said, and MJ did.

"Hmm," he said. "Not bad. It's not a speaking part. Five hundred."

"Fifteen," MJ said, wondering what kind of brain this man had. Didn't he realize Lalande would have told her how much she had been getting?

"Not for half a day."

"Yes," MJ said, amazed at her own temerity, "for half a day." *He's got all these people waiting around here, and the dollars are just burning away. . . .*

"All right, get over there."

"Not until we get a contract signed."

The director shrieked some more at that, but she stood her ground, and after a few minutes a shoot manager materialized and handed her a template contract. There were no unexpected waiver clauses; MJ made sure the amounts were filled in correctly, and signed it after the director did. It called for "one business day," which in the business meant nine to five, or a fraction thereof.

The next eight hours were—well, indescribable. Lalande had been right about that. One thing it took MJ a little time to get used to again: the makeup going on and coming off, going on and coming off, time after time, a hundred times. Then a layer of moisturizer and a break so that the lips could recover a little—and then the whole process started again.

All through this, Delano the director went plunging around, endlessly yelling. MJ hadn't thought that anyone could yell so interminably. He yelled at the lighting technicians, the camera operators, at the ADs and the script girls, and the DGA trainee, and most of all, he yelled at MJ and the makeup artists. The lipliner was too broad, too thin, the lighting wasn't right, the lipstick shade needed to be corrected, the skin tone was bad. And this accusation he lodged against MJ as if there were something she could do about it. Her pores were too big, she couldn't hold still, she didn't look moist enough, her tongue was too red. . . .

For a very long while, MJ asked herself the question that Lalande had asked her: *Do I want this job?* Then she thought about a bill for $4,689.72 and decided that yes, she did want it. So she sat still, and opened and closed her mouth a hundred times on order, while the lipstick was put on and taken off—and the place began to smell entirely too much like skin and toning lotion and moisturizer and lipstick melting under the heat of the lights. And the powder made her sneeze.

The hours dragged by, accompanied by the sound of screaming. MJ began to wonder whether her ears might actually be damaged by this constant noise. Certainly other people didn't spend any time nearer it than they could: the parts of the crew not actively shooting seemed to spend most of their time out of the room, leaving MJ and the poor long-suffering script girl to take most of the abuse. *Honestly, now,* she said to herself around four-thirty, *this is bad—but it's not as bad as coming home to your apartment and finding Venom waiting for you. Now,* that *was bad.*

The screaming continued while she was filmed with an "unseen hand" applying lipstick to her somewhat down-pouted lower lip. MJ held quite still through that, momentarily transfixed by the vision of Venom meeting the director, or the other way around. *You want to scream?* she imagined herself saying. *Here. Here's something to scream about. . . .*

"Are you listening to me?" Delano screeched, practically by her ear. *"Don't you pay attention? If you don't at least get conscious, I'm going to throw you the hell out of here!"*

MJ opened one thoughtful eye and looked at Delano out of the corner of it. Some of the makeup crew near her saw the motion. One of them froze where he stood, watching. *You make it sound good,* she thought. But for the moment she said nothing, and her eye slid to the big clock across the room.

It was two minutes of five.

Delano ranted in her face. She shut the sound out, catching only occasional excerpts.

A minute forty, she thought.

"Useless, redheaded bimbo—"

A minute and twenty.

"—brains of a duck—"

Forty-five seconds.

"—dragged in off the street like a—"

Thirty.

"—waste of my valuable time—"

Eleven. Ten. Nine.

"—don't know why I don't just go down to Bloomingdale's and hire a dummy—"

Three. Two. One.

As the second hand hit the twelve, MJ shot straight up out of the cramped little chair, almost into Delano's face. He staggered a step backward, banging into a light; it swayed, and for one naughty moment MJ prayed that it might fall. But it steadied itself.

"You silly little man," she said sweetly. "You distasteful, arrogant, stupid man. You don't have enough talent to grow grass on a lawn. You've got about as much brain as a retarded billiard ball. If you had another brain, you'd *still* have just one. And what's more, you're *cheap*—I bet you'd walk miles in the snow for the chance to cheat an orphan out of a nickel.'' She was scaling up now. ''You're a legend in your own mind, Delano. I bet you speak very highly of yourself. What makes you think you have the right to abuse these nice people the way you do? You're a heel. You're a lowlife. You barely know which end of the camera to look into. If I saw you being mugged in the street, I'd offer to hold the muggers' coats and cheer. If I saw you drowning, I'd throw you a boat anchor.'' MJ noticed, in a clinical sort of way, how Delano's mouth was working open and shut. He looked like a flounder. ''You look like a flounder,'' she added, at the top of her lungs, unwilling to let the chance observation go. Then she paused. ''Did I call you a fish-faced moron?''

Delano, his mouth still working, said, ''No.''

''Well, I meant to. I quit.'' She stalked past him as if he were a recently anointed fire hydrant, marched over to where the shoot manager was standing with his clipboard, and said, ''Give me my money!''

''Uh—''

''Cash, right this minute,'' she said, ''or I'm going to take that rap sheet there, the one with the overinflated budget on it, roll it up very tight and small, and shove it in the first orifice that presents itself!''

The shoot manager's eyes went appreciatively wide. He came up with an envelope and handed it to MJ.

Steaming happily, she opened it and counted the cash. Delano was muttering again, something about a lawsuit. MJ ignored him, waved good-bye to the crew, and headed for the door.

One last scream, of pure wordless fury, came echoing from behind her. She smiled. ''Last refuge of the illiterate,'' she said softly.

A couple of men stood near the door, smiling slightly at her. As MJ approached, one of them opened the door for her, almost reverently. The other, a small cheerful-looking man with dark hair, dressed in casual clothes, spoke. "Excuse me," he said, "but I couldn't help over-hearing—"

MJ chuckled. "They probably overheard me in Nyack."

"Yes, well." He handed her a business card. "Would you give me a call tomorrow, if you have the time? I'd appreciate a chance to talk to you."

She glanced at the card. It had a yellow, smiling-sun logo, and said SUNDOG PRODUCTIONS and under that, a name. JYMN MAGON.

"Well, certainly, Mr. Magon," she said. "Glad to. Please forgive me, though. I have to go off and spend my ill-gotten gains."

"Right. I'll look forward to hearing from you."

Outside, MJ hailed a cab, climbed in, and as it drove off, immediately began to blush and practically to vi-brate with embarrassment. She hated temper tantrums. She valued the ability to talk your way through a prob-lem almost more than anything else. Nonetheless, some-times it felt really good to blow up—and this was the second time in a month that she'd done it. *I wonder if I'm coming down with something,* MJ thought. *But then again, there were extenuating circumstances.* She sat back in the cab. *And now I've got all this money, too. Maybe I should lose my temper more often.*

She looked at the card again. Sundog Productions— some kind of film or TV production group, maybe? It had been a long time since *Secret Hospital,* the soap opera on which she had a recurring role for a time, and the luxury of a steady paycheck. This could be very interesting.

She decided to stop in the store on the corner and pick up some things for dinner, and make herself a snack. She hoped Peter would be back from the mafiosi in good time—but she didn't know what kind of hours mafiosi kept. Probably better not to wait up. Meanwhile,

she thought happily about all the money. Money always
gave her a good appetite.

And with this kind of money, I could eat a horse!

The long dark limo with the blacked-out windows met
them at the *Bugle* at about seven. Peter and Mel climbed
in, and Mel said amiably to the driver, "Hi there."

The driver glared and said nothing—just waited until
they closed the doors, then gunned the car around the
corner a lot faster than it should have gone. He started
to drive, fast, toward the Midtown Tunnel.

"I don't suppose it would be wise to ask where we're
going," Peter said.

Mel shrugged. "Brooklyn, somewhere," he said.
"You know and I know that the greater part of the Rus-
sian-language community is down there in Bensonhurst
and Coney Island and Brighton Beach. I won't be looking closely at any street signs, and I don't recommend
that you do so, either." He squinted at the windows.
"But I don't think we'll be able to see any."

He was right; the glass was blacked out on both the
inside and the outside, an interesting effect that left them
with nothing much to do but sit back and enjoy the ride.
It was a very plush car, a stretch Mercedes limo with all
the extras: champagne bucket, television, phone. "I'd
suspect this thing of having a pool," Peter said.

"His other one does, I hear."

"His other one?"

"Yeah. Just the Russian love for hot water, I guess.
But also, Dmitri is a little, well, flamboyant. That's why
you're along. He likes publicity—within reason—and
he'll find the presence of a photographer nice. He'll feel
more like we take him seriously."

"Oh. And don't we take him seriously?"

"Absolutely. But a little coddling never hurts when
you know there's an ego involved. Which there is. Try
to avoid his bald spot."

Peter chuckled.

After about forty minutes, the car began making a lot of turns. "Oh," Peter said, "this is the part where we get disoriented."

Mel laughed. "I was disoriented the minute we went through the Battery Tunnel."

"It wasn't the Battery. Had to be the Midtown."

"See? What'd I tell you?"

Outside, the car engine noise seemed to change—got closer, more immediate—then a lot more echo-y. "We're inside," Peter said.

Mel nodded. The car stopped, then both the doors opened from the outside.

Peter and Mel looked at each other. Then carefully, keeping his hands in view, Mel got out. Peter did the same on his side.

They were in a parking garage, no telling on what level. There was nothing to see but unbroken concrete walls in all directions. All around the car stood a group of big, serious-looking men, some dressed more like bouncers than anything else, some dressed fashionably enough in dark pants and windbreakers or casual jackets. All had lumps here and there under their jackets, and all were holding guns, too, some of the biggest ones Peter had ever seen.

Mel turned to one of the men, who reached inside his jacket and removed his gun. There were a few grunts of admiration before the gun vanished. Then the men looked at Peter.

He held out his camera to the nearest of the large men. The man took it from him, examined it closely, and gave it back with utter unconcern. Then all of them turned toward one of the nearby doors in the concrete wall, and some of them began to head that way. Peter and Mel followed them.

They went up several flights of stairs, their many footsteps echoing together. They came to the door. One of the suited men pushed it open, and Peter and Mel went in after him.

116

They came out in a long hallway of what looked like an apartment building. The hallway had no windows, only doors, and all of them shut. The leading bodyguards led them down to the last door in the hallway and opened it.

Peter and Mel went in, looked around. It was an apartment, and a beautiful one: high ceilinged and very modern, with big windows, except that all the big windows had their venetian blinds down and shut. Tasteful lamps were on here and there, sitting on handsome antique tables and among old overstuffed furniture. The room was eclectic without looking designed. The way they were kept, the things in it obviously belonged to someone who liked them and took care of them. And sitting on one of the overstuffed couches was a little man in a light shirt and dark twill trousers, reading a copy of the German newspaper *Die Welt*.

Peter looked at the man, and thought that he had never seen anyone who looked so much like a weasel. It was partly the shape of his skull, partly his odd kind of widow's peak receding hairline, partly the reddish cast of his hair. The rest of the effect was produced by little, bright, close-set eyes and a small delicate mouth. A bit of a surprise, that—Peter expected something bigger, somehow. The overall effect was of being looked at by someone who lived entirely by calculation, wits, wiles, and plotting.

As he saw them come, he tossed his newspaper aside and held out a hand for them to shake, Mel first. "Dmitri," said the little man, "Dmitri Elyonets." His voice was a light, pleasant tenor, not heavily accented at all.

Peter stuck his hand out. "Peter Parker."

"Welcome. Please sit down."

Peter looked around. "Before we get started," he said, "I'd like to know what the ground rules are. Am I allowed to take pictures in here?"

"In here, yes. One warning: of me, take the back of my head only."

That's going to make it interesting trying to avoid the bald spot, Peter thought, but this kind of challenge was what made photography interesting, especially with vain, image-conscious celebrities. "One-third profile from behind?" Peter suggested.

Dmitri considered. "Which side?"

Peter went around the back of him and had a look. "Right, I think."

"Very well. You're a smart young man, you handle it that way."

"What about your people?" All the men who had accompanied them up from the parking lot were now in the room with them.

Dmitri looked around and then waved some of them out. "Anyone here, them you may photograph."

Peter was glad of that. If all he'd had to take pictures of was the back of Dmitri's head and his furniture, it would have been a pretty bleak and limited shoot, even seen as an ego exercise. The bodyguards, by and large, had interesting faces, and looked like the population of a James Bond movie before the hero had shown up—a bunch of grim people seemingly ready to produce flying bowler hats with a sharpened rim or steel teeth at a moment's notice.

Peter began to move carefully around the room, taking pictures of the contents and the men, trying to show, without emphasizing it, the gangsterish look of them as they stood in classic bodyguard pose, hands folded in front of them. "So," Mel said. "You called for this meeting. I was glad to come. I've known about you for a while."

Dmitri laughed. "Yes, I know you have. Sooner or later we would have had to meet. I prefer it this way."

"I'd be curious," Mel said, "about exactly what the cause of our meeting is. If rumor tells the truth, you're doing well enough in business."

"More than well enough," Dmitri said. "The usual things endemic to this part of the world. Gambling." He shot a quick glance at Peter to let him know he was included. "A little asset shifting."

"You mean the laundry," said Mel.

Dmitri rolled his eyes a little. "And some newer areas. Wire work—"

"Electronic fraud, you mean," Mel said.

Dmitri laughed again. "Always the semantics, with you. Well, business has been doing well enough. But it never does exactly as well as you'd like, so one is always looking for new ways to expand, eh?"

"True enough," said Mel. "But I get a feeling that you've found some people involved in some kind of expansion that makes you nervous."

Dmitri said nothing for a moment, simply gave Mel a long cool thoughtful look. "There," he said at last, "you would be right." He hunched over a little, his hands clasped in front of him, and Peter got one of those "back of the head" shots that was still very eloquent of the man's personality: his tension, the liveliness of the man.

"There are people in my business," said Dmitri, "who are not as cautious as I am. When you're here for a while, you learn that any business, whether one like mine or not, is a renewable resource. Yes? You have to treat it with respect, not stretch it too far, not overextend it. Push it too far, it dies. But don't push it hard enough, it stagnates. Always a question of balance.

"But right now," Dmitri continued, "there are people out there who only see the push. And their dealings are somewhat—" Dmitri shook his head. "They push, but they're not afraid. They don't care about the balance. They don't look forward, not past tomorrow."

"Do you know who these people are, specifically?"

"Ah," Dmitri said, "well. You must be clear: my concern is not to go straight." He waved a hand dismissively. "If I did straight business in this town, I would have to work ten times as hard to make a third, a quarter, of the money I make now. I know what I like.

But I want things stable." He leaned over to thump the coffee table in front of him. "I want things to stay the way they are. In the old days, on the collective farm when I was a boy, the world itself would show you what had to be done. Milk the cow too hard, too often, its poor old udders get sore, and the milk dries out. Milk it much too hard, and it dies, or someone takes it away from you. I don't want that—dead cows, or missing ones. I want it to give milk for a long time yet. But there are people doing things that make that impossible. So—" He threw his arms wide, an expansive gesture. "I come to you. I come to the press. Here freedom of the press is everything, and what the press says is listened to. I want people to know. So I call you, and ask you to come listen to me, while I tell you about the people who are going to kill the cow."

"What you're saying, if I understand the agricultural idiom correctly," said Mel, "is that there are people becoming affiliated with your—organization—who are pushing for such high-profile scams or amounts of money being shifted, that they would be impossible to hide. That they're likely to attract the attention of the really big law-enforcement agencies down on you: the FBI, the CIA—"

"Oh, the CIA, they're here: we know them, they know us," Dmitri said. Peter wondered briefly just what that meant. "These people, they aren't careful—they're going to make business bad for all of us. They're greedy—or else something worse than greedy, and I am not sure what that might be. But this I feel sure of: something else is going on in some of the other organizations which I do not understand."

"Well," Mel said, pulling out his notebook and a pen, "let's hold that for a moment. Let me be clear, too. Some of these people are not friends of yours—there are old feuds. I am thinking in particular of the organizational head called Galya Irnotsji."

Dmitri sat back on the couch again and rubbed his

nose a little. "Well, he is an enemy of mine, yes. But that is not the reason I want to stop him. I want to stop him, and his people, because they are going to do something bad to," he waved around him, "this place. Which is my home now, which has been good to me." He shot a sidewise glance at Peter, who was taking another picture. "You'll think perhaps it's odd. I am—you know what I am." Dmitri shrugged. "But still I want to be good to the place that was good to me. I'll take what I need to live. I'll make money from the fat banks and the big companies, and hide it where it can't be found. But past that, people should live the best they can."

Peter nodded, getting the feeling that here was a modern version of something he had thought had died out in the Middle Ages: a genuine robber baron, who nonetheless had started out as some kind of skewed gentleman.

"Now let me tell you what you ask," Dmitri said to Mel. "Galya, yes. A thorn in my side for a long time now. He's started dealing with somebody, not one of us—not Russian or Ukrainian, not at all from the other community, the Italians, or any of the Chinese. This person that Galya deals with—I don't know who he is or where he comes from. Now, lately, my eyes and ears"— he waved outside, suggesting that they were everywhere—"my people tell me he's been bringing in a little hot stuff."

"Nuclear material," said Mel. "From where?"

"I cannot say. Not that I won't tell you—I don't know. I have to tell you, I have handled some of this myself, but not for here. To send away. There are always buyers for that. But the stuff that Galya's handling is not going out of the country. It's coming in, and it *stays*. Not just coming in and staying in one place, either, but being shipped many places. New York, Detroit, Chicago, Atlanta, Los Angeles, Denver—all the big cities. Everywhere, small shipments have been moving around for the past couple of months. The shipments, they're labeled 'industrial waste' or something else—it doesn't matter. We know what they are. When I started hearing about this, I didn't know what Galya was shipping. I found out eventually. It's hard to keep a secret in our business.

"Then, the other day, we hear that upstate, in the Adirondacks—here, in our state, our home—someone has blown up an atomic bomb. A little one, but a bomb. And I think about all those cans and packages of 'industrial waste,' and I wonder, What does this mean? For a while, I'm not sure that this means anything. Then, yesterday, I hear that Galya, several days ago, had a big payment—*big* payment—so that he's having to launder it all over the place. And now I hear he's gone down to the Caribbean, to Mauritius, I think it is, to see about the finishing touches, the last work on his new house. A big house, a lot of money spent on it—like a little town. You know what real estate costs down there. It must have cost a fortune, even by our standards."

Dmitri leaned forward again. "At first I thought he just wants a house on a little island so he can run drugs easily. Everyone does it down there. You rent a flying boat, it files some fake flight plans—it's easy. But I just don't like it, don't like the way it feels. All these things, together, at once—I think Galya is involved in something that's going to be bad for business, bad for my people, bad for people in this country, this good country where we came to make a life for ourselves, a living."

Peter raised an eyebrow and took another back-of-head shot.

"I want him to be stopped. I want to tell"—he almost choked on the word—"the police what they need to know to stop him."

Mel and Peter looked at each other, and Mel began making neat small shorthand notes. "Names and dates?" said Mel.

"Names and dates."

"Then let's start."

It took a long time. Dmitri was a tireless talker, who would not let Mel tape anything. Shorthand was all right, though, and for the next three hours Mel wrote as tirelessly as Dmitri talked, taking down names of nearly every crook, major and minor, who was working with his enemy Galya—phone numbers, fax numbers, details about what they were doing, numbers and illegal betting shops, legal betting shops that had been infiltrated by illegal "private entrepreneurships," candy stores that were cash laundromats, supermarkets that were too, several big banks with "pliant" managers on the take, who falsified the cash transaction reports required by the IRS, or failed to file them altogether. The recitation went on and on.

When Dmitri started talking about the businesses in Peter's part of town, Peter's eyes widened. Many protection rackets were in force: false invoicing was going on at the grocery around the corner where he liked to shop, the one with the really good cheese case, plus dry cleaners, drugstores . . .

Peter shook his head as he moved slowly around the room, taking pictures of an old portrait here, a bodyguard there, half-dozing as he watched his boss, or the back of Dmitri's head again, as he gestured earnestly. It was amazing how much expression the back of a head could have. And on and on, until Peter found himself unable to count how many businesses in his area were *not* on the take. And Mel just wrote it all down, nodding and asking a question every now and then.

Three hours. Peter sat down, finally, unloaded his camera and reloaded it with fresh film, but it was a token gesture. There was simply nothing left to take pictures of in the room. A little while later, Dmitri sat back and fell silent.

Mel sat back too, flipping through the pages of his notebook. Then he looked up. "How's your security these days, Dmitri?" he said.

Dmitri looked around him, waved confidently at the

(admittedly, somewhat sleepy-looking) men standing around him. "I trust them with my life."

"You're going to have to. You know how news travels in this town. It's going to be a matter of hours before Galya knows I've been here. He'll know what we've been talking about. After that—"

Dmitri shrugged. "The Communists knew where I was, too," he said. "I survived them. I'll survive this too. This is important," he said, leaning forward and tapping the coffee table again. "This is business. *Galya is bad for business.*"

"He'll be bad for you now," Mel said. "Even if he doesn't sneak up behind you one dark night and do you in, he must have some of the same kind of information about your doings that you have about his."

Dmitri laughed again. "Not nearly so much. He's not a subtle man, our Galya: he doesn't look behind things. I look to my future, and to the inevitability of betrayal— and so I make it as hard as I can. But we shall see. And you—what will you do with this?"

Mel looked at the notebook. "Transcribe it first," he said. "Then start fact-checking."

"You would check *my* facts?"

Now it was Mel's turn to shrug. "Dmitri, freedom of the press doesn't mean we get to print just anything we like. It needs to be true, in all minor particulars as well as major ones. We just need to check. Money laundering is one thing: information laundering is another."

"Well, all right. But," he checked his watch, "you should go now, yes?"

"I suppose we should. I'll be in touch, Dmitri. And listen—" Mel stood up. "If all this is as you think it is, you could be doing the city, the state—maybe the country—a big favor."

"It did me a favor," Dmitri said. "It gave me a place to come and do business." The glint in his eye was cheerful, and feral, and funny. "I scratch America's back: it scratches mine. *Da?*"

"Da," Mel said.

"And you, young Pyotr," Dmitri said, turning to Peter. "Those pictures better be good. I have a reputation to maintain."

"These'll be the best pictures of the back of your head that you've ever seen," said Peter.

Dmitri roared with laughter. "Too bad you can't do something about the bald spot. Hey?" He jabbed Peter in the ribs cheerfully. "Never mind. A long night, you did a good job. You get in the car, they'll take you where you want."

"I'll take the subway in," Mel said. "If your guy just drops me near a D or F train, I'll be fine."

Dmitri led them to the door, shaking his head and looking at them strangely. "You *are* a madman," he said.

They went back into the garage, got into the limo, drove around Brooklyn for a bit, then stopped, presumably near a subway stop, and Mel got out.

"All right," he said to Peter. "You want to come back with me? Safety in numbers."

"Sure, why not," Peter said, and went, for he wanted to keep an eye on Mel on the way home, unable to shake the notion that something untoward might happen to him.

They went down the stairs into the subway station—

—then straight back up the stairs on the far side of the station and across to where a couple of gypsy cabs were waiting by an all-night grocery for late fares. "This'll do," said Ahrens, hopped into the first cab, and told the driver, "First and Eighty-sixth, please." They sped off.

"Mel, would you mind dropping me off along the way?" said Peter.

"No problem. Where?"

"Which bridge are you going to take back?" he said to the cabbie.

The man scowled a bit at the odd question, then said, "Probably the Williamsburg."

Peter thought for a moment. "Grand Street and Union Avenue, then."

The cabbie glanced at him in the rearview mirror and raised his eyebrows. "Not a very safe area, this time of night."

"It's all right. I'm meeting somebody."

Mel looked at Peter with a half-amused, half-disapproving expression. "Does your wife know about this?"

"As a matter of fact, she does."

"Okay, then. Suit yourself."

They got to Grand and Union, looking deserted and desolate under the yellow sodium glow, and Peter got out. Mel leaned forward to peer at him out of the still-open door. "You'll be in tomorrow with those photos?"

"Yeah. About noontime."

"Great! I'll see you, then. Be careful."

"You're telling *me* to be careful!" Peter laughed, closing the cab door. It headed away down the street and left him alone on the curb.

Quickly and quietly he slipped behind a unit of stores on the corner, scanning the alleyway to make sure the alley really was as empty as it seemed. It was, and he got busy changing.

Half a minute later, a long, slender strand of webbing shot up to hit a high-tension tower not too far away, and Spider-Man went scrambling after it, swinging onto the next building and heading after Mel's cab. *Just to be sure,* he thought.

The atmosphere of danger he had been feeling all evening had sharpened abruptly when he came out. It hadn't been his spider-sense, but something else. Probably just good old-fashioned worry.

The cab, well ahead of him by now, was indeed heading onto the Williamsburg Bridge. He went after it, sending webbing in a long shot toward one of the bridge superstructures, and swung in a wide, fast arc out into the night. They were exhilarating, these big jumps. Sometimes even working from skyscraper to skyscraper down the concrete canyons of Manhattan could seem a little constricting. Swing too wide there, and there was always a vertical solid surface sixty stories high to get abruptly in your way. The feeling of openness as he looped and swung between the structures of the bridge was like a breath of fresh air.

And all the time, he watched the cab. There wasn't much other traffic on the bridge, except for a few cars heading the other way, toward Brooklyn. *Two-thirty in the morning, so I suppose—*

His thought stopped at the roar of a fast-revving engine below him. He looked down and saw a white minivan go tearing onto the bridge in what had to be hot pursuit of Mel's cab. Spidey swung lower as the van poured on speed, its engine bellowing in protest through a muffler whose packing had seen better days. There was a brief tire squeal as it changed lanes, then another burst of speed to bring it up alongside the cab. It changed lanes again—

—and this time sideswiped the cab hard into the railing.

Once, and there was a screech of grinding metal. A long tail of sparks went stuttering across the tarmac surface before the cabbie recovered and pulled away.

Twice, and something gave. It was the railing, lengths of metal popping free of their sockets like pins in wet clay and tumbling down toward the waiting river. Spidey swung down, shooting webbing from his free hand at first one support, then another. More webbing slapped against the shattered railing as the cab slewed to a teetering stop right on the edge, and as he hit the bridge and bounced, he sent a final jet across all three strands to give them a common anchor, pulled everything as tight as he could, and turned, gasping to see what would happen.

The web stretched, and the cab tipped over sideways.

Then it stopped stretching, and the cab caught. The minivan, whose driver had slowed to watch, gunned its engine and accelerated away on over the bridge. Even though the web was holding for now, Spidey clambered hastily up the bridge support and shot a couple more lines over the cab.

Okay, spider-strength—do your stuff!

Then he heaved, and heaved again. The cab shifted, bouncing in the hammock of web strands that surrounded and supported it, then slowly leaned back toward the bridge and dropped with a crash onto all four wheels again. There was a burst of noise from inside: two voices, one yelling, the other swearing. Which was which, he couldn't tell.

Anyway, Spider-Man didn't have time to attend to them right now. But anyone capable of that much foul language at such a volume couldn't be much hurt. As he webbed away down the bridge in pursuit of the white minivan, he saw Mel stagger out of the cab, stare at the webbing, touch it, and then gape around in all directions but the right one in an attempt to see what had happened.

At the other end of the bridge the minivan had gone lurching off at the first exit, swinging around onto the approach road so as to recross in the opposite direction. Spider-Man took himself up one of the supports and out of sight, watching in case the side or rear door opened to reveal the muzzle of a Kalashnikov. If they did, he could web either or both doors shut too fast for a gunman to react.

Mel watched it approach and shook both his fists in a rage as it drew level, then ducked as a hand came out of the driver's window with a pistol in it. The gun barked a few times, a quick volley of badly aimed shots from the wildly swaying vehicle that spanged and ricocheted most impressively, but came nowhere near him.

The van had no plates, and there was no point in Mel bothering with it any further. He turned back toward the cabbie and began waving his fists at *him*, instead.

Excess tension, Spidey thought. *Wonderful thing.* He watched the white van roar away beneath him and back toward Brooklyn. *Now then,* he thought, and went in pursuit.

It led him on a merry chase, all the more so because he was taking particular care not to be seen. It was a bit of a trick as they got off the Brooklyn-Queens Expressway, but he managed it, and followed the white van south. After a mile or so the driver plainly decided he was safe, because the van slowed right down, almost too much in Spidey's opinion. Any vehicle being driven that carefully was as likely to rouse a traffic cop's suspicions as one being driven too fast, particularly this late at night, and though they hadn't used an AK-74 in the drive-by, that didn't mean there wasn't one inside.

At one point, near Flatbush Avenue and Church, it actually pulled off into a side street while two men jumped out and used cordless electronic screwdrivers—he could hear the thin whine—to bolt New York plates back onto the front and rear of the van. Spidey took a careful mental note of the numbers; they probably belonged to another car, stolen or otherwise, but then again they might prove to be some kind of help. The van started up again, and so did he.

At Foster Avenue the van veered sideways, then after a few long blocks turned south onto Ocean Parkway. *Aha!* Spidey thought, for down at the bottom of Ocean lay Bensonhurst, and after that Brighton Beach and Coney Island.

Russian country.

He swung from building to building, keeping up the best speed he could and grateful that, even at this hour of the morning, there was enough traffic to keep the van from simply blasting out of sight and losing him. They headed into the depths of Bensonhurst, turned briefly toward Ocean Avenue, then headed down a side street.

There the van pulled up in front of a brownstone, turned its lights and engine off, and sat quiet.

Hmm, thought Spidey. *Are we waiting for someone?*

Farther down the street he could see an apartment building with an underground parking lot, and suddenly he began to wonder. Hurriedly dropping from his vantage point on the roof of the brownstone, he landed on the roof of the van. There were muffled exclamations from inside, but nothing that worried him particularly.

But instead of webbing the doors shut from the convenient position of the roof, he jumped to the ground before applying his own brand of external lock. It was just as well. Even before the occupants realized that they couldn't get out, some smart guy emptied half a clip of full-auto through the roof, right between where Spidey's feet had landed.

There were a couple of metallic squeaks and clatters as the doors were tried, then another three rapid shots turned the laminated windshield into a piece of sagging modern art. It was shoved from its frame, and people started climbing through the hole.

"Oh no," said Spidey in a disapproving voice, and started webbing them as fast as they got out. Their gunfire was what newscasters would usually call *sporadic;* it made an encouraging noise but otherwise didn't do much good. One after another, as though there were a stamping-press inside, the van emitted big men in dark clothing, and one after another, as they emerged, Spider-Man hit each one with a generous squirt of web fluid.

This resulted in the utterance of several words like *svoloch* and *chyort*—which Spidey assumed to be some manner of Russian swearword or other—as they cut themselves on glass, or kicked each other in the soft parts before they realized that there really *was* only space for one to get out at a time, and they swore even harder when they found themselves trussed securely by the lengths of webbing.

Four of them, finally. It had seemed like more. When

people stopped climbing out of the van, Spidey carefully peered inside in case anyone else had seen what was happening outside and decided to stay under cover. No; it was empty.

But on the back shelf of the van were four cell phones.

As he looked at them, and a grim smile spread across his face beneath the mask, one of the phones began to ring. The men lying webbed on the ground all glared at him, and one of them growled something that sounded like *"prokleenyesh sookeen-sahn . . ."*

"Yeah, yeah, army boots to you too," Spidey said as he reached in and picked up the phone. He tapped the reply button, and a voice that seemed too big for the little handset speaker started yelling at him in Russian. "I'm sorry," he said in a fair imitation of the annoying CellTech voice mail, "but the party you are calling is all tied up right now."

That's a joke so old it appears in cave paintings, he thought ruefully, *but what the hey? Besides*—he glanced at the well-webbed Russian hoods lying at his feet—*how often is it true?*

There was a long pause at the other end of the phone, and then laughter. It was a shrill, high-pitched, and unpleasant sound that could never be a genuinely merry sound like Dmitri's guffaw. "Who is this?" said the voice at last, speaking in good though accented English.

"Spider-Man," said Spidey, just to see what the reaction would be. It was more laughter, even more shrill, even less pleasant, and on a hunch he said, "Galya?"

"Oh, very smart, Mister Super Hero. You have been talking to Dmitri Il'yevich, have you not? That was a bad mistake. And somebody else has been talking to him. That reporter—"

"Who your people just tried to kill."

"Yes, well, if they missed him this time, they'll get him some other day. Or someone else will. He doesn't make a lot of friends, your Mister Ah-rens." He pronounced the name in two distinct syllables. "Not that he will matter in the long run. Or you.'' There was more laughter. ''After all, in a hundred years, who'll know the difference?'' He laughed harder. ''Or in a hundred days.''

Then the line went dead, and a moment later Spider-Man was listening to a busy signal. He looked at the phone, thought about dumping it, then decided not to and secured the phones in a pouch made of webbing—but only after using one of them to call 911 and report automatic gunfire just off Ocean Avenue. The lights of the first blue-and-white were already riding their siren wail toward him along Ocean Parkway as he webbed away.

But he was unable to get rid of the sound of that laughter, the sound of a man who didn't have a care in the world—even about being caught in the act of attempted-murder-by-proxy. Who didn't care about anything because he knew that it wouldn't matter in a hundred days.

Whatever that meant.

Elsewhere in town, inside a huge apartment—a nearly unfurnished place where the curtains were kept closed all day—a big-shouldered, broad-bodied man sat behind a large desk, going through some paperwork. In front of him on the marble floor stood a slender red-haired man in a black jacket; not quite standing at attention, but giving that impression anyhow.

''Report,'' said the man behind the desk.

''Operation Stifle is going along nicely,'' said the red-headed man. ''The last few—sanctions—are being taken care of. No one who knew about the Miami processing plant will be left alive within two days.''

''Very good. It's not just a matter of 'loose lips' and possible betrayals. Loose ends are so untidy. . . .'' He turned over some of the paperwork on the desk with one hand, leaning his chin on the other, pausing for a moment to listen to the faint rumbling from outside. ''I would do something about the soundproofing,'' he said absently, ''except that, in a little while, there won't be any point, will there? How are the container shipments going?''

''They've almost all reached their secondary destinations. Our teams will be breaking them down into their final sizes over the next two days.''

''Very well. Keep an eye on the timing of this phase, the pickups and so forth. It would be very annoying if the authorities discovered one of these shipments by mistake. Or detonated it, for that matter.'' The big man smiled slightly, turned over another page.

''Oh, and the guest suite is ready, sir.''

''Excellent. I would hate to have Spider-Man miss this denouement; it will be so delightful to watch him realize that, for once, for all his meddling over all these years, there's genuinely nothing he can do to stop the process.'' A metal tentacle arched slowly over the man's back, bent down to tap, like someone's drumming fingers, on the table. ''We'll see if it's true what they say, that heroes break hardest when they break. Are we sure the sanction teams are properly equipped?''

''Yes, sir, and there are six of them. We'll have no trouble bringing him in for the big blowoff.''

The big man chuckled. ''Blowoff. Yes. I do so love the vernacular. Very well. Anything else that needs my attention, Niner?''

''Not at present, sir.''

Sitting back in his chair, the big man smiled. ''It's always so satisfying,'' he said, ''to be in the last stages of a project, watching all the pieces come together. You can go, Niner.''

The redheaded man left quietly. The four metal tentacles attached to the big man's waist descended to curl and wreathe around him in a contemplative way as he folded his hands, closed his eyes briefly.

Day Hundred is coming.

FIVE

Peter woke up to the smell of coffee. He had come to bed very quietly, but MJ had been sprawled under the sheets, so fast asleep and looking so wrung out that she probably wouldn't have noticed if he'd played himself a lullaby on a tuba. His last thought before closing his eyes was that her day had apparently been pretty much like his.

Now, with the scent of fresh coffee filling the apartment, he rolled over and yawned. "Aha," came a voice from down the hall. "I know that sound." MJ was already fully dressed and made up, and not just the usual casual-but-pretty. This was the full nine yards.

"Where are you going?" he said, blinking the remains of sleep from his eyes.

"Work!"

"But I thought your hand—"

"Not my hand. My voice."

"Wait a minute. Wasn't lipstick involved in this somehow?"

"Yes, it was. But that unhappy episode seems to have borne a different sort of fruit. Come on and have some breakfast, and I'll tell you all about it. But first, you'd better look at the news."

Peter yawned again and got out of bed, wrapping himself in his bathrobe as he padded toward the kitchen. "The way you say that, I'm getting tempted to put an ax through the screen."

"Oh, I dunno. It's not the TV's fault."

He wandered in just as the morning newsreader was repeating her headline stories. "—muggers are now in hospital at Bellvue, suffering from serious injuries—" she was saying, but it was the placard behind her head that caught his attention. It showed Venom's tongue-lolling, grin-distorted face.

"Oh, wonderful."

"Yes," said MJ, pouring him coffee. "I don't like having to be away from you when he's around."

137

"It's not like we haven't tangled before, and I'm still okay—"

" 'Okay,' he calls it," said MJ and snorted derisively. "With your ribs broken and your head bashed in half the time, and lumps and bumps and bruises all over your body, and cuts and scrapes and scratches and dueling wounds, this is some new definition of 'okay' that I'm not familiar with."

Then she sighed and sat down, looking at her own coffee cup. "I don't like it, Tiger. What if he's come back to settle things? He's had plenty of time to recover after the last fight."

"And so have I. But there's no way to tell with him. And I can't worry about him right now; I've got other things on my mind. And you? What was your day like?"

"Oh, please." She told him about meeting Lalande and the others at Baja, about the lipstick shoot, and finally about the small, smiling man who had come up to her and given her his card. She pushed it across the table to him, and Peter grinned.

"Film and television? Steady work, maybe?"

"I don't know yet. I called him earlier this morning to set up a meeting, and it turns out he's a voice director for this studio. They do animation, and he wants to audition me, to see"—she smiled—"that should be, to hear, if I'll be good for some series that he's working on."

"It could *be* steady work, then. How does voice pay?"

"Well, I'm still a SAG member after *Secret Hospital,* so there's no problem at the union-card end. If he wants to hire me, I can start right away." MJ picked up the business card and put it away again. "And after yesterday, it would be a real pleasure to work at something that didn't involve bright lights, and people running around screaming, and having to do the same shot over and over again because last time it wasn't just quite right. In fact, after yesterday I'd seriously consider ditch-digging.''

She finished her coffee and eyed him over the rim of the cup. "You were out late. How did it go?"

"Yes, well . . ." Peter gave her a much-edited version of the interview with Dmitri, and its aftermath, then watched her nod dubiously.

"At least the shooting didn't break out while you were actually there," she said. "But I don't like the idea that this guy immediately tried to kill Mel. What's to say he won't try to kill you, too? After all, you both heard the same things."

Peter raised his eyebrows. "I'm not sure that his people even knew that I was there. But they sure knew that Mel was—and they knew he'd taken a cab even after that little shuffle in the subway station. He was being watched, but I must have gone unnoticed. Not important enough, maybe."

"A backhanded compliment, if you like. Let's keep it that way. There are some kinds of importance nobody needs." She checked her watch. "Gotta go, Tiger. Where'll you be today?"

"I've got pictures to develop, and then I thought I might follow up on the lead that Sergeant Drew gave me. His source of cell phone information. After yesterday we're gonna need some other source of help, because we're not gonna get it from CellTech."

"Right," she said and kissed him. "I'm off."

"Only a little, and it hardly shows."

Her eyes twinkled at him as she headed for the door. "We should try to get you on *Letterman* sometime," she said and shut it behind her.

Peter chuckled. He got up, washed, shaved, dressed, and did some morning maintenance for Spider-Man, mostly involving refilling the web-shooters. Then he took out the cell phones from the van last night and stared thoughtfully at them, especially the one on which the call from Galya had come through. Just ordinary cell phones; brand differences, design differences, model differences, and otherwise no different from every other cell phone in the city. Peter put on his Spider-Man mask to muffle his voice, picked up the ordinary phone, and dialed for Sergeant Drew.

The sergeant was up to his neck in work, as usual, and was just on his way out to a court appearance when Spidey got through. "Listen," he said, "just call this number," and he rattled off a seven-digit number. "Got it?"

"Got it. That's a 212?"

"Yeah. If there's a problem, say I cleared you. Then wait." And Drew hung up.

Peter dialed the new number, and waited. A moment later, a very soft feminine voice said, "Doris Smyth."

"Uh, Ms. Smyth, my name is Peter Parker, and I'm a friend of Spider-Man, who—"

"Oh yes. Sergeant Drew called me to say that Spider-Man might be in touch. Or have someone do so on his behalf." Peter noticed the phrasing, and was briefly, cautiously intrigued by it. Did Drew suspect? Or was he likely to, after finding out just who Spider-Man had assigned to make the visit in his place? Well, there was nothing for it now but to press on—though not regardless. Rather more cautiously than that. Ms. Smyth continued, "The sergeant didn't say much more than that this involved a very interesting problem. Would you like to come up to my place and discuss it?" The voice was warm and friendly.

"Certainly. That is, if it's convenient."

"No problem at all." And she supplied him with a posh East Side address.

"Is there an apartment number?"

"Just forty-fifth floor. You'll know it when you see it." There was a small chuckle. "The building ends quite soon afterwards."

"I'll be there in, uh, twenty minutes."

And in twenty minutes, Peter was looking up at a

sleek and expensive forty-five-floor apartment building and muttering "Good grief," under his breath. A sleek and expensive doorman opened the sleek and expensive door for him, and Peter stepped inside.

As he passed, the doorman said, "Apartment?"

"Uh, I was only told the floor. Forty-fifth."

"Ah, that would be Mrs. Smyth. Right this way, sir." He directed Peter to an elevator—as sleek and expensive as everything else he had seen so far—then reached inside, punched 45, and smoothly withdrew from between the smoothly closing doors.

When it stopped, and the doors opened smoothly, he was looking out into a small private lobby with only one door leading off it. Then the door opened.

Peter wasn't quite sure what he had been expecting, but it certainly wasn't this. Standing in the doorway was a genteel little old lady, with pale, fine skin that was barely wrinkled, except for the demure pattern of smile and laughter lines around her eyes and mouth. Wearing a dressy little green tweed jacket-and-skirt set, with a dark, high-necked blouse and a discreet string of pearls, she looked as if she were going out to take tea somewhere nice and swap gossip with a couple of duchesses.

"Ms., er, Smyth?"

"Mrs.," she said, "but call me Doris. And you're Peter Parker?"

"That's right." They shook hands, and she gestured him in. Peter walked into one of the biggest and most beautiful apartments it had ever been his pleasure to see, wonderfully furnished with antiques and expensive porcelain: the Irish Belleek that MJ lusted after, the Meissen that Kate Cushing liked so much, beautiful old couches upholstered in crimson and gold Regency stripe, with wood that gleamed with the same deep, lustrous patina as Mel Ahrens's old typewriter, polished breakfronts and bureaus, and behind all of these, floor-to-ceiling windows with a truly astonishing view.

It was not at all the sort of place where he expected

to find help for his and MJ's cell phone problem.

"Forgive me," Peter said, "but—Well, I'm just blown away. This view goes right 'round, doesn't it?"

"Oh yes. I have the whole floor. My late husband used to be in shipping. He was quite successful, but, well, George isn't with us anymore." She cleared her throat. "Anyway. Sit down and have a cup of tea, and tell me what your problem is."

They sat down at a handsome glass-topped table at one end of the huge main living room, and Peter explained what had happened to MJ's phone. "Yes indeed," said Doris. "There's a lot of that nonsense going around. Very nasty. And of course, the phone companies aren't wildly eager to do anything about it. All they want is to cover their assets, so to speak, and expenses too, of course. They'll happily take it out of their subscribers' pockets."

"I've noticed that," Peter said.

"Yes, quite. So much easier than trying to find a way 'round the problem. But then, *that* might cost money. You don't have the phone with you at the moment?"

"No, I don't. My wife's got it, and she's out on business."

"All right," Doris said. "Well—"

"Forgive me," Peter interrupted, "but I'm not sure that you—I mean, what do *you* do about this kind of thing?"

"Come back this way, Peter Parker, and I'll show you."

She led him out of the living room and across the kitchen, out the far side, and into another room that was as big as both the first two rolled into one. Bookshelves were here, and more beautiful old furniture, and a corridor that led along one side of the building, walled with more floor-to-ceiling windows looking out over the cityscape below.

"I just can't get over the view," Peter said again. It was true; he'd been as high, or higher, when out web-slinging, but that had never been an activity conducive to rubbernecking.

"George always said I should be comfortable in my old age, and I've always liked to see what's going on around me. This seemed to be the best way to combine both wishes. And here we are." She opened up a door on the left that might once have led into a guest bedroom.

Now the guests would have to be communications experts from the CIA. At the very least.

What had once been a bedroom was now packed with more electronic equipment than he had seen in one place since the last time he passed through the Fantastic Four's headquarters. From floor to ceiling along every wall, mounted in studio-quality instrument racks, were banks and banks of scanners, fiber-optic phone connections in bundles as thick as packs of spaghetti, ISDN linkages, phone-band radios, what seemed to be short-, medium-, and long-wave radio receivers bristling with buttons. Everything was black, very expensive, and very professional.

"George always said I should have a hobby," Doris said to Peter, "and I never could get the hang of knitting. And as for casting off, I must have created the longest single sock in history. But he left me quite a bit of money—"

That's an unnecessary observation, Peter thought, looking again at the cool, dark racks of equipment and feeling them gaze back at him with tiny LED eyes.

"—and I always did like keeping in touch with people. Listening to what was going on. And what comes through here is so much more interesting than most talk shows, don't you think?"

"But isn't it, er, sort of illegal to listen in on private communications?" he said, staring at yet another floor-to-ceiling wall of equipment, this time so complex that he couldn't even guess at what it was meant to do.

"Not if the government gives you everything they want you to listen with."

"Um," said Peter. There were some statements that went beyond words.

"You know, I had one of the first cell phones sold in New York City," Doris said. "And about ten others. I got cloned, too. It made me cross." She said it quietly enough, but there was something about the glint in her blue-gray eyes that suggested it wasn't a good idea to make Doris Smyth cross.

"I started doing some research into hacking, and phreaking, and all the other ways a phone company could be cheated. It got very interesting. So I started buying equipment to look into the problem myself, and quite soon after that I tracked down the people who had cloned my own phone. It was easier then: they left a track through the ether half a mile wide. Once I had done that, I contacted the phone company and passed the information along. They were so impressed that," she smiled up at him, "they hired me. I do fairly well. Something like a ten percent identification rate, which I gather is pretty good. The end result is that all three of the major cell companies here—including CellTech— use me as a security consultant. I charge them what the market will bear, and in some cases I do work *pro bono*. That will be you, young man. Or rather, your wife. They socked you for—how much was it?"

"Four thousand and change."

She tutted disapprovingly. "A young couple like you can't be expected to pay that kind of money. We've got to do something about these regulations. They're hurting people. It's not *your* fault that half the criminals in New York are making cell phones work for them. It's only to be expected, though. If something is worth money, then someone, somewhere, will work out a way to steal it." She led the way out of the room, and closed its door behind her.

"Surely there have to be other consultants working

144

on this kind of thing,'' Peter said as they walked back up the glass-walled corridor. "So how come you're doing so well? It could just be natural talent, of course."

Doris glanced up at him again, and smiled. "Flatterer. If your wife finds that you're wasting perfectly good compliments on eighty-year-old grannies, you're going to get in trouble!"

"Eighty?"

"But I don't look a year over sixty, right?"

"Really, you don't. What's your secret?"

"Snoopiness, and having something to do. Something really interesting. Everyone should have something really interesting to do, even if they have to keep it a secret. Have you?"

"Er, I do a lot of freelance photography, for the *Bugle* and for—"

"Oh? Would I have seen any of your pictures?"

"You would have seen some in the *Bugle* over the last week, yes."

"Then you're a celebrity! Well, you have to come and sit down, finish your tea, and tell me all about it."

"I'm not a celebrity, not really," Peter said. "It's my wife—" But it was no use. He got to sit down again with Doris, and tell her all about his wife, and especially about MJ's stint in *Secret Hospital*.

"She's in *that!* Who is she? The nurse? Why, she's famous! And her phone was cloned. The very idea! Well, we're going to do something about that." Peter smiled slightly. MJ was going to love this. "And you tell her she has to come up and see me. She has a *fan*. Why, she must meet such interesting people, and do such interesting things."

Peter let her rattle on. It was plain that one of the reasons Doris was so good at her job was that she loved gossip. No scrap of information, not the most petty detail, was too insignificant for her attention.

He sat with her for what must have been the better part of the afternoon, and after the rather dodgy company of last night, she was a pleasure. But more to the point, the more he talked to her, the more he realized that under her little-old-lady exterior she was a serious professional, and a power to be reckoned with. She told him about ways that cell phones were being illegally used in the city that even he, with his daily exposure to the criminal element, had ever dreamed of. Not just drugs and gambling and money-laundering, but coordinating times for burglaries, bank robberies, and even simple street muggings. One criminal gang had even been using them as detonators to blow up the gas stations they had just robbed.

"A lot of people just don't understand electromagnetics," said Doris, "much less what the various frequencies can do." She eyed Peter keenly over the rims of her glasses. "But some of us do understand. That's one of the reasons why I bought this place."

Peter glanced around him. "Well, it's a really nice apartment," he said, "and the view—"

"No, not that. Come out this way." They stepped out onto the terrace together. Doris's terrace went all the way around her penthouse, and it had emitters, microwave receivers, and relays that made the setups on the Empire State Building and the World Trade Center look seriously inadequate. Peter had never seen so many antennas together in one place in his life.

"I've got line of sight into three states," she said, "and from here I've also got line of sight down into three-fifths of the city's streets. That means a lot of the time I can do a direct ambient-radiation trace on any cell phone in use. It's really very useful."

Peter was feeling much better, reassured as well as slightly awed after seeing the quiet room that had looked so much like a starship's bridge. He was still thinking about MJ's phone bill, but also about the other phones that he had taken from the Russian thugs last night— and Galya's bizarre, threatening laughter. *I wonder, is there any way to get her to look at that one?* he thought as they went back inside to sit at the table again.

"More tea?" said Doris, already reaching for the pot.

"Uh, thanks, Doris, but I really think I should be going."

"Well, bring that phone up for me—as soon as you can get it away from your famous wife." She smiled at him. "I really would love to meet her sometime."

"And I'm sure she'd love to meet you, too. I'll get the phone just as quick as I can. By the way, there was a sort of crank call to it, just last night. Is there any way to find out where it came from?"

"That's fairly simple, as a rule. Once I've got the phone itself, I can look into it." She saw him to the door, shook his hand, and told him to have a nice day— then went back inside to resume her secret identity as a senior-citizen spook.

Peter shook his head. Little old ladies just weren't what they used to be.

Sundog Productions was a small, four-story brownstone in the middle Forties, near Third Avenue. She buzzed the door, and a voice said, "Yeah?" It sounded like Jymn Magon.

"It's Mary Jane Watson-Parker, for Jymn Magon," she said.

"Oh, hi there, Mary Jane! Come on up." The lock buzzed, then clicked, and MJ pushed the heavy wooden door open. She swung it shut behind her, then proceeded to climb four levels of stairs straight up from the street. There had been other doors leading off on each floor, but those were all boarded up.

The topmost door had another buzzer, and a glass window overlooking the reception area. A friendly-looking woman waved at her through the window, and buzzed the door open as she approached. MJ was fairly fit, but even so she was panting a little as she stepped inside.

"Some climb," she said.

"Yep," said the other. "But it tires the burglars out as well. Come on in. I'm Harriet."

"Pleased to meet you."

The door of one of the inner offices opened, and Jymn Magon came out. "Hi, Mary Jane," he said. "Come in, please."

"Call me MJ if you like."

"Glad to. Now, if you'll just step this way, into our corporate lair." He led her through the reception area and out to the back of the brownstone. One side of the room had a spiral staircase leading down from it into the areas beneath, and this upper floor had been partitioned into offices.

"We keep the studios downstairs," said Magon. "All the doors and windows are sealed. It's not just for security; we had to install a lot of anechoic insulation for the voice recording, because of the usual traffic noise—and because we're real close to Grand Central and all five gajillion trains that use it. Even so, we've got some of the quietest studios in the city here."

He ushered her into a comfortable office whose walls, where they weren't covered with framed animation cels, were decorated with children's drawings, and offered her a chair. "Sit down, and tell me what you've done." Behind his own desk was a big poster entitled THE SIX STAGES OF A PROJECT. MJ glanced at it briefly, then gave him a quick verbal résumé of her work.

He was most impressed with the *Secret Hospital* work—less for the work itself than because she had survived in one piece. "I've heard what a zoo that place was," he said, grinning. "I hear about it every time I meet someone who was ever on the show." They also talked briefly about yesterday's lipstick shoot, and about the "director of death."

"All right," said Jymn, "so the field has a tradition of eccentric, egocentric directors. But they're not all De Mille, and they certainly don't all have his talent. So

148

they've earned the occasional dressing-down by irate lipstick models.''

MJ smiled modestly.

Jymn went on, ''But, while everyone appreciated the words, I also appreciated the voice that uttered them. You've got really good timbre. When your voice drops, it gets very dry, and there's a strong sound to it. Too often, female talents think they need to shout when they're voicing a strong character, and they end up sounding like early Margaret Thatcher, all squeaky and nasal. It took years to get her to drop her voice low enough to get the men to listen to her, apparently; and once she got it right, they hated her twice as much. She was too good at making them do what she wanted.''

''What exactly did you want to audition me for?'' MJ said.

''Well, right now we're starting work on a new syndicated series: sixty-five episodes. It's a super hero show called *The Giga-Group*.''

MJ raised her eyebrows. ''I thought the super hero trend was getting kind of old.'' With so many super heroes making headlines and lead news stories, people seemed to have grown tired of the fictional versions.

''No, the pendulum's swinging back again. Go figure. In any case, we've got a nice syndication deal, so *someone* thinks the trend's not dead—and insists on giving us their money as a proof of confidence—and I for one have no objection to finding out. Right now it would be 'casual' or 'fill-in' voices that we'd want you for: not running characters, but ones who appear in specific episodes as one-time characters, super-villains, things like that. Do you think it's something you could do?''

''I could certainly audition for you, and we'll see how it turns out. But,'' and she smiled, ''I've always been kinda fond of the super hero thing.''

''Good. Character identification already. Come on downstairs. We'll do a brief set of readings from some scripts that have either been shot, or are about to be, and see how you sound. Oh, and one last thing: your SAG membership is current?''

''Yes.''

''One less thing to worry about, then. Let's go.''

She followed him down the spiral staircase and into the reception area for the third floor, a central windowed area overlooking four separate recording suites. Two of them were already occupied: people were sitting inside manipulating soundboards, and beyond, through yet another set of glass windows, other people were sitting in director's chairs with music stands in front of them, microphones hanging from the ceiling, and intent expressions on their faces.

''Some of our leads, in there,'' said Jymn, pointing to the suite on the left. ''Mike Bright, Chris Clarens, and Orkney Hallard. They're three of our good guys. The bad guys are out to lunch. Anyway, come over here into Four, we'll get you comfortable, and then you can read some stuff for me.''

MJ went along happily enough. This was the least tense audition she could remember having for a long time. Jymn brought in a stack of scripts and riffled through them, pulling pages out.

''Since we're working on such short notice,'' he said, ''and you haven't had a chance to read any of this material ahead of time, I'm not going to give you anything too substantive. I'm looking for emotion here, the kind of crazy voice that you were doing yesterday when our friend was yelling at you. Big reactions, over the top; don't be afraid to shriek.''

She gave him a wry look. ''Would you believe that shrieking is the one thing I've tried to avoid most in my entire life?'' she asked.

''Good. Then you'll do it here, and get it out of your system—and if this works out, you'll get paid for it.''

Now there's an interesting concept. MJ smiled. She was liking this better and better all the time.

''Most of these characters are bad guys, so don't be

afraid to 'nyah-hah-ha' a little. Unfortunately, our broader viewing public is not yet *au courant* with the concept that bad guys don't necessarily *sound* bad, but it's gotten into the culture and right now we're stuck with it. Please God, twenty years from now when everyone's reading Tolstoy and Kipling again, all this will seem very silly. Okay, I'm going to shut you in here for the sound. Do you have any problems with claustrophobia?''

"Not at all. I live in a Manhattan apartment."

Jymn chuckled. "Just thought I'd check."

MJ spent the next hour reading what seemed very fragmentary lines in various funny voices: high, low, mean, menacing, scared, funny. It was surprisingly easy—or maybe it was that the director was surprisingly good. Jymn had a talent for drawing out tones and colorations of voice that you didn't know you had. It helped that he had quite a talent in the voice line himself. If you couldn't actually understand the sound he wanted, even after five minutes of explanation that could vary from earthy and graphic to highly technical, he would make it at you. Then all you had to do was imitate, and you were home free.

"Aha!" MJ would cry, pronouncing it with more or less exclamation marks as required; and "Now I've got you!" in every shade of meaning, including some that were highly inappropriate to a children's animated show; but there was something about the way she said, "Resistance is useless!" that on at least one occasion, Jymn pitched face-forward onto the mixing board and pounded it with his fists.

"I'm sorry," she said. "Should I read that one again?"

Jymn hit the talk button that let him be heard inside the soundproofed studio, and though more or less back under control, MJ could still hear tremors of laughter running up and down his voice like a piano hit with a brick. "Yes," he said. "Oh yes. The same way as last time, but louder!"

So it went, for a cheerful hour and more, until Jymn stopped, keyed his talk button, and said, "Are you thirsty? Can I get you an ice water or something?"

The thought had occurred to her in midcackle of some villainous laugh or other, about ten minutes or so ago. "Oh, yes, please," she said. "I'd love it."

"Sit tight," said Jymn. "I'll be right with you." He got up from the mixing desk and vanished out through the sound-room door.

Trapped, thought MJ. *I'm trapped.* Not so, of course. The heavy baffled door wasn't even locked, staying tight shut as much by its own ponderous weight. But the studio was so quiet, its anechoic tiling soaking up every sound. She sat for a few minutes and just listened to it. New Yorkers forget, sometimes, just what real quiet is, and if taken out into the country they lie awake at night, missing the distant or nearby sounds of subway and traffic, and the endless subliminal roar of ten million other human beings packed together into the confines of the city who were just getting on with their lives.

In here, you could almost believe that human beings weren't outside anymore. Almost, but not quite: the listening ear could detect a truck going by or the rumble of a deep train, even though it was a sensation more felt than heard. She put her hand on the tabletop nearby, but there was nothing. Complete stillness. A total lack of noise.

I wonder, thought MJ with a grin, *if we could get these people to redecorate the apartment.* The grin went mischievous. *Or at least the bedroom.*

Jymn came back in, carrying a Coke for himself and a tall cup of ice water for her, and brought them through to the studio. "Listen," he said, his voice oddly dull and lifeless as the tiles flattened all the subtleties out of it, "we don't need to do any more today if you don't want to."

"Okay. Whatever you like." She took a drink from the Styrofoam cup and glanced at him over the rim.

"Sorry about these things," he said. "Déclassé, I know, but we haven't been able to get up to the Gristede's for the good plastic ones." He sat down in another of the director's chairs. "You're very flexible," Jymn told her. "You take direction brilliantly—and you're very good-natured. It surprised me yesterday when I saw you in that madhouse. I was wondering what someone so calm could be doing there."

"Toward the end of the day," said MJ, "I was beginning to wonder myself."

"Anyway, are you available?"

"How soon?"

"Tonight."

"To*night*?" MJ blinked. "So soon? I presume you're not talking about dinner."

Jymn laughed. "No. We're taping a *Giga-Group* episode tonight, and we lost a couple of our voices. Business, sickness, the usual annoyances. I can use you as an interim voice. I'd like to do that, and I'd also like to have you work with our people a little bit, because I suspect we could use you as a regular. Semi-regular, at least. Our main character voices are all spoken for, but we've got some recurring villains, and one of them is female."

"Villains? Hey, fun!"

"Yes, I thought I heard that when you were screeching before. You don't get much chance to be *baaad,* do you?"

MJ chuckled, but couldn't really tell Jymn why. The thought running around in her head right at the moment was that, being a super hero's wife, you mostly concentrated on being *goood,* just as good as you could be. It meant maintaining your own career, while attempting to make sure that a man largely unconscious of his own needs—and especially his own stomach, even when it was growling the loudest—got enough food, enough rest, and enough love to make up for what he didn't get in the violent dark world outside that he inhabited.

"No, and I don't see that tonight will be a problem."

"Okay. As far as I can tell right now, we'll be starting at the usual time. That's around eight; it gives the city a chance to get quiet. I have to warn you, these taping sessions do run late, usually eight to midnight or a little over. We contract in four-hour blocks, we pay Guild scale per four hours, if we run past midnight, we pay Guild-and-a-half. Does that suit you?"

She did a brief bit of mental math and realized that at the moment, Guild scale for four hours was about $500 per hour. "That's fine," she said. "Do we need to sign the paperwork?"

"C'mon upstairs. We'll cut it, get the signatures—do you work through an agent?"

"Not for voice."

"You may want to look into that at a later date. If you start working with other companies"—he smiled slightly, as if remembering something—"you'll find that some of their terms aren't as advantageous as ours, and it could be in your own best interests to get an agent with great big teeth and a loud voice to do the screaming on your behalf. We can recommend a couple if you like; otherwise talk to the talent. They'll be more than happy to tell you horror stories." Jymn rolled his eyes. "Endless horror stories. Other than that, let's go write you a contract and sign it. Do you need an advance?"

She opened her mouth, closed it again, shrugged, and said, "Why not?" Then added, carefully, "You're awfully, er, easygoing about this."

"Oh, absolutely. We know where you live. If it doesn't work out—we'll sue your butt. In the meantime, I've got work to do; I'm clear that you like this work, and I know you're good at it. We'll see how you work with a group, but I'm confident enough to advance you one night's salary. We'll go down to the cash machine and fish it out, give you a chance to do your shopping before we start work.'' He gave her a look. ''I know how awkward it is. Arranging the rest of your life gets rather interesting when you've neither days nor evenings free.''

''Well, thank you,'' said MJ. ''Thank you very much. Has anyone ever told you that you're very, well, *nice?*''

He gave her a look that was appreciative of the compliment, but somehow ironic. ''Not recently. But then, after our friend yesterday, Attila the Hun would look *nice.*''

Chuckling, she agreed, and followed him out.

Elsewhere in the city, other people were also arranging their evening. Eddie Brock had been a busy man since the previous night. He was staying in a small, quiet hotel on the Lower East Side and had spent the better part of the afternoon going over the paperwork and copies he had brought back from the Bureau of Records.

Hunting down the actual ownership of a company can sometimes be deadly dull work; at other times it can be a good deal more exciting, especially when the trail starts heating up. There are shells within shells, share percentages, and beneficial and beneficiary owners in a paper trail that can sometimes lead halfway around the world in twenty different languages. And if it should involve one of the countries that *really* take their banking secrecy seriously, like Liechtenstein, then the trail can run up against a wall that no amount of digging will ever penetrate, and the ownership of a given firm will never be truly known.

Ownership and control are only rarely the same.

Eddie Brock was nothing if not methodical. His background as a reporter had tended to make him so until, late in that reporting career, issues had so blinded him to the truth of one business he was investigating that he jumped the gun and printed material that could be proved untrue. The rebuttal . . .

He shook his head, hating to let the thoughts into his head again, but unable to keep them out.

Another authority had stood up in front of the world, embarrassed him, called his integrity into question—a questioning that had been applied retroactively to everything else he had ever written—and caused him to be blackballed from the one profession he had ever really cared about. But that other authority, and the person behind it, would be dealt with soon enough.

But right now, he had other fish to fry.

CCRC was being audited by the government. Everybody knew that. The IRS, the DEA—and for all he knew, the FBI, the CIA, and even the FAA—were all on its tail. And Eddie Brock was still enough of an investigative reporter to know that a company involved in the laundering of millions, and perhaps *billions,* of dollars of illegal funds is not just closed down like a bankrupt shop putting its shutters up. There is almost always warning that there's trouble in the wind and, almost always, the money goes away.

Specifically—and it was practically the standard method—other companies would be purchased or established and clean money already laundered through other sources would be channeled into them. Any companies that had previously been founded as intermediaries to service the laundering pipelines would themselves be closed down. In military terminology, it was a "withdrawal to prepared positions."

Eddie sat now in his little hotel room working on a laptop computer whose present program allowed you to construct complex graphical expressions of relationships between completely abstract factors. Those could be anything you liked, but corporate entities was what he was looking at right now.

The New York Securities and Exchange Commission and the Bureau of Records had begun to work very closely together since the days when insider trading first reared its head. There was now more information available about companies opened in New York, the United States, and, though to a lesser extent, overseas than there ever had been before.

In particular, Eddie was looking into those overseas connections, searching for large amounts of money that had been moved out of CCRC or its accounts—and especially money that had been removed from the United States—during the period immediately before the audit had been announced.

The period when Venom and Spider-Man had been tearing the place apart.

Compared with other countries, even those that didn't make an issue of it, banking secrecy in the U.S. was little more than a joke. If you had friends in the right places, say the IRS, the DEA, or even some local police departments, and you knew the right phone numbers to call, then you could access databases that would tell you far more than any private citizen had a right to know about the movement of funds in and out of the country. Put that together with the SEC's register of newly formed companies and corporations—onshore or off, it didn't matter—and you had a powerful tool for levering your way into corporate secrets. Always assuming you knew how to sort the data.

Fortunately, Venom knew how. The copies he had made yesterday in the Bureau of Records were all New York based. Some of them were hard copy because they were already too old to be worth keeping online. Say, three months old. That was how fast corporate formation turned over in New York State. Not as fast as in some offshore havens, certainly—where if you lingered too long over lunch you could find your morning's harvest of information already well on the way to obsolescence—but fast enough.

Venom was looking for corporate formations that were immediately bolstered by large transfers of funds. Certainly bank managers, and banks in general, were required to report suspicious transfers of any value, and all transfers above a certain threshold, to the government. But if your bank manager was pliant, as it were, and kept that way by regular applications of folding grease, then such reports would never be made. He would know you, would certainly know what you were capable of doing if he let you down, and wouldn't be *suspicious* of your money because he knew full well that it was dirty.

His search was for newly established companies without a track record, whose names appeared in no previous register—but who suddenly sprouted large bank balances that they promptly wire-transferred offshore. New York being what it is, he found plenty; the difficulty was in determining which were more or less innocent, and which were the ones he was after.

Almost all had addresses of record in lower Manhattan; hardly surprising, since that was where almost all the really good corporate formation attorneys had their offices. By correlating the records of the SEC and the IRS, an interesting picture was assembling itself. Again and again he was turning up references to a company called Rothschilds Bank Securities S.A. He knew immediately that it had been purchased off the shelf and that the name was no accident. Most shell companies invoked the name of some encouragingly large and well-established concern, trying to sound legit whether they were or not, and whether their reasons were nefarious or just good business sense.

Rothschilds had a brass-plate address which was the same as that of a well-known lawyer in South Street, near the seaport. It had opened for business about three days after the break-in at CCRC's New York headquarters during which a fission-eating life-form had killed two homeless people. Even then, paranoia or merely guessing at which way the wind might blow had caused them to jump.

Rothschilds was formed on a Tuesday. By Friday of the same week, it was showing a deposit balance at

Chase Manhattan of $180 million. By the following Monday, that had already dropped to $60 million, and the rest of that week saw further deposits of $240 million come and go. Venom knew a pipeline when he saw one.

He also knew what most people did not, the actual names of the company directors. The SEC required those on the registration documents, U.S. banking policy being what it was. He noted their names and addresses, but paid most attention to one in particular, a name that had also appeared far down the list of CCRC's directors.

There may be others, he thought, *but that one will do to start.*

"Time to go," he said aloud to the symbiote he wore as a second skin, and it responded at once. The tank top and shorts he wore changed shape, and blackness wrapped itself around him. Blackness with fangs.

Twenty minutes later he was in lower Manhattan.

It was getting on toward dinnertime, and those offices not already shut were showing signs of doing so. Venom, high above it all, was calmly wall-walking up the side of another of Wall Street's latest crop of steel-and-glass monstrosities. He had never cared for the newer schools of architecture. Its soullessness appalled him, and it probably cost hundreds of thousands of dollars each year just to keep those acres of glass clean. It did, though, make it easier for a wall-climber with the proper technique to go straight up the side of a building in a big hurry, pick a window, and get inside unseen except by their potential victim.

In this case, Venom knew the window very well. He had called earlier, and the building's security people had been more helpful than they knew about which floor and which office he was most interested in. After that it was just a matter of sticking his head quickly down from above window level for a peek inside, to see who and what were in a given office. Now, in a south-facing corner suite with a nice view out over the Battery, he was correctly positioned, and he was waiting.

A man came in and closed the door.

The office was a handsome chrome-and-steel affair, late Industrial Modern. Very sleek, very Memphis. Venom had difficulty with the Industrial style of interior design. It looked, well, *industrial,* and there was no point in saying that was the intention all along. There were other, subconscious intentions being pandered to, and as for the people who willingly embraced it . . .

He smiled, and the symbiote smiled with him. They were hardly *people* at all.

The man sat down at his desk, and there was a long moment of stillness before Venom extruded several pseudopods and punched the window in. He was careful to strike hard enough that all the glass went inward, rather than falling on the innocent bystanders down below whose business this wasn't.

The man sitting at the desk, who had just taken off his jacket and tossed it onto the couch, jerked around, mouth and eyes wide, his curly hair practically standing on end. He was a tall man, broad shouldered and built big.

But not big enough.

Venom was on him in two pounces, and only a few seconds after that the man was well-wrapped in alien tentacles, with several others waving their razory tips in front of his face.

"We may as well call you Mr. Rothschild," said Venom conversationally, "since that name is only slightly more fake than your own, and a good deal more pronounceable."

As Venom swung in the window, a second man was coming in through the door. He stopped in his tracks, staring. The first man looked at him, then at Venom, and yelled *"Bistrah! Ookhadeetyeh!"*

As this second man turned to run, "Rothschild" threw himself straight at Venom's huge, dark figure, struggling. This didn't discomfit Venom in the slightest, though the collision of his heavily muscled body was enough to stagger even him. And that stagger was enough for his flurry of extra pseudopods to miss the fugitive. Not by much, but by enough for him to get clean away.

There were, if that was possible, even more fangs and drool on show than usual when Venom turned his attention back to "Rothschild." "You seem unusually eager to keep us from meeting your friend," he said grimly.

"Innocent guy." The English had only a faint hint of Russian. "Nothing to do with you."

"Innocent indeed? You've been watching too much television, Mr. Rothschild. What makes you think that anything you could say would make us consider him— or you—innocent? Now then. You're evidently a well-educated man with an excellent command of language. Do you understand the meaning of the culinary term 'julienne'?"

There was a long silence, broken by gasps, whimpers, and the occasional thin scream.

After a few minutes, Venom said, "Don't imagine that anyone is going to call the police, or that even if they do, that New York's finest would be so foolish as to come in here. We really think not. Now, let us tell you why we've made this little visit. We want to know—"

"CCRC," gasped the man. He was bleeding from dozens of long, thin cuts, and what remained of his shirt wasn't white anymore, but he was still comparatively unharmed, and knew the reason for it only too well. Venom was making him last.

"No, no, nonono," said Venom, shaking his head and spattering drool all over the carpet. "The answer we want is nothing so simple. For instance, we already know that you're involved with CCRC's, er, reconstruction. *Perestroika,* isn't it? A shame to leave all that perfectly good money in a country. And we also know all about the setting up of several new foundation trusts in Liechtenstein and Switzerland. And Hungary. Interesting choice, Hungary. The country with the tightest banking laws in Europe at the moment. The country least likely to tell you where *anything* is. They know what side their bread's buttered on; they're looking to pick up where Switzerland now leaves off.

"That said, there's other business of much more interest to us. Someone has been moving large amounts of, let's call it 'cargo,' but we both know what it really is, don't we? And it glows in the dark. So this 'cargo' is transported from a processing plant in Florida, all the way up to a location in upstate New York that's not too far from the southern boundaries of the Adirondack State Park. Details are hazy, as the eight ball would have it, on where exactly that storage location is. But we're not going to ask again later. We're asking you now. And we want to know, or we will continue our investigation of cooking terminology. Julienne, until we're bored. Then frappé. Then puree, or sauté, or maybe just plain old shake and bake. Your choice, *tovarish*."

There was more stubborn silence, and then another shriek.

"Yes, we imagine that would have hurt," said Venom. "But then, you so obviously didn't hear us that it can't have been working properly anyway. However, we think we should warn you, we really *are* getting impatient. Oh—we almost forgot. Besides everything else, we also want the name and address of your friend."

"Friend?"

"The fast-moving gentleman whose escape you were so eager to cover just now. Interesting, that you would protect him with your life."

"But I—"

"Oh, but you are, you are," said Venom softly.

There was another silence, punctuated by more screams, and then a sobbing voice said, "558 First Avenue. 1-D. I don't know his name."

"Then his nickname will do. He has to answer to something, we would think. Or do you just whistle?"

"He's—he's called Niner. Niner." The voice gasped, and choked, and said nothing more.

"My," said Venom. "We didn't think it would spurt like *that.*" He spent a few minutes arranging the limp body against one wall of the office, then picked up the phone, dialed 9, then 911, spoke briefly to the recording, and hung up.

Ignoring the sound of shallow breathing from the far side of the room, Venom stalked about, opening files and drawers, looking here and there. The bottom drawer of the big steel and smoked-glass desk was the one that interested him the most. As he opened it, the lock gave way with a small metallic crunch and he looked down at five cell phones.

"Well, now," he said. "Let's pack these up and take them away, shall we?" The symbiote obligingly produced several pockets in its costume, and only a few minutes later, a black shape slipped quietly out of the broken window and was gone.

Later, in a quiet, shadowy place among the sewer tunnels under the Union Square subway stations, Venom sat calmly going through the cell phones. He would key each one to bring up its home number, the little screen would obediently display the digits, and he would dial. Every time he did so, the reply was in Russian. It wasn't a language he had ever studied in depth, but he didn't need to understand what was said to understand well enough how these phones were being misused. One by one, he set them aside. For later.

He repeated the same procedure for the fifth and last time: activate, read, dial, listen. But this time when he held the last phone to his ear, it didn't speak to him in Russian.

Instead a cheerful voice said, "Hi there! This is Mary Jane Watson-Parker. Either I'm out of cell right now, or the phone's switched off, or it's throwing another hissy fit. Don't ask me. Just leave a message after the beep, and I'll call you back as soon as I can.''

As the phone beeped at him, Venom pressed the hang-up button and briefly stared into space with those huge pale eyes. ''Well,'' he said. ''Well, well, well.''

His grin was ghastly.

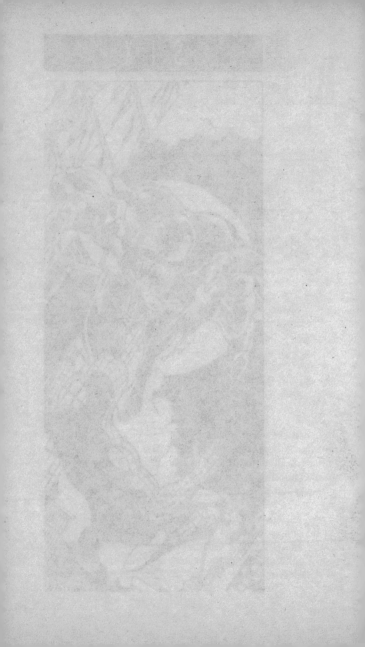

SIX

A bout an hour before, Peter walked out of the door of Doris Smyth's apartment building. He had dropped off the phone with her, and promised to talk to his "famous wife," and even get an autograph for her.

Just where is my famous wife right at the moment? he wondered. There were other things to think about, though. He badly needed to be up among the tall buildings and about his business of taking care of the city. He ducked into an alleyway, changed, and went straight up the face of a building not too far from Doris's place.

He swung a little way around the neighborhood just to loosen up, then clung to a building just across from Doris's penthouse, hiding a little around the corner to peer at her. Through the floor-to-ceiling windows she was quite easy to see. The size of the apartment was still quite startling, and right around from the living and dining area he had already seen was a small office complex with a connecting door into the electronic inner sanctum.

There, Doris hammered away on a PC, pausing now and then to stare quizzically at the screen. She was one of the fastest typists he had ever seen. *God, could we use her in the newsroom,* he thought. She might be eighty but, plainly, arthritis wasn't something that she worried about too much.

Go get 'em, Doris. Find out what you can.

He swung away, heading for midtown and parts south.

It was an excellent, bright, sunny day. A breeze was blowing—down among the trees he could hear the song of an occasional bird, and as he swung around the corner of the building he met yet another monarch butterfly, going about its business with great purpose thirty stories up.

"What are you *looking* for?" he said to it in passing as he shot another jet of webbing at the next building along and paced it. "Girl butterflies? Boy butterflies? A good pollen pizza, extra nectar, hold the anchovies?"

Apart from food and mating, he couldn't begin to

167

guess what might be on a butterfly's mind, especially when that mind was hidden in a brain smaller than the head of a pin. Yet this butterfly seemed to have an appointment, and moreover was running late.

Crash!

He hit something—or rather it hit him, something black that left him hanging from the web, dazed and reeling. Then he realized it was swinging back at him, hard. He clutched the building to keep from falling, slapped his hands and feet against the walls, and saw what was heading for him again.

It was Venom, of course—anyone or anything else would have alerted his spider-sense. But, as a by-product of the brief time when Eddie Brock's symbiote had bonded with Peter Parker, Venom did not trigger the early warning sense that Spider-Man depended on.

Venom came at him, all claws and pseudopodia, tongue and teeth and dribble, and that enormous mocking, hungry grin.

"Okay, *that* does it, I'm losing my temper now!" Spider-Man snarled. He leapt clear, no web of his own to hold him up, only a superheated jet of his own anger at this repetitive, constant, stupid, inconclusive feuding. It wasn't just painful, it wasn't just an interruption to a crime-fighting career that was dangerous enough already, but it was also getting seriously tiresome.

Spidey slammed into Venom, wrapping himself around the barrel-chested upper body while the pseudopods wrapped themselves around him, and concentrated entirely on pummeling Venom's head.

"I didn't start this!" he yelled furiously into Venom's ear. "I didn't start this, and right now I don't need it!"

"What you need," said the dark voice, "and what *we* need, are two entirely different things." Pseudopodia wrapped around Spidey's throat, and choking, he tore at them. "And this is a need that has remained unsatisfied for far too long!"

They slammed into the side of a building and glass

shattered. Even through his daze, Spider-Man found time to wonder how the people inside were going to explain that particular claim to their insurance company. Fortunately the impact wasn't as destructive as he had feared—the wrapping that the symbiote was trying to fling around him had acted as a blunt-trauma pad all down his spine.

But the high-frequency crash as the massive sheet of plate glass gave way was enough to make it shiver away from him a little. Spidey took the opportunity, thrusting out with all his limbs in an attempt to shake it loose. It let go of his legs and arms, but still clutched him by the throat, and Venom's leering face wasn't far away either.

They dropped a dozen feet as Venom's own organic webbing stretched under the double burden, and Spider-Man used the distracting jolt as they stopped to add a little more distraction, by doubling up, arching around, and doing his level best to kick Venom in the back of the head with both feet.

One heel skidded off the rounded skull, but the other hit home square and solid. This time it was Venom's turn to reel and, as they swung out and down in another descending arc, they finished against yet another window and another explosive crack of breaking glass.

"The insurance companies in this town are just going to love us," Spidey said. As the huge slabs of shattered glass shifted and screeched, the sound loosened the symbiote's grip still further. He managed to shake himself free of its grasp and jump sideways onto the vertical surface of the building. "Would you mind telling me what brought this on?" he demanded.

"You brought this on," rumbled Venom. "All of it." Strands of darkness wreathed about him as the sound-shocked symbiote recovered what passed for its equilibrium.

"You'll be claiming I bombed Pearl Harbor next," sneered Spidey, scuttling around the corner of the building. Like a huge, black steam train, Venom came around after him. It was what Spidey had been expecting, and he was ready.

A great wad of webbing from both web-shooters hit Venom full in the face, head, and upper body, and together he and the symbiote went down, spinning more webbing behind them to break their fall.

Spidey followed, bounding down the glass wall. It didn't last; these things never seemed to last. Venom shot out another stream of webbing that anchored on the corner of the building; he recovered, turned the speed of his fall into a swinging arc, and came back up and around fist foremost.

It caught Spider-Man right in the pit of the stomach. No matter how good-looking, how well-defined, or how just plain hard the human abdominal muscles might be, they remain only muscles. Flesh, not armor plate. Spidey folded over like a half-closed penknife, coughing and winded, and the next blow took him in the side of the head.

Only reflex took him out of harm's way, because he had no idea how he had wound up clinging to another building twenty feet away. Apparently his autopilot must have cut in at the right time.

Venom came at him again. Spidey leapt to meet him, wrapped his arms and legs around him, and sent them both tumbling out and down toward the street. They turned as they fell, web shooting out from Venom to anchor on a building cornice as they plummeted past it. The strand didn't just stop their fall, but snapped them back up several stories as if they had been bungee-jumping. They hung at the end of the line, not even doing anything so structured as trading punches but just flailing at each other.

Then another fist caught Spidey on the forehead. "You just don't *get* it, do you?" he shouted, shaking another incursion of stars away from his vision. "I don't want to *fight* with you." He hammered each word home with a quick left-right-left sequence into Venom's lantern jaw.

"You do a good imitation," Venom snarled, punching back. They were swinging to and fro by now, a great, thrashing, furious pendulum of kicks and punches, the soggy sound of impact and the grunt of breath. One massive punch hit Spidey in the side, and there was a single new noise, a sharp, whiplash crack as one rib gave way.

That's the third time this year, said a surprisingly calm voice in the back of his head. *The doctors at the University clinic are never gonna believe this one. What are you gonna say? "I walked into a door." They're already sure that MJ beats me up!*

Then spider-sense went sizzling along his already-outraged nerve endings and made him flinch sideways—just before something that had nothing to do with Venom or the symbiote whizzed past his ear. Spidey knew exactly what it was, because he had heard the same sound too many times before: the tiny sonic boom of a high-velocity bullet, then a perceptible instant later, the slam of the shot.

Already shooting webbing for his getaway, he glanced down and saw the man with the gun. Even at this distance its long, curved magazine was unmistakable. Another AK-74 Kalashnikov. Another puff of flame bloomed from its muzzle. This time, a spout of dust and fragments exploded from a little crater higher up the building, the snap of the bullet's passage drowned out by a more Hollywood-authentic whining ricochet.

Then even that was lost in the flat, all-too-real hammer of automatic fire as the gunman lost whatever passed for patience. He flipped the Kalashnikov's selector to full rock-and-roll and tried to use quantity where quality had failed. The bucking, juddering gun proved at once that it wasn't as easy as it looked in the movies.

"Now what?" Spidey panted bitterly as he swung high and wide for a safe, solid corner. A cluster of full-metal-jacket slugs chewed masonry in his wake and left a series of appropriately spiderwebbed holes through yet another long-suffering window.

"It would seem we have company," said Venom. He was laboring a bit himself, and his chest was heaving. Spider-Man's last kick had caught him squarely over the breastbone, and the symbiote's arms were boiling around in a seethe of undirected fury.

"Anyone I know?"

"Russians," snapped Venom, trying to get his breath back. "CCRC."

"Oh really?" The gunfire stopped briefly as a magazine was replaced, then started up again. It was back to single shots again, each one probing and picking like a needle at possible hiding places. "Truce?" suggested Spidey. "For now, anyway?"

"Not much choice," Venom gasped, plainly reluctant as always to take the course of good sense. "We'll continue this discussion later." He looked down and pointed at a man in a peculiar floppy dark hat with grommets in it. "There. We need him. His name is Niner."

"I'll do what I can," said Spidey. The rib felt bad. "You take the batch on the left, I'll take the batch on the right? Okay, then *go!*"

They leapt together and bullet strikes spattered around them; but always above. It's harder to shoot at a falling object than one might think: it's a near ninety-degree deflection, and the lead required keeps changing with the acceleration of the fall. And that's only with a steady thirty-meter-per-second-squared descent. These two targets kept splaying their limbs as air brakes or balling up tight to drop faster.

Where other jumpers from tall buildings only strike the pavement and splat, these two struck the pavement and bounced. Feet and fists lashed out, and the men on the ground, who might have thought that safety lay in distance and ballistics and weight of firepower, were rap-

idly taught that their only true safety lay in distance
alone.

The gunmen had all of their Kalashnikovs on full automatic now, spraying bullets everywhere with a complete disregard even for their own safety, never mind the
locals who were scattering in all directions. The lack of
blood in the street was only due to the fact that most of
the firing had been directed upward.

"These people are going to get hurt!" Spidey shouted
at Venom. "The innocents, remember? Save them!"

But the innocents were already doing a good job of
saving themselves. They were New Yorkers, after all,
and not entirely unfamiliar with the sound of gunfire,
though not with gunfire that was rapidly approaching the
noise level of a small war, nor of battles involving super-
powered beings on the street. They knew to get under
cover when they heard it.

"Him!" Venom shouted, pointing at the man in the
strange dark hat, and took off after him. Niner dashed
into a building and was gone, with Venom in pursuit.
And that left Spider-Man all alone, facing four or five
gunmen, all of them firing rather chaotically at him. Or
at least in his general direction. Being given a big, shiny
assault rifle was one thing, but possession didn't auto-
matically grant mastery, and wherever these guys had
been recruited, it wasn't a marksmanship school.

Spidey gave thanks for that—and also for the fact that
the sight of Venom's fanged maw and his cloud of whip-
ping black pseudopods would have been enough to un-
settle even the coolest, steadiest shot. These characters
were like reeds in the wind.

He bounded toward the gunmen, never moving in the
same direction for more than a split second at a time,
leaping up the sides of neighboring buildings for the
added advantage that came when he jumped back down
again. Once again it proved true that shooting at a rapidly moving, rapidly foreshortening target could quickly
ruin anyone's aim—though never so much or so fast as

when that same moving target finished its last leap with both feet full in your chest. Or your stomach.

Or the one man Spidey took out simply by landing on his head.

He hit the ground rolling, swung out one leg at ankle level, and neatly chopped both of another Russian's own legs right out from under him. The man's AK-74 went one way, his legs went another, and the mafioski's head hit the pavement with a satisfying, if rather hollow, *clonk.*

Two others were running toward him, firing from the hip in the best traditions of all those old newsreels from World War II. That was fine if the purpose of firing was to keep a lot of enemy heads down; it was rather less effective when trying to hit a bouncing, elusive, rubber ball of a super hero. And whether running, jumping, or standing still, using any gun on its full-auto setting guzzles ammunition and empties one of those long banana magazines in just three seconds.

That was something else films tended not to bother with, except for dramatic effect. Spider-Man had frequently been grateful for the ignorance of crooks whose knowledge of firearms came mostly from bad action movies.

As Spidey ducked behind a row of parked cars, most of them already the likely subject of yet more insurance claims, he could hear first one and then the other gun stop firing. Yet the footsteps kept on coming. Either this pair were very brave, or very stupid. And he'd seen no sign of bravery so far today.

Or maybe they were being very crafty instead. There was always the chance that they had managed to pry their fingers from the triggers before all their bullets ran out. Or maybe they had reloads, though he hadn't seen any extra magazines so far. But like traffic, it's the one you didn't see that gets you, and he wasn't about to take any chances.

Yet when the muzzle of one Kalashnikov came poking gingerly around the end of the nearest car, it was too good an opportunity to miss.

Spidey raised his arm and webbed the weapon all over its barrel, then gave the length of webbing a good, hard yank. The gun jerked from its owner's hands and went spinning high into the air. Spidey heard it come down with a skidding clatter thirty or so yards away, and he also heard the footsteps of the now ex-gunman running away even faster than he had approached.

That left one.

Spidey was glad he hadn't risked standing up too soon, because there was a hollow metallic slap that he'd heard before: the sound of a fresh magazine being smacked home. An instant later there were three quick, spaced shots, and three heavy bangs that rocked the car on its springs. Spider-Man hadn't thought the Kalashnikov could put a bullet clear from one side of the vehicle to the other, except through the windows, but the ragged, bright-edged holes that were appearing on *his* side changed his mind.

He moved along the row of cars in a spider-scuttle far faster than the gunman could have been expecting, letting the guy keep thinking he was still four cars from his present position. That suited Spidey. He squeezed between a Lexus and the 700-series BMW beside it, thinking, *Who teaches these people to park so close?* and peered out from the shadow of a convenient wheel-arch. Spidey then waited for this last one to follow his friend's lead and come too close.

He didn't. Instead he hunched down into a position that, though it looked awkward, allowed him to see right underneath each car. If he looked underneath and saw no one hiding beyond, then he slammed four bullets through the bodywork. Two went through the front door at seat and foot-well height, then two more through the back. Then he duckwalked along to the next and did it all over again.

Spider-Man didn't like the look of this one bit. All

the others had been rock-and-roll players, subject to what some reporters on the *Bugle* called ''Beirut Syndrome'': if it puts out enough noise and enough bullets, then it must be doing *some* good.

But this guy was good, and the parking row wasn't very long. It wouldn't be more than a minute before Spidey ran out of cars that weren't in the line of fire. But then, inside his mask, Spider-Man smiled. The solution, as usual, was an obvious one.

Totally focused on someone who had to be hiding almost at ground level behind the cars, the gunman's attention couldn't shift quite fast enough to realize that a sudden flicker of movement up and over their roofline might be more than just a pigeon. Pigeons didn't jump like that, pigeons didn't bounce like that, and most of all, pigeons didn't have fists like that.

Thud!

Spidey massaged his knuckles gently, spared just one glance for the unconscious body that had skidded several feet away, then looked about for Venom and the elusive Niner. No chance; they were gone.

He winced, and pressed one careful hand to his side over the damaged rib. *Did he just crack it, maybe?* he wondered. Yes, no, or maybe, it didn't really matter. There was no time for a checkup or an X ray, or indeed anything much except to go back to the apartment and strap himself up—a first-aid skill at which he had way too much practice—then get back out and get busy.

Spider-Man headed for home.

That night, about eight, MJ headed off to Sundog to do her first night's voice work. It was a little strange, now, to feel the nervousness that she hadn't felt during the audition. *I've never really done this before,* she thought as she got out of the cab. *What if I screw up in some weird way? I'd really like to do this work—oh, please don't let me screw up.*

She pushed the doorbell, and a friendly voice said,

"Hi, MJ! Come on in!" The door buzzed open.

"Hidden camera?" she said to the voice from the little grille.

"Yup," said the voice. "You wouldn't believe how many people I get to watch standing there in the daytime, picking their noses."

She chuckled and went up the stairs, a little more slowly than last time so that she wouldn't arrive out of breath. At the top of the stairs, the owner of the friendly voice, Harriet the receptionist, was waiting for her with the second door held open. "You're working on *The Giga-Group* taping, huh?"

"That's the one."

"Okay. They're all down in Six: that's the biggest room. Two levels down from this one. You want some coffee or something?"

"I wouldn't mind a Coke."

"Caffeine by any other name," Harriet said, with a lopsided grin, and went off to get it.

MJ went carefully down the spiral staircase, amazed at the complete difference of tone between this job and her last one. *Maybe making cartoons sweetens your disposition or something,* she thought. Certainly Jymn was nothing like most of the directors she'd seen lately.

Two levels down, as Harriet had said, she found Recording Room Six, which took up the whole floor. The design was interesting: the inner recording room, where the cast sat and worked, was a large U shape with a very thick bottom. On the nonmicrophoned side, in the middle of a huge semicircular mixing board, were several seats for the mixer, voice director, and so forth. When MJ came in, there was already somebody working at the board, a chunky man with a graying ponytail and a beard; next to him Jymn Magon sat, going over some pages and using a scalding-pink highlighter on them. At the sound of the door opening, he turned. "Oh, hi, MJ! Any first-night flutters?"

She laughed just a little. "Now that you mention it—"

"Don't worry about it—none of us bite. This is Paul, our soundman."

"Hi," Paul said and turned his attention back to his board.

"He's always very focused during a session," Jymn said. "Don't mind him. He loosens up afterward. Come on and meet your fellow voice talent."

He pushed the studio door open for her. "Guys? Here's your new coworker."

Three men and a woman looked back at her from the director's chairs where they perched. "Halsey Robins— he's several of our good guys." A middle-aged man with a shock of startling white hair nodded to her, smiled. "Marion Archangel." She was a petite middle-aged woman, pert and blond; MJ recognized her name as that of someone who had done a lot of commercial work in the last few years, so that there were some products, specifically a brand of margarine, that MJ associated with her. She smiled at MJ, gave her a little wave. "Doug Booth." A slim handsome young blond man dressed all in black, he waggled his eyebrows at her. "And Rory Armistead." The oldest of them, a portly man possibly in his late sixties, he nodded gravely to MJ and said, "Welcome."

"Thank you," MJ said. "I hope you'll all bear with me: I'm very new at this."

Marion chuckled. "You've done live TV, though. You'll do fine—this is a lot easier."

"MJ auditioned wonderfully," Jymn said, "and she's going to be super, no pun intended. Now listen, group, let's get our act together here. MJ, you had enough time to look over the script for tonight, and the other material?"

"Sure." Jymn had given her several copies of scripts for *Giga-Group,* and the series bible; she had read it avidly after getting home from the food store. Only

Jymn's high good humor during the audition had later kept her from wondering whether she was making some kind of awful mistake, for as MJ read the bible, it became plain that *Giga-Group* was probably the most politically correct super hero cartoon she had ever seen—and she thought that because of this, the concept suffered somewhat. You could not have found a more, well, *homogenized* group of super heroes anywhere: speaking racially, sexually, and culturally alone, there was at least one hero in the group of every imaginable kind. They all had "sexy" names that were supposed to be evocative of their individual super-powers: Hotshot, Tripwire, Roadblock, Wrecker, on and on. She privately wondered how (if such a group of characters ever existed) they would keep each other's nicknames straight, let alone their normal names. *There would have to be a point,* she had thought, *where, when you're forming a new super hero group, everyone has to wear name tags for a few weeks until they get each other sorted out.* All the heroes also had (to judge by the bible) periodic outbreaks of extreme *angst,* and appeared to be cursed by the show's writers to speak almost entirely in clichés. When she finished reading through the first script she had been given, MJ was laughing so hard she practically started wheezing—and not because it was *supposed* to be funny.

"Well, you get the general idea," Jymn said. "Ten super heroes, battling more or less constantly against a rotating group of super-villains who are either in jail, executing devilish schemes, or sitting at home in their secret hideaways *hatching* devilish schemes."

"They're not villains," Doug said, grinning. "They're just ethically challenged."

"Oy," Jymn said. "All right, it's true enough. This show is an ungodly hybrid between the caring-and-sharing shows of the early Eighties, and the irradiate-'em-till-they-mutate-then-put-costumes-on-'em-and-let-'em-all-fight-it-out shows of the late Eighties. That said, all we have to do is try to make it sound good."

"Frankly, Jymn," said Marion, "we couldn't do that with a rewrite by God, and the Archangel Michael running a digital mastering board. As it is, we have to make do with Paul—" Paul, outside the window, gave them an enthusiastic raspberry. "Okay, okay. *Saint* Paul."

"Better," Paul said.

"Oh come on," Jymn said, "this script isn't so bad."

"You mean, it won't be when we're through with it," Halsey said in his soft drawly voice: and MJ paused for a moment, recognizing it suddenly as the voice of a famous cat in a cat food commercial.

"You people are going to teach MJ bad habits," Jymn said, despairingly.

"At least she'll learn them from professionals," Rory said. "We haven't seen a good script for this series yet. But then it's just getting started, and that's normal. Still, we'll know one when it comes along. Meantime we'll make them sound the best we can; that's what we're taking the King's Shilling for. Here, MJ, you come sit by me and look over my shoulder while you work in."

MJ took the offer gladly, perching on the next director's chair over, and putting the marked script for that evening's work on the music stand beside it.

"Okay, people," Jymn said. "You all have your parts marked. MJ, I want you to read the part of Tripwire, the one I marked for you this afternoon; she's one of the villains. And also there's a part for a cat. Can you meow?"

MJ laughed out loud, taken by surprise, and emitted her best imitation of the loud cat that lived in the garden of a brownstone a few doors down from their building.

"Not bad," Jymn said. "Paul, you get that level?"

"Yeah, it was good."

"Okay. MJ, can you make it sound like it's talking?"

"Noooouuuuw."

"Hey, that's good," Rory said. "We've got another Frank Welker on our hands here."

"Always steady work for people who make animal noises," Marion said, smiling at MJ.

MJ smiled back. "Okay, come on, people," Jymn said, "let's get settled. From the top of Act One . . ."

From that affable start the evening got strange, and continued to become stranger. The script they were reading was really so bad that, at first, during the read-through rehearsal, one or more of the actors was likely to break up at any moment. Rory seemed most affected by this problem, which astounded MJ, since he seemed the oldest and most experienced. But when it came to actual recording, the guffaws were nowhere to be found. MJ found herself surrounded by people generating the voices of super heroes, ringing voices full of commitment and power. She *believed* them when they spoke. It astonished her. She tried to work to make her voice resonate that way. "A little more of that, MJ," Jymn would say from outside the recording room, and she would do it again, breathing deeply, as the other actors coached her, and setting herself into the voice.

"Don't let it make you crazy, MJ," Marion said at one point. "I've seen your commercial work. If you can act like you really believe a dishwashing detergent is going to be kind to your hands, then this isn't that much of a jump." And Marion was right. It got to the point where she could cry, for her super-villainness character, "Resistance is useless!"—and believe that it *was* useless—and no one laughed. The others nodded and looked serious, and got ready to read their own parts.

There were occasional bouts of hilarity, primarily when MJ did the cat voice, and another one when Doug, playing the villain called Optimum, suddenly seemed to get his voice confused with a bad imitation of Charles Laughton doing the Hunchback of Notre Dame, and half fell out of his chair to slouch and stagger around the room shouting, "The bells! The bells!" These things always seemed to happen when there was a little tension in the room, MJ noticed. Too many errors in a take, too many takes on a line, then something would happen to let the tension loose, and the next take would go all right. A couple of times, MJ caught Jymn provoking one of these releases; other times, the actors themselves would cause them. It was the sign of a team that had worked together amicably for a long time, on and off, and who trusted one another, and had fun together.

The session went by in a hurry, this way. About halfway through the evening, Jymn said, "Marion, I'd like Glaive's voice to be a little more different from Lasso's. Let's let MJ take her." So MJ became, however temporarily, the voice of a guest super heroine, Glaive, and spent the rest of the evening enjoying learning how to produce on demand what Jymn referred to as "the right hero-style delivery," and claimed she had a naural talent for. For about the millionth time that night, she bit back a reply about occupational hazards. She was almost sorry when, by midnight, they were almost through with the script, except for some patching and relooping of lines that Paul didn't like the sound of. Finally even that was done, and at twenty after twelve Jymn came into the studio and said, "That's it, crew. Next session's tomorrow night." To MJ he said, "Nice work. You'll be back tomorrow?"

Truthfully she said, "I wouldn't miss it for anything."

"That's great. A good first night, MJ! Go home, get some sleep—we start a little earlier tomorrow. Six o'clock, everybody."

So they all departed, to a line of cabs waiting outside the studio for them. "MJ," said Marion, "you're just down the block from me, aren't you? Come on, we'll split the fare."

They did, and MJ walked into the apartment, not too much later, feeling utterly on top of the world. Another couple of weeks of work like this, and the phone bill could do what it liked. "Peter?" she said, heading for the bedroom. "You up, honey?"

The bathroom light was on. He leaned out to look at

her—and MJ gasped. "Oh, jeez, honey, what *happened* to you? You're one big bruise!"

"Venom," he said, sounding rather resigned.

She stared at the elastic bandage wrapped around her husband's chest. "Oh, no, he didn't break your rib again, did he?"

"No, it's just sore. But how was your evening?"

"Terrific. I am a happy, happy woman," she said, not sounding at all happy for looking at her injured husband. "But never mind that! Come sit down and tell me what happened."

"You won't like it."

And she didn't.

In the barren luxurious apartment, not too far from there, the big-shouldered, broad-bodied man who was born with the name Otto Octavius sat behind the desk again, going through some paperwork. In front of him on the marble floor, waiting, stood the red-haired man.

"So," said Doctor Octopus, the nom de guerre he preferred. "How are our various laundries doing, Niner?"

"We washed about eleven million dollars last week alone," said the man in the black jacket. "The cell-model recruitment for laundries has worked out very well. The problem was always finding enough people to do the legwork. That's solved now."

"Good," said Octopus. "We have a lot more to do yet over the next couple of months. I want to accelerate this process so that it's finished well before Day Hundred. Have Galya look into it—his people seem to be acting like real go-getters at the moment. What's the status on the currency situation?"

"About four billion in counterfeit is now in circulation in Europe," said Niner. "The Union's economies are going to have a nasty shock in about sixty days when their governments notice the surplus."

"Just before the Dublin summit," said Doctor Octopus. "That's excellent. The yearly G7 conference is barely a week later. They'll be at each other's throats, and whatever economic coalition remains between them and the Russians will fall apart on the spot."

A long metallic tentacle came arching over, seized one of the pieces of paper in delicate grippers, and turned it over. "Our last shipment of 'emplacements'—" said Doctor Octopus.

"They're ready to roll, sir. If we ship them during the G7, every one of them will be in place within two days. That leaves nearly thirty days of the Hundred to make the final settings."

Octopus nodded, turning over the last piece of paper, and looking keenly at Niner. "And that last emplacement I entrusted to you," he said, "that's been successfully completed?"

"Yes, sir. It's right up there, where they'll never look for it, and never find it until the sky lights up."

"Excellent. Go get in touch with Galya, Niner. I want the rest of that cash dealt with while cash still works."

Obedient, Niner went. Doctor Octopus got up from behind the desk and slowly crossed the bare room to where the curtains hung down. One of his metal tentacles reached out and twitched one of the curtains aside just wide enough to let him look out. Below him, Manhattan lay in the sun: shouting, stinking, pulsating with noise and life.

"Not for much longer," he said softly, to the stones of the city. "A hundred days or so, that's all. Just be patient. A hundred days."

The tentacle withdrew. The curtain fell.

S·E·V·E·N

T he next morning, Peter got up and tiptoed out of bed, leaving MJ still snoozing there, to find an early call waiting on the answering machine. "This is a call for Peter Parker," said a soft woman's voice. "It's Doris Smyth. Would you be able to come see me sometime after ten this morning? No need to return the call unless you can't. I'll be home all day."

Has she found something already? he wondered. *Wow!* As quietly as he could, he washed and dressed and had a hurried breakfast, left MJ a note to tell her where he was headed, and then left for Doris's.

When she opened her apartment door for him, Doris looked up at Peter with an expression that was slightly more muted than the sunny smiles she had been giving him when they first met. She was still smiling, but the look had a slight edge of caution to it. "Peter! Good morning, come on in. Would you like some tea?"

"Uh, yes, I'd love some, thanks."

She led him to the dining room table, where a teapot, a cozy, and silver tea service were set out, incongruously next to a partially disassembled cell phone, various delicate tools, and a small black box with a liquid-crystal readout on the top. "Here, sit down. Milk? Sugar?"

"Sugar, please." He stirred it in and peered at the phone. "That's our phone?"

"That's the phone you brought me," Doris said mildly, sitting down herself and taking a sip of her own tea. She reached out for the bottom half of the phone's shell, the part with the most electronics in it, and turned it over thoughtfully in her hands.

Then she glanced up at him. "I've been looking for this for a while," she said.

"You've lost me."

Doris made a slightly regretful expression. "Let me be plainer. This phone is one that both its home phone company, Americell, and the police in several states have asked me to look out for. Its present calling records have been hacked several times, with great virtuosity, by

187

someone whom the police are most eager to find. But more—look here.''

She picked up one of the tools on the table, a little slender metal rod with a hook at one end and a little slanted, slotted screwdriver head at the other, and pointed into the body of the phone with it. ''See that little chip there?''

''Uh, yes. It's awfully small.''

''True enough. Here's another.'' She picked up from the table a twin to the first chip, a tiny wafer slice of green-and gold-patterned plastic no bigger than her smallest fingernail, and with great care, using her own thumbnail, split it apart. Nestled inside it was an even smaller chip, about the size of two pinheads. Peter squinted at it.

''You are seeing,'' said Doris softly, ''one of the better-kept secrets of the telephone industry. It won't remain secret forever, but it's doing its job pretty well for us at the moment. This is a 'covert' chip, one that the phone companies are increasingly having installed in their phones without even the manufacturers being entirely sure what it does—or most of the people at any given manufacturer, anyway. The phone companies have been so concerned about the rampant cloning of phones that they came up with a microchip whose only purpose is to secretly record all the numbers that have been pro-grammed into a telephone as its 'own' number, for the duration of its lifetime. It doesn't take a lot of memory or power, and when a professional gets their hands on a much-cloned phone, its whole audit trail is laid out for you to see. Very useful.''

She put the phone down, gazed at it for a moment in a slightly unfocused way. ''Very few phreaks or hackers know about the existence of the chip, and even those who stumble across it aren't going to be able to repro-duce the algorithm that makes the chip dump its data, much less the one to erase the data trail. This one hasn't been tampered with, I'm certain, and its trail indicates that over three hundred different numbers have been cloned into it over the past year and a half." Now she looked up at Peter, and the expression was a little challenging.

"What I need you to tell me now," she said, "is exactly where you got this phone in the first place."

"Uh," Peter said. Those gray-blue eyes looked at him, and he said, "Uh, Spider-Man passed it on to me."

Doris looked at him. Then she nodded. "I thought so," she said and glanced over toward one of the coffee tables across the room. Peter followed the glance, and saw, somewhat to his surprise, a copy of *Webs,* the coffee-table book of Spider-Man pictures he had gotten published not too long ago.

"Yes," she said, "I did just a little checking up on you. I tend not to take things at face value, in my line of work." And she smiled slightly: that sunny look again. "Where did your web-slinging friend find it?"

"At a crime scene of some kind. A robbery, I think."

"Hmm. Yes, that would fit in." She got up and went over to an escritoire by the wall—yet another beautiful antique—and pulled its doors open. A computer and printer were hidden inside, and by the printer was some stacked-up paperwork. She brought it over to the table. "Here," she said, "is a list of all the phone numbers that this phone has 'owned' in the last year and a half. All stolen from other, legally held phones belonging to the three New York companies, and two of the Connecticut ones, and some from Pennsylvania."

She turned back to the escritoire. "And here," she said, coming back to Peter with a ream package of paper and plumping it down on the table in front of him, "is a list of all the numbers called by this phone during that period."

He stared at the wrapped package. "This is a *list?*"

"Four hundred and fifty-three pages," Doris said. "The numbers are ranked most-used to least-used. It's interesting reading. A lot of calls to betting shops, hun-

dreds of calls to a corner grocery not far from here."
She looked rueful. "I used to shop there all the time.
I've stopped now. But almost all of them are calls to
places that are the subject of an ongoing police investigation. So if your friend Spider-Man is interested in
this kind of thing, you'd better pass this information on
to him. I hope he's a fast reader." She thought a moment
and added, "If he has a computer, I can give you this
data on disk. It'll be easier to sort."

"Uh, he has access to one, yes."

She went to the escritoire again, did something briefly
at the computer's keyboard, then left it to its own de-
vices. "That'll be ready shortly. Now what I need you
to do is let me know where the phone that your famous
wife was having trouble with is. Naughty of you to slip
me this one without telling me. If it hadn't been for your
wife, I would have called the FBI."

Peter gulped.

"But then I found out about this other connection,"
Doris said, glancing at the copy of *Webs,* "and after all,
Stevie Drew said you were all right to work with."

"Stevie"? Never mind. . . . "Uh," Peter said, "thank
you, Doris. I should have told you, really, but—"

"You were being circumspect for reasons of your
own," said Doris. "I'm not going to pry. Let's let it
pass. But bring me your wife's phone, all right? If your
problem is solvable, I want to see if I can solve it. For
one thing, if her phone has the covert chip in place, we'll
be able to see some other data—time and location information, other things—which the phone company's
own records won't necessarily reflect. There may even
be recordings of some voice material."

Peter's eyes opened wide at that. "Recordings?
How?"

Doris smiled at him. "Our snoopy government. Peter,
there are more intelligence-gathering bureaus running
around in this country doing their gathering than most
of the government would ever like you to know. They'd

quote you 'national security' as a reason for it—and to some extent they might be right. But the truth is that governments are just naturally nosy, and big ones are much nosier than others, and we have one of the biggest. A lot of calls are monitored, though everyone denies it. There's no use in them denying it, really. The technology makes it easy now, especially since our cell phone systems are still almost all analog, which any kid with a scanner can listen in on. And one of the most basic human vices is the desire to look through the keyhole and see what the neighbors are *really* doing. When things go digital, the monitoring may lessen a little. The signal is harder to break, and consumers are getting more sensitive to the issue. Which is as it should be. But governments will still fight back, doing their best to fight tight voice-encryption methods. By their own lights, they're right to do so, they feel they're protecting their own interests." Doris sighed a little. "The NSA in particular monitors a lot of calls all over the country. Computers do it for them, taking random samplings of band width and searching for certain keywords in conversations—guns, bombs, drugs, that kind of thing. If something dangerous-sounding turns up, a little bell goes off somewhere, and a live monitor quietly comes into the circuit to determine whether the threat is real. Other countries do much the same. In fact, the NSA learned the technique from the British, a while after the troubles started in Northern Ireland. As far as I know, every call from Britain to Ireland and vice versa is still routinely computer-sampled for suspect content. And I think they do the same, just for general interest—and again, with an eye to Ireland, and their own drug-smuggling problems, and so forth—with everything that comes in from the U.S. and Canada via the transatlantic cable and satellite downlink stations on the south coast of the U.K. GCHQ passes on anything interesting that they 'hear' to the NSA, and the NSA returns the favor at its end."

Peter shook his head in astonishment. "Is that legal?"

Doris gave him an excessively wry smile. "It must be, dear. They're the *government,* aren't they?"

"But what about freedom of speech?"

"The Constitution guarantees you that, all right. But it doesn't guarantee that no one will be on the other side of the wall with their ear pressed to it, does it?"

Peter opened his mouth and closed it again.

"As I said, when the U.S.'s cell phones go digital, it'll be harder for the eavesdroppers, 'legal' or otherwise," Doris said. "But I don't expect to see that before well into the next century. Assuming I *am* still around to see it. All the phone companies are arguing about what standard to use, and I think they will be for years. But for the meantime, when you're on a cell phone, exactly as with a portable phone in your house, you need to *assume* that what you're saying is being overheard and recorded by someone who means to do you dirt.

"In any case, all this may work to your benefit. It's just possible that in the NSA tape archives there is some evidence pertaining to calls made on your wife's phones. I have access to those archives on a need-to-know basis, and, well," and Doris smiled that sunny smile again, "as regards this, I just need to know, that's all."

The glint of the gossip lover showed briefly in Doris's eyes, and Peter laughed. "Okay, I'll call her later and ask her to drop it off for you. You two can have a chat then, and you can cross-examine her about *Secret Hospital.*"

Doris nodded. "More to the point, though," she said, "if I can link that phone to police work presently ongoing, that will get you off the hook with CellTech." She smiled, a slightly feral look. "They listen to me. But then, they *have* to, considering what they pay me on retainer. So have your wife give me a call."

Peter thanked Doris and headed out. As he walked down the street, at one point he paused and looked back at the top of her apartment building, all discreetly crowned with antennas, and he found himself thinking,

*Did I ever say anything on that phone, anything, to MJ,
that might suggest to a casual listener that I was someone else besides just Peter Parker? And forget casual
listeners—that might suggest it to a little old lady who
could probably make toast just by sticking a slice of
bread out her window?*

He sighed. There was no point in worrying about it
just now. Meanwhile, he had places to be. He headed
for them.

Other people, also, much later that day, were going
about the town on their business.

The offices of Bothwell Industries, housed in a refur-
bished office building downtown, had closed for the day
a couple of hours ago. It was a small new company, still
in the process of moving into its premises: furniture was
still shoved up against the bare walls in its three rooms,
and boxes were stacked everywhere in the near-
darkness.

Among the boxes, a lithe dark shape moved quietly,
reading labels with a tiny flashlight, and making sure
that the light was always shielded by his body. A handy
pseudopod cupped around it, to make doubly sure.

Venom had been there for about an hour, mentally
sorting out the boxes into ''check it now'' and ''don't
bother'' categories. The chaos in the place at the moment actually worked to his benefit somewhat—it
meant, among other things, that there had been no time
to lock files away securely. That suited him very well
indeed.

He paused for a moment, glancing around him. The
symbiote sent out a few questing streamers in the direction of boxes it obscurely knew he was interested in.
''No, no,'' he said softly, ''patience. We'll do this systematically. We may not get another chance, and we
cannot afford to lose this one.''

Venom went to the first of about twenty cardboard
file boxes in which he was interested, opened it, and

started going through the files inside. Most of them were innocuous, as he suspected they would be, but he was in no hurry at the moment. Security in this building was on the lax side; he had been watching it for the better part of the day to make sure, and not half an hour ago he had seen the lone security guard for the place lock the back door and head down the street to a local bar. The laxity amused Venom, and rather pleased him; he had no desire to slice up some poor hired lackey while doing what he had to do tonight. And by far the *best* thing that could happen, as far as he was concerned, was that one of the company directors might use his own building key, and come in alone. Then he and Venom would have a nice little chat.

Niner, he thought, going through the files, seeing correspondence about some shipment of oranges from Spain, passing it by. Bothwell appeared to be an innocent enough import-export firm, but the research he had done at the Bureau of Records, cross-indexed with the SEC information, made it plain that vast amounts of cash had been through Bothwell's accounts in the past couple of weeks. Now, there were legitimate firms for which this might have been true, but also many illegitimate ones. He had looked over a number of them today, in a cursory fashion—either from the street, in ''civvies,'' or from the rooftops. Heaven only knew what some of those other firms were up to—where their money came from, what they were doing with it. But this firm had distinguished itself, in midafternoon, when Venom had seen the man called Niner, the man who had gotten away the other day, walk out its front door, dressed like a businessman, with a briefcase full of what was doubtless fascinating material.

Venom wanted to talk to that man. The symbiote's tendrils writhed a little with anticipation at the thought. ''Patience,'' Venom said again. ''We'll have a chance to ask him our questions eventually. But first I want to have a better idea of what questions to ask.''

The next hour or two were weary ones. Eddie Brock had been more than capable, as a reporter, of the long slog through reams of boring information; this was very much the same. Invoices, impenetrable bank statements, letters in several different alphabets (many of them Cyrillic)—none of them told him any of the specific things he wanted to know about Bothwell. The symbiote began to make little movements that Venom had long since learned to translate as the alien version of, "I'm bored, can we go now?"

He ignored it. For the time being, he had to. He opened another box, and another, and carefully and patiently went through them all. The frustration of the whole business was that vital evidence might be right under his nose but in coded form, and he might not recognize it. Many firms, even now, used various commercial or industrial code books and software to hide their immediate intentions. There was no way to tell whether "Your inquiry about the condition of the last shipment is being investigated" actually meant "Tell the chief operative we want him back in the main office, fast" or "That last deposit for twelve million has gone through as promised." All you could do was look.

He shut that box, opened another one, went through it. Nothing. Shut that box, opened another one. Went through it—

—and suddenly found himself looking at a letter regarding more oranges from Spain—with a sticky-pad note attached to it saying, in a neat precise hand, *Cross-ref with tacticals/delivery systems schedule for DO.*

Venom looked at it thoughtfully. Whatever oranges might need for their safe shipment, there would be nothing "tactical" about it—and the word "tactical" linked with "delivery system" made his hair try to stand up on end under the symbiote, and its tentacles wreathe and flutter. He put the letter aside, noted the date, and started digging through that box with ever-increasing interest.

Two files farther in, behind some more back statements with entirely too many zeroes, he found a piece of cream-colored letterhead that he lifted out of its file and held up to the light to check the watermark. Original. At the top of it appeared the letters CCRC/IN-TERNAL.

Transfer instructions, the heading of the letter said. *Sensitive materials—see file 886, 887—*

He laughed out loud. In the hurry of their move, someone had put this file in the wrong box. The box labeled 800 was across the room. He went for it.

"Aha," Venom said softly, as he opened the 800 box. There were several locked metal security-deposit–type boxes in it, of a size to take files.

The symbiote put out several willing tentacles and levered the steel box open. The lock gave with a tiny screech of metal and a loud snap. Other pseudopodia came down, lifted the files out, opened them.

Delivery system disposition—Missile launchers have been positioned near: Boca Raton, Winter Park, Miami; Atlanta, Peachtree, Mobile; Solid emplacements: Chicago: Tower, El 1, El 2, O'Hare.

Venom began to growl softly under his breath. The symbiote shuddered with his reflected, growing rage. *Fissionables transport. Miami reprocessing plant has been shut down, but Tuscaloosa remains operational and will finish present inventory. Shipments otherwise proceeding according to schedule.*

"Shut down," Venom said to the symbiote. "We should say it was. You had fun that night, didn't you? Well, it looks like more fun is coming."

"Light bombs." ERWs are now 60% emplaced for Day Hundred. Previous difficulties with the timers have been worked out. Tests on the satellite detonation system have been abandoned as too uncertain with so little time remaining in the program.

"So little time," Venom thought. *What are they planning?*

And then the last note, a sticky-pad note on the cover

letter of another report on "deliveries of inventory." *I am not entirely pleased with the quality control on shipment 18: rad count is below optimum. Have it recalled and replaced—we have more than enough fissiles to do so within schedule. Please remind all staff that there is no room for error: the usual sanctions will apply.—OO*

Venom stopped growling—a sound more frightening than the growl had been.

OO.

Otto Octavius.

One of the world's leading experts on radiation and its various and sundry applications.

He remembered the earlier reference to "DO," which, Venom now realized, likely referred to the name under which Octavius tended to operate since his metal tentacles were bonded to him and he embarked on a villainous career:

Doctor Octopus.

Indeed. Now it all begins to fall into place.

Eddie Brock was a methodical man. He went through all the other boxes he had deemed pertinent before he left. But his silence then, some two hours later, was more profound and terrible than all the silences before it. He stood up, stretched—even a man with a symbiote to massage his tired muscles gets stiff after a long time hunkered down among files—and headed for the stairway to the roof, working hard to contain his fury. He was going to have to be especially careful to keep the symbiote in check. There was someone he needed very much to kill but wanted more to see.

MJ went back to Sundog that evening in a very cheerful mood. She had still been worried about Peter when she got up, but when he came in carrying about a ream of paper, whistling, and told her why he was feeling so cheerful, she felt much better too.

It was pleasant not to have to get up too early, and she took her time about getting ready for the day, while

Peter pored over the stacks of paper he had brought home. She then went out with both her cell phone and Peter's, and dropped hers off with Doris Smyth. She was glad she had taken Peter's phone with her; she and Doris got into one of those like-at-first-sight conversations that people sometimes have, a conversation that ranged over everything from personal philosophies to sordid gossip from the *Secret Hospital* set, and they both drank enough tea to float themselves away. She and Doris were still talking when MJ realized that it was five-thirty, and she had to go to work.

MJ promised to come back another time and continue the conversation, then she hurried downstairs and caught a cab over to Sundog. She had just enough time to call Peter and let her know what had happened to her. "It's okay," he'd said. "I thought you might have done something like that. Listen, I've got to get out and do some night work."

"Okay, Tiger. When do you think you'll be back?"

"Not too late. Probably about one."

"Okay, see you then."

She bounced out of the cab in good spirits, and headed in and up the studio stairs. When she got down to Studio Six, the same crew from last night were mostly in their places when she got there, laughing and chatting among themselves. They welcomed her like an old friend. *These are such nice people. I hope this job lasts!*

Jymn Magon came in and started trying to get everyone organized. As MJ was beginning to suspect was usual, it took a while. Finally they settled down to start the recording of the next *Giga-Group* script. "This one has a little more stuff for Glaive in it," Jymn told MJ, "and her part is somewhat bigger than the last time— she's more important to the plot. So get in there and swagger a little. Don't be afraid to go too far over the top."

"Why should she be?" said Doug Booth. "Who would notice?"

Much laughter ensued, and they started. MJ swaggered it as best she knew how, thinking of the occasional super-villains she'd run across in her career, and less heroic but generally decent folk like the Black Cat. The others cheered her on, seemingly impressed, and MJ started just unashamedly enjoying the part and the way she was playing it, bold and flamboyantly heroic. It seemed to work, at least for Jymn, and even to MJ's untutored ear, the more hackneyed lines in the script seemed somewhat improved when you delivered them as if they were the truth that would save the world. The night flew by, punctuated by one bout of laughter so severe that she could scarcely breathe, when Rory (playing a character who had for some obscure reason been temporarily regressed into a Neanderthal) suddenly started refusing to come out of character when taking direction from Jymn. "I need a little more weight on the 'Me afraid—me not know what to do,' " Jymn had said, casually enough. But Rory's reply was, in character, "Oh, okay, me screw that up the last time, me do it again," and he remained stubbornly Neanderthal for the better part of an hour.

Later, in a cab on the way home, MJ wondered whether it had really been all that funny. *It seemed so then.* But it didn't matter. She felt wonderful. She had come striding out of Sundog, after a whole night of rampant heroism, feeling nine feet tall, covered in adamantium, invincible and invulnerable, and feeling pretty good about herself—especially at five hundred bucks an hour for six hours.

She looked up at their apartment window as she got out of the cab and paid the man. The light in the third window over was on, which was Peter's code meaning that he was still out web-swinging. *Well, he said he wouldn't be late. I'll fix something light for him to eat when he gets in. And boy, I could murder a sandwich, myself.*

MJ headed upstairs, strode on down to their door, unlocked it, stepped in, and locked up behind her. There, for a moment, she paused. She felt a draft. A window was open somewhere—not the bedroom one, not the one Peter usually came in by after a night of spidering around . . .

Someone cleared his throat. MJ's head snapped around. Her first thought was *Oh Lord, I've disturbed a burglar.*

It was worse than that.

Over against the living room window, black pseudo-podia wreathing gently around him, stood Venom.

The blood started rushing around inside MJ, but not to her fear-clenched stomach, as she would normally have expected—instead, it went to her face with anger. Hardly knowing what she was doing, she chucked her keys over onto the telephone table and strode straight over to him.

"I'm sorry," she said, in ringing tones, "but I must have messed up my appointments calendar again. I wasn't expecting you. Or *did* you call to make an appointment first?"

That dreadful grin looked somewhat fixed at the moment—as if by brief surprise. "We did call," he said. "Your cell phone, we believe. But we fear we did not leave a message."

"People who hang up on answering services," MJ said, looking Venom up and down, more with Glaive's scorn than her own, "are a symptom of the downfall of civilization. If you're rude to machines, you'll be rude to people, too. And breaking into people's homes is also fairly rude, by the way. But now that you're here, won't you sit down? And can I get you something?" Venom opened his mouth. She didn't give him the chance. "And no wisecracks about my husband, please, since that's doubtless the cause of you giving me the pleasure of your company. Tea? Coffee?"

"Nothing right now," Venom said. MJ looked pointedly, as if expecting something. Very slowly, the pseudopodia wreathing around him, Venom added, "Thank you."

He sat down.

MJ turned her back on him, something she would never have done—but Glaive would have. She strode away from him into the kitchen, opened the refrigerator, and got out the baloney and some mustard. "If you called my cell phone," MJ said, "I would guess it has something to do with the fact that someone cloned the poor creature. Ran up a four-thousand-dollar bill, too. Did *you* have something to do with that?" She stared at him. Venom opened his mouth, and MJ turned away again, ignoring him. "No," she said, getting out a knife for the mustard, "even you wouldn't sink that low. I apologize for suggesting it. Are you sure you won't have a sandwich?"

"What I would like," Venom growled, "is to see your husband."

"He's not at home," MJ said. She composed her sandwich, put it on a plate, got herself a Coke, took them both to the little dining-room table, put them down, and sat down. She did not eat. Her mother had always told her it was rude to eat in front of people who weren't also eating, unless they were family. She looked at Venom.

He actually twitched—he, not the symbiote.

The sound of a key in the lock came from outside. All the blood in MJ attempted to relocate itself, again, in relief, but she refused to make any other sign, except to lounge back in the chair a little. The other key went into the other lock. The door opened, and Peter came in. "Hey, MJ, did you—"

He stopped. He saw his wife sitting at the table, with a slight smile on her face, and Venom sitting on the couch.

Venom stood up. "We have a guest," MJ said. "Or guests."

Peter moved slowly toward Venom, his face going

dark with anger. "What are *you* doing here—"

Venom stood up, seeing at last a reaction that he understood, and headed toward Peter. "Your wife's phone number," he growled, "appears among numbers belonging to some Russian criminals who are working in town at the moment. They appear to be involved with the covert restructuring of CCRC—and with Doctor Octopus."

Peter stopped, his mouth open. *"Ock—"*

"It is difficult to say," said Venom, "but he may be one of the owners of CCRC. Or *the* owner. Unfortunately, much of the pertinent information is concealed by Liechtenstein banking laws, and many shell companies."

"Lord," Peter said.

Venom's pale eyes turned in MJ's direction. "Is it true that your wife's phone was cloned—"

"Ask *me*," MJ said, the Glaive voice again, and it was the character, not her, that made her shake her hair back when Venom turned to her, and lift her head defiantly. "What makes you think I would bother lying to you?"

Venom simply looked at her, then turned away. "So— a false trail. Well enough. We would personally much prefer the leisure to finally settle up accounts with you here and now. But there is other information much more important to be discussed, and a much more important reason why we've come here."

He quickly told Peter about his evening's foraging in the Bothwell offices possibly belonging to the man called Niner—or, on the other hand, to Doctor Octopus. MJ's eyes got wide as Venom told of what sounded like extensive shipments of covert nuclear material making their way around the country. "Useless as they often are, this must be dealt with by the authorities," Venom said. "Spider-Man has certain connections in the AEC offices in New York that we do not—and we think he had better alert them, and seek their help."

Peter eyed Venom suspiciously. "You could call them yourself. Why put me on the spot?"

"As if they would listen to me," Venom said. "While you—"

"—are as involved as you were with the near explosion of a nuclear device under Manhattan, as far as they're concerned. Why should they listen to me, either? There are still people in the office there who suspect I might have been at the bottom of the whole thing." Then Peter paused. "Well," he said, "I suppose it's worth a try. The stakes are too high not to try, anyway. And the worst that can happen is that they'll chuck me out on my ear. But Doc Ock—" He brooded a moment. "If all the events of the past few months are somehow traceable to him . . ."

"That will have to be looked into as well," Venom said, "but right now the main priority is that all this atomic material be found and made safe before millions of innocent people are caught in some kind of disaster— accidentally, or on purpose."

"I'll call them first thing in the morning."

"Very good. And we want you to understand that that information had best be shared with us promptly." Venom turned a long look on MJ. She returned it, with interest, as coolly as she could. She refused to look at Peter at the moment, who was already doing a slow burn. The last thing anyone needed right now was for these two to go for each other's throats. "Otherwise, we should dislike having to call on you at home again."

"The feeling's mutual," Peter said.

"We will call you in the morning, then," said Venom. He turned toward the window he had come in by, and then left.

It was a few seconds before MJ could move; then Peter's arms were around her. She hugged him back, wordless, as Glaive suddenly became just a character in a bad script again, and her stomach clenched with sudden postponed fear, and her appetite left her with a rush. "Oh, Pete—!"

"It's all right," he said, hugging her. "It's all right."

"No, it's not," she said mournfully. "My sandwich is getting all curly at the edges."

Peter shot a glance at it. "If you don't want it, I'll eat it. Tell me about your day, which obviously was a *doozy*, and then let's go to bed—'cause we're going to have a busy day tomorrow."

EIGHT

The next morning, about ten, Spider-Man swung quietly down onto the roof of the New York City offices of the AEC. A small, stout man in a quiet business suit was standing there, a little ruffled by the wind, waiting for him.

Spidey walked over to him. "Mr. Laurentz?"

"That's right," said the little man. He looked at Spider-Man in a considering way, and Spidey considered him back: bald, an olive cast to his complexion that suggested the Mediterranean, bushy mustache. "Please call me Rob. Do you want to come down to the offices? Or would you rather talk up here?"

"Which would be wiser?" Spidey said.

Laurentz smiled suddenly, a surprisingly loopy grin. "It's a nice morning. Let's sit up here."

Spidey looked around for chairs, saw none: but Laurentz had already strolled over to the parapet that ran around the edge of the building, and sat down on it, with considerable disregard for the effect of roof dirt on such an expensive suit. Spider-Man went after him and sat down too.

"You'll understand, I guess," said Laurentz, "that there are some—doubts about your bona fides here and there in the organization. I'm not overly concerned, though. I know enough about what happened down in the tunnels not too long ago to make me glad to shake you by the hand. And if there's anything I can help you with, it's my pleasure."

"That's a relief." Spidey looked out across the city and started to explain what was on his mind.

Laurentz sat quiet for a while, letting Spider-Man expound, particularly regarding the large amount of fissionable material that seemed to be running around loose. "Well, you know," he said at one point, "there was always a lot more of it than we're generally told about—or that the public is generally told about—being shipped here and there. All under tight government control, of course. The Commission is supposed to be informed about them all, but, well, we're a *civilian* organization, and the military, which handles its own shipping, doesn't always tell us everything. One of the aspects of this job that occasionally makes it a little interesting.''

''I just bet.''

Laurentz sighed a little. ''We've been investigating CCRC, of course—or what's left of it—ever since those first barrels of toxic waste were found downtown. To date we've found six other stockpiles scattered here and there around Manhattan: smaller ones, but significant enough. And they weren't just of waste—they were enriched uranium and processed transuranics.''

''Bomb-grade transuranics?''

''Some refined plutonium, yes, but not a whole lot. Enough to cause a disaster if it got out into the environment, though. You couldn't make an H-bomb out of it all if you tried.'' Laurentz's brow furrowed. ''But light bombs, yes. And if I were a terrorist, that's what I would go for. They're the wave of the future.''

Spider-Man gulped. ''Excuse me—'light' bombs?''

''Sounds like a marketing ploy, doesn't it?'' Laurentz's smile was mirthless. ''I'd love to kick the man or woman who came up with that asinine name. For a while, the other name for them—not much better—was 'neutron bombs.' ''

''Oh,'' Spidey said softly. ''Why are these the preferred flavor all of a sudden?''

''Cheaper,'' Laurentz said. ''You need less trigger material. Just be sure you understand what we're talking about here. There was a lot of confusion about this end of weapons technology—the idea that these weapons wouldn't destroy buildings, only people.'' He laughed, a bitter breath of nonamusement. ''The first models of this bomb were designed as a tactical weapon, a battlefield nuke. The idea was this: If you're in the middle of a large armored combat and you drop a conventional nuclear weapon over or on it, obviously everything at ground zero is going to be destroyed. But out at sort of ground one-and-a-half, things won't be quite so grim, at least for a while. Soldiers in tanks are afforded some protection by their tanks from the blast and heat of the direct explosion, and so afterwards they're likely—so the generals would think—to just keep on soldiering for a day or three longer until the symptoms of radiation sickness start catching up with them. Well, the generals didn't like that idea much, so they got behind the idea of designing a bomb that would release such a massive blast of neutrons that the tanks would be no more protection than tissue paper, and the soldiers would die at least within hours, if not right away."

"Nice people," Spider-Man murmured.

They sat quiet for a moment, watching a flight of ducks make its way up the East River in a vee. "Yes," said Laurentz. "Well, anyway, as it always does, word got out. There were some astonishingly mishandled press briefings about the 'neutron bomb' in '78, followed by some astoundingly sensationalistic coverage in the media. Such a stink went up from the public that the research was very quietly dropped in late '78, and for a long while nothing else was heard about it."

Spidey nodded. "I take it, though, that now, for whatever reason, people are getting interested again."

"Budget," said Laurentz, "what else? And additionally, there have been enormous leaps in technology since 1978, making the 'light bombs'—'tidies,' they also call them—a lot more practical. And the concrete technology on which to base them is already everywhere, in the storehouses of every atomic power. NATO has a lot of artillery-fired atomic projectiles—'hundred-pounders,' they call them. They use pretty small amounts of fissile material, and they're very flexible and easy to use. They're not much bigger than a mortar shell. You can shoot them or just hide them with a timer, and when they go off, their normal output of radiation is increased many times by the tamping and pumping techniques that we've invented over the years to reduce the size of much larger bombs.''

''We're so inventive,'' Spidey said.

''We are,'' said Laurentz, ''and it gets worse. It would be—well, not easy, but certainly feasible—to build such bombs so that they were much more effective than the NATO weapons. Radiation 'tamp' hasn't been extended to anything like its maximum efficiency as yet, and materials technology continues to produce alloys and metals that are more and more effective for tamping. You could boost one of those battlefield nukes to thousands of times its present rad output—possibly *tens* of thousands of times. Blow something like that up in a large city, and you wouldn't notice any more of a bang than you might get out of, say, a couple of tons of chemical explosive. A few buildings would be flattened, a lot of windows blown out. But a hundred-pounder with a little imaginative augmentation . . .'' Laurentz looked off toward the river with a grim expression on his face. ''Put something like that where we're sitting, and you could leave half the population of Manhattan with LD50, the lethal dose, in a flash. Three days, they're dead. Less, for most of them.''

''Do you really think that many terrorists have this kind of weapon?''

''Have it? Maybe. But would they use it?'' Laurentz shrugged. ''I've had a little training in this—most of us at the Commission have. Their feeling, and I share it, is that, at the moment, I doubt most terrorist organizations—ones with a plan, that is, a goal to achieve, I don't mean random crazies—I don't think they would dare. I think most of them have the sense to know that the first person or country to use nuclear weapons against a target is going to have the entire rest of the world community—most especially including the nuclear powers—come down on it like a rock. That organization would then have open season declared on it. They'd be hunted down mercilessly and wiped out—possibly their host country as well. By and large, I think terrorists want to inspire *terror,* not rage. Rage makes people fight back; terror is supposed to make them tired, to make them say 'Let's give up and go home.' At least, that's how I think the logic would go. But all it takes is one person who doesn't understand the logic, and—*whoomf.*''

"It must be a constant worry."

"Oh yes. And worse than ever, after things broke loose in what was left of the USSR, and fissile material started making its way out into the hands of people you really wish didn't have it." He smiled, just a little. "Fortunately, the laws of nature are working with us a little bit on this one. Most people who try to work with trans-uranics don't have the training. They're working on a shoestring, in secret. Most of them are so lacking in expertise that, very quickly, while taking apart a shell or trying to build a bomb, they get contaminated by the fissile, and it kills them and everyone around them fairly quickly, and very painfully. It's something of a deterrent."

Spidey gulped again. "I just bet," he said softly.

A barge made its way down past the Delacorte Fountain's white plume of water: they watched it go, hooting at an approaching tug. "The point at which you get into trouble," Laurentz said, "is when you have *good* scientists working with the fissiles—people who *won't* have the good grace to drop a canister and LD50 themselves. People with access to money, and to the expensive specialized equipment that you need to work with fissiles safely. This is why the U.S. has been trying to hire as many former USSR scientists as it can, at the best rates, to keep them away from other countries who might be interested in building a little surprise for their neighbors."

Spidey nodded, saying nothing. His mouth was dry.

Doctor Octopus, he thought.

Ock was one of the premier scientists in the world, it had to be said, and radiation was his area of expertise.

There was no ignoring the man's genius. He would not drop any canisters, nor would he hire anyone who was likely to—or keep them on, after they'd done it once. His perfectionism would be offended, and he'd have them taken out and "neutralized" on the spot. And if there was anything else that Ock did have, it was money. Lots and lots of money, some of it earned from his career as a scientist prior to the accident that bonded him with his tentacles, most of it from the countless thefts he'd masterminded in the years since. He would have more than enough to buy himself, openly or covertly, all the machinery he could possibly need for this kind of work. And all the helping hands he'd need.

"What kind of luck have you had tracing the material that you know of being illegally shipped around the country?" Spidey said.

Laurentz shook his head regretfully. "Not a great deal. Our normal sources have dried up rather dramatically over the past few months, as if someone had put the fright on them pretty conclusively. One piece of information did slip out: some fissile, which we're still trying to locate and seize, was given to a couple of small midwestern right-wing 'patriot' groups, for 'protection.' " That mirthless laugh again. "Some members of one group got curious, and peeked into Pandora's box— tried to take one of the bombs apart. Unfortunate. Only for them, anyway; the thing didn't detonate."

"And that bomb upstate?"

Laurentz looked at him and shook his head. "That, interestingly enough, was a tamped device. Very effectively tamped, too. It developed a lot of radiation and did little actual destruction—though that's little consolation to the poor people in that tiny town. They're probably going to have to move now. The thing has irradiated the area's plants pretty conclusively, and the damage is going to make its way into the food chain."

"Any indication, as yet, who was responsible?"

"No. No one's taken responsibility, anyway."

Spidey stood up and began to pace a little. A few seagulls wafted by overhead in the wind and the sunshine. "One thing we have noticed over the past few months," Laurentz said, "the last six months, anyway. Our own technology is improving too, as you might imagine, and we're getting better at analyzing ambient and background radiation than we used to be. We've been noticing an increase in the city ambient. Bear in mind, Manhattan is founded on basalt and granite, which usually have radon associated with them. But we know what *that* ambient ought to be, and the radiation we've been sensing lately is higher—as if Manhattan was running a slight fever. The only place you normally get readings that high is over by Fourteenth Street, where the earthquake fault is."

"*What??*"

"The earthquake fault. Didn't you know about it? It's only a longitudinal. It's not all that geologically significant, though every now and then it burps a little. Cal-Tech keeps an eye on it for us, because when it burps, sometimes it leaks a little radon, we have to do street monitoring to make sure that people are safe."

"Burps, huh? How hard?"

"Almost not worth speaking of. One-point-two, one-point-three Richter—you'd notice a heavy truck going by sooner. In fact, Cal-Tech sometimes has trouble reading it because of the traffic vibration, but fortunately the transverse wave is diagnostic."

"The things you learn about this city," Spider-Man said.

"There's an underground river there, too. Not naturally submerged, though—I think they diverted it artificially in the 1800s. At any rate, the last analysis of the radiation figures seems strongly to suggest that there's a stockpile we haven't located yet, somewhere in or on Manhattan—more likely, in it—and it's beginning to affect the ambient of the substrate around it."

"Any way to tell where?" Spider-Man said.

"Not specifically. The equipment is kind of obvious looking, and even in this town it's hard to walk around the city streets with it and not be noticed." Laurentz then added with a sad smile, "Not that we have the money to do it. Congress has cut our appropriation again this year. But there's something down there. So far we haven't been able to find anything, while investigating the CCRC records, that would cast any light on the problem."

"Well," Spidey said, "let me cast a little light of my own."

Briefly he told Laurentz about Venom's certainty that Doctor Octopus was involved, and the extent of the involvement. Laurentz looked thoughtful, then nodded.

"I think I remember seeing a couple reports from the FBI and Interpol," he said, "possibly SHIELD as well, that he was connected to incidents in which material was being smuggled in from other countries. The problem's been proof, until now. Octavius seems to have been fairly good about keeping himself from being connected to whatever's going on." Laurentz looked at Spidey. "Are you going to be investigating this yourself?"

"I don't see that I have much choice. You guys can't do it—and if the situation is getting sufficiently dangerous then someone's got to do something."

"Heroism," Laurentz said, and gave Spider-Man another of those thoughtful looks. "Well. Maybe I can help. We have some fairly effective radiation sensors—sort of the great-grandchildren of the Geiger counter—though I have to admit that they're best at close range."

"That's where we're likely to be," Spidey said.

" 'We.' Two of them, you'd need?"

"Yes."

"You're in luck," said Laurentz, standing up, "because two of them is all we have. Just make sure you bring them back. I can sign them out for you, but if you lose them, I'm going to have to put off getting married for about thirty years—that's how long it'd take me to pay back what they're worth.''

Spider-Man nodded. "Sounds good," he said.

"Wait here," said Laurentz and went off toward the building's roof door.

About twenty minutes later he came back with a pair of harnesses, to which were attached small ''black boxes'' with LCD readout panels. Laurentz turned one of them on and showed Spidey a surprisingly complex readout panel, with a tie-in to a satellite navigation "finder" system. "Here. And here's the manual." He handed Spidey a small fat book about as thick as the Yellow Pages.

"I have to read all this?"

Laurentz grinned. "Just the first couple of chapters. The rest is detail."

"Couldn't you just give me the Cliff Notes?"

"This is a government document," Laurentz said dryly. "Count yourself lucky that no one's already arrested you."

"It's the story of my life," Spidey said. "Mr. Laurentz—thanks for your help. And please get the government to pay attention to what Ock's doing."

"It's always a struggle," Laurentz said, "but I'll do my best. Good luck, Spider-Man."

"I'm going to need it," he said as he webbed up the two harnesses and the instruction manual, shot out a webline, and swung away.

Spidey went home to change, sat down, and spent the rest of the afternoon going through paperwork. Doris's great sheaf of numbers still needed his attention, and the manual would have to wait.

He riffled through the pages for a couple of hours, until figures and signal strengths were all blurring together in his eyes. He had long since given up looking at the "most frequently called" numbers, and was now concentrating on the numbers least frequently called, and the cloned numbers that had been least frequently used.

There were, in particular, eighteen of these that were used only once. Peter looked carefully at all their associated readings—not able to make much of them—but there was one set in particular that matched up, for each of the cloned numbers.

He reached out for the phone and called Doris Smyth. "Hello?"

"Doris, it's Peter Parker."

"Hello, dear! I'm sorry I haven't had time to call you today; business has been unusually frantic. I don't have anything new on MJ's phone, I'm afraid."

"That's okay, that's not what I'm calling about. I'm looking through those printouts you gave me."

"Oh, dear," Doris said, "I hope you're not getting eyestrain."

"I am, but it doesn't bother me. Doris, what exactly is 'Ssth' in this one column? The fifth column over?"

"Signal strength."

"Hmm," Peter said. "Am I imagining things, or do I remember you telling me that sometimes you could get *location* information from that little covert chip?"

There was a pause. "Sometimes," Doris said, "yes. If the signal strength is sufficient, the covert will try to locate itself in terms of the nearest cell emitters. If you know the emitter locations, you can work out where the phone was."

"Can you do that for a few of these?"

"I'll try for you. It may take a while. What page of the readout?"

He told her, identifying the specific numbers. "One more thing before you go," he said. "Am I wrong in thinking that it's hard to get a bad cell phone signal in New York?"

Doris laughed at him. "Dear, I'm amazed we don't pick up conversations on our *fillings*. There are emitters every block and a half, it seems. If you've got a bad signal, it usually means that you're in a building with an unusually effective Faraday cage, or one with a lot more girders than they usually use these days, or you're down in the subway.''

"Faraday cage?''

"It's a network of wires or metal mesh that people use to protect computers from ambient RF radiation that might hurt their data. For example, I know one shopping center that had to build a Faraday cage around its two biggest department stores, because they were close to a big radio station, and every time the station came on in the morning, it would wipe out all the data in their cash registers' computers. You don't get many buildings here that need to be purposely caged, though. RF of that kind is rare in the States—the store I was thinking of was in Europe.''

"Okay," Peter said. "Doris—thanks lots.''

"You're welcome. I'll call you back as soon as I have something. Bye!''

She hung up. Peter stared at the printout.

In an old building—or in a cage—or in the subway. Underground.

Peter thought about Hobgoblin's hideaway, where the bomb with which he intended to nuke New York had been kept.

I wonder—did he build that? Or was it just lent to him—or built for him?

By Doc Ock, for example?

Peter wondered. Before he started wearing the Hobgoblin suit, Jason Macendale was a mercenary called Jack O'Lantern. Macendale had always been willing to work for anyone if the price was right.

No question but that Ock's price would likely have been right, if he actually owned CCRC.

Underground.

He reached for the phone again, called the number that Venom had left on his answering machine earlier that morning, and talked into it rapidly for a few minutes, stating that he would leave a web-wrapped package for Venom on the roof of his building, telling him what it was, and where (in a general way) he intended to be.

Then Peter hung up and started studying the manual, preparing for a night on the town—or, rather, under it.

NINE

A famous architect once said, "New York is an iceberg." He was not talking about the friendliness, or lack of it, of the inhabitants or about the climate in the winter. He meant the infrastructure, in the original form of the word: the structure below the city, under the streets and the buildings. At least as many "built things" lay below the ground as above, and possibly more.

Between thirty and two hundred feet below the streets of New York lies the biggest, most intensively built infrastructure of any city in the world. Miles of electric cable and fiber, tons of steel and iron in the sewers old and new; water mains, access tunnels, and conduits for steam and gas; and deepest of all, the skyscraper foundations, reaching in some cases four to five hundred feet into the bedrock. There are cellars and subcellars, passages between buildings, some used for years and forgotten, some newly built; train tunnels still being used by the mainline stations, and others long forgotten; the incredible tangle of subway stations, reaching from one end of the island to the other; and here and there, a secret that only two or three people knew.

Down in the dark, in a subway access tunnel, Spider-Man was making his way toward one of them, on a hunch that Doc Ock might be there—or better still, that his stockpile of radioactives might be. Spidey had strapped one of the two AEC radiation sensors to him; his camera was in its usual belt-buckle holder, and he was as ready as he was likely to be to deal with Ock. Whether he would be doing it alone or not, he had no idea. One possibility—that he might have Venom's help—was almost as bad as the idea that he might have to take on Ock all by himself. *But,* he thought as he leaped and sprang through the darkness, *this is what heroes do.*

MJ had said it to him, when she came home and understood what he was going to do. "Maybe I won't go in to work," she said.

"No point in that," he'd said, holding her close. "I don't even know if I'm going to find anything tonight. You go ahead and make money—we've still got that phone bill to think about."

She rolled her eyes. "Well, if things keep going on this way, not much longer! All the same, just one night off—"

"No. They need you. They like you. You told me so. And you like working with them, *and* it's good money, so you go on and do it. After the nightmare you had the other night, I think you deserve a little enjoyment. I'll call you if anything exciting happens."

"On what? Doris still has my phone."

"Oh."

She chuckled and kissed him. "See how preoccupied you are. Go on, my hero, and do what must be done." She threw her head back, looked at him levelly, and said it in her super heroine voice.

He laughed. "Hey, pretty good. Just don't get bitten by any radioactive bugs or anything now, okay? One of us in the house is enough."

"If you were in the house more often, I'd like it more," she muttered. "And not chasing around after— Well, it's not the chasing that bothers me. It's the being chased. Venom—"

"Honey," he said, looking into her eyes, "we can't do a thing about him. He's here. If he comes near me with intent, I'll do everything I can to clean his clock, but worrying about it just wastes energy. Right now I've got other problems. The city's sitting on some kind of powder keg again—"

"And here you come with the matches."

"Not me," Spidey said. "I've got the extinguisher. I think."

"Go on, then," she said and pushed him away gently. "You and your gadget there. Go do what you have to— and don't be back late."

"Being late," he said, "in all senses of the word, is the last thing on my mind."

It was still on his mind, though not last, as he paused in the subway access tunnel and looked out on the tracks of the Lexington Avenue local. Far down in the distance he could see the lights on the platform of the Sixty-eighth Street station. He was not headed that way, though. There was someplace odder he had to find again, and it had been a while since he had been this way.

Doctor Octopus, over his long affiliation with the city, had become as familiar with its buried side as most people become with the parts of it that stick up in the sunlight and air. He had had several hideouts here and there, some of them obvious, some of them less so. Two of the more obvious ones, large subcellar spaces found or built under old office buildings, Peter had already checked. They were, as he had suspected, empty. Ock was too smart to return to spots that were so easily accessible. Spider-Man had wanted to look at them anyway to see whether there were possibly any radioactives stored there, as much to test his sensor as anything else. So far it hadn't given so much as a peep. Nor would it, at the moment—Spidey had it set on silent running, so that it would vibrate against him like a hypertrophied beeper set on quiet if it felt anything. But this left other opportunities to be investigated.

Ock was an avid reader of history, a pastime that had led him to some interesting discoveries, and the place to which Spidey was now heading was one of them. He looked both ways before crossing the tracks, jumped them and the third rail, and made his way down to the next access and maintenance tunnel leading away from them.

About half a mile down this tunnel, he found what he was looking for: an old opening with thick sheets of heavy metal, like the kind they put down on the streets while doing repair work, riveted up over it into the masonry of the walls. The masonry here looked older than that elsewhere, and there was a good reason for this.

I'll have to let someone know about this, Spidey thought, and reached up to grab one edge of the metal sheet. He got a good grip, then slowly pulled. The metal groaned and began to bend, and masonry around it crumbled; screws and rivets popped out of the steel sheet as the whole business leaned toward him. Then suddenly it gave way. Spidey leapt aside as it crashed to the floor of the access tunnel and lay there, rocking and scraping against the wall.

Slowly and carefully he stepped in through the doorway he had revealed and switched on his spider-signal to look around in the darkness.

It was still pretty much as it had been: the matte-masked glitter of dusty crystal reflected back filmed rainbows when hit with the red light of his spider-signal. Spidey stepped into the oldest subway station in New York City, and his footsteps echoed back from marble carvings and the inlaid terrazzo of the floor.

He hadn't believed it when he saw it the first time: a little station, with mosaics and beautifully carved bas-reliefs, and one track running away under the ground to a point about three blocks away. There was another little station, identical to this one. Both stations had crystal chandeliers and vases built into the walls for flowers. The other one had had a grand piano.

During the 1800s, there had been a very wealthy businessman who had the idea that New York should have a subway system. He had taken this idea to Tammany Hall, from which Boss Tweed effectively ran the city, and set it out for the Boss himself. The Boss had laughed and said a crazy idea like this would never catch on—whoever heard of streetcars underground? And besides, the open-trench digging that would be needed for such a project would disrupt everything for years.

The businessman did not have open-trench digging in mind. He proposed to tunnel completely underground and remove the spoil gradually from one end of the hole.

The wits at Tammany Hall laughed louder than ever at this idea, and refused the businessman permission to even try.

Being, however, a New Yorker of a particularly robust period, he acted typically. He went ahead and built the thing anyway, secretly, and at his own expense. Two years later, he invited the dumbfounded Tammany fat cats to come and see his subway.

They did, and they were (against their will) impressed. They were willing to start building more such subways, but the rampant corruption of the Tweed administration had used so much of the city's money that there was nothing to spend on such a project, and soon enough the Tweed machine was out of office. The new administration couldn't be bothered with subways, and the businessman's little project was boarded up, shortly after his death, and forgotten—except by one super-villain who read his history books very closely. Doc Ock found it, used it as a hideout for a time; and in the middle of a particularly nasty and lively running battle, Spider-Man had followed him there, and they had fought. For a long time after, Spidey had thought with affectionate regret about how, if things had gone just a little differently, all New York subway stations might have had chandeliers and grand pianos.

Now, though, the chandelier was somewhat the worse for wear—as a result of that old fight—and the dust lay thick. No one had been here for a long time.

Something poked him gently in the ribs. He whirled to see what it was.

Zzt.

Huh?

Zzt.

"Oh," he said, and then almost laughed out loud, and stopped himself. It was the sensor, buzzing sporadically against him.

He took a couple of experimental steps down toward the platform.

Zzzt. Zzzzzzzzt. Zzzzzzzz.

Spidey headed that way. The buzzing got stronger. He headed farther on down, until he ran out of platform and had to jump down onto the ancient track. *Zzzzzzzz.*

It was getting stronger, the buzzing, and more prolonged. This was definitely not background radiation; he had the sensor set well above that. Spider-Man leaped on down the tracks, going as silently as he could—

Zzzzzzzzzzzzzzzzzzzzzzzzzzzzzzzzzzzzzzzzzzzzzzzzzzzzz.

When he got down to the other end of the platform, the buzzing simply wouldn't stop. He stood still for a moment, looked around him cautiously with his spider signal.

Nothing. Bare walls, bare floors.

Marks in the dust on the terrazzo floor.

He went over to the marks, bent to examine them more closely. The strength of the buzz got as high as it would go, and a soft light flashed on the sensor to indicate that he needed to decrease the sensitivity setting somewhat if he wanted the buzzer to work properly again. He didn't move to do so, still looking at the marks.

Little barrels. Little drums, like we found in the CCRC buildings. And radioactive as heck, if I'm getting this much reading just from the floor and the dust they were standing on.

The thought was rather intimidating. For the moment, he tried not to breathe. Gone, though, and no way to tell how long ago that happened. *Though not a lot of dust has fallen in the scraped places where they were moved. So maybe it didn't happen too long ago. And they were taken out another way, otherwise I would have seen markings down in the dust at the other end, not to mention picking up the radioactivity.*

He looked to see where the marks led. Down toward the farthest end of the platform. *There would have been a stairway here,* Spider-Man thought, *when it was originally built.*

Maybe there had been; now there was just a wall that had been sealed up the same way as the one he had come in through. The buzzing continued here.

He reached up to the riveted-on sheet of metal, pulled at it slowly. It gave way, very gradually—finally fell, clanging and echoing, on the marble floor beside him.

Spider-Man looked through the doorway, into the dark. *Zzzzzzzzz,* said the radiation sensor.

"All right," he said softly, "let's see where this leads."

It led a long way into the dark. The ceiling of the tunnel was low, and the masonry was old at first, then newer. Then the masonry stopped and rock began: plain black basalt, the roots of the city. And then the tunnel sloped downward, often twisting and turning sharply as it went.

Spider-Man trailed a gloved hand along the wall for a short way. The wall was surprisingly smooth. *Laser drilling?* he wondered. That kind of thing was incredibly expensive.

It occurred to Spidey that there were, once again, entrepreneurs in New York willing to spend a lot of their own money—well, *somebody's* money—on private construction projects. And the way the tunnel twisted, sometimes almost back on itself, suggested that someone had been using satellite guidance, or some other similar system, to avoid the foundations of other buildings, entries to other, older tunnels, cable conduits, etc.

Spider-Man went on at the best speed he could, trusting his spider-sense to allow him to maneuver safely in this darkness. He had been making his way along for about a mile, he thought, when the tunnel's downward slope increased more acutely, and its run straightened out a good deal. At this point, Spider-Man stopped and listened very hard. Nothing. His spider-sense had nothing to say to him, either.

It was getting damp. *Surprising how the summer humidity can make it even down here. There's just no es-*

cape, is there? And it was cooler, too. Slowly Spider-Man started on down the tunnel again, going softly, listening.

Sound began: water. Far off, very soft, a tinkle and drip and splash of water, like the sound you hear in subway stations in wet weather—except that the subway stations, as far as Spidey could tell, should be far above him at this point. *Zzzzzzzzt,* the sensor sounded against his chest. It had been maintaining a fairly even tone all this while, picking up the traces of where the barrels had passed though this tunnel, here and there spiking a louder *ZZZZ* when it passed a place where some barrel might have banged against a wall. *The contamination,* Spider-Man thought, *must have been horrendous. If all the barrels were leaking radioactivity like that . . .*

He shuddered as he went along. Spidey had a healthy respect for radioactivity, both in its positive and negative aspects. The negative one was most on his mind at the moment, though. It took only a speck of plutonium in your lungs to kill you dead, and not even from radio-activity: the sheer toxicity of the metal was more than sufficient.

Spider-Man went on, and the sound of the water slowly grew and grew. Then, ahead of him, away down the tunnel, he saw the slightest glow of light: a pale greenish glow, as if from fluorescent tubes. Very quietly, he made for it.

The pale glow slowly defined a doorway, quite liter-ally a light at the end of the tunnel. He came to the end—

—and simply had to stop and stare.

Off to his right, the pathway that flowed into the tun-nel he had left continued off around some outcroppings of rock, out of sight. Spider-Man stood at the edge of a wedge-shaped natural cavern nearly three hundred feet across. From high up one of its walls, off to his right, water poured down in a thin stream of waterfall, into a shallow pool. Water splashed up high from this, and flowed away off toward the side of the cavern directly across from him, down and out of sight. The floor was a pincushion tumble of stalagmites, mingled with powdery stuff that had probably fallen from the stalactites above; some of this was a powdery fungus that glowed a faint golden-green. Down the middle of the cavern ran a deep fissure with many shattered stalagmites on either side of it. *Maybe not the fault itself,* Spidey thought, *but a symptom of it.* The ceiling was not level; it arched up in a sort of earth-Gothic style, hung with innumerable stalactites, some two hundred feet sheer to a highest, narrowest point, and from that area, though he couldn't see it directly, came just a spark of real light. *Some grille on the sidewalk?* Spidey thought. *This must be the river they diverted.*

He half wished he had a cell phone, so he could test the cell. *I bet the signal would be pretty weak down here.*

Zzzzzzzzzzzzz, said the sensor insistently. It felt stronger than it had since down in the almost-a-subway-station.

Obediently he turned to see in which direction the signal would increase. Off to the right, it got stronger, following the level path that had been cleared through the stalagmites nearest the cavern wall.

He went cautiously along the path, quietly listening. The water made it hard to hear; the echoes were confusing. Now, though, they began to fade as the cleared path led him through into another tunnel, this one much straighter than the previous one. It ran on straight for nearly a hundred yards and there were lights in it, at intervals.

Zzzzzzzzzz, said the sensor. *Zzzzzzzzzz. ZZZZZZZZZ-ZZZZZZZZZ.*

It vibrated so hard that it felt slightly indecent, and Spidey stopped briefly to turn its sensitivity down a good ways. Then he went on, but the adjustment lasted only a short time. *ZZZZZZZZZZZZZZZ, ZZZZZZZZZZZZ!*

He came to a door. It was made of extremely heavy

metal, like an airlock door in a submarine, but the door-
knob seemed simple enough. He turned the knob and
pulled. Very silently, on well-oiled hinges, the door
slowly leaned open.

*ZZZZZZZZZZZZZZZZZZZZZZZZZZZZZZZZZZZZZZZ-
ZZZZ!!!!* bellowed the sensor, and with good reason.

Spidey looked into a room nearly the size of the cavern he had just left, all carved out of the living rock. It
was piled high with metal drums. Every one of them
had a stenciled number on it. Some had old lettering as
well: WASTE, CHEMICAL WASTE, TOXIC: DISPOSE OF AP-
PROPRIATELY. One, not too far from Spider-Man, said
COOKING OIL.

I don't care what it says, Spidey thought to himself
grimly, *this ain't no Mazola!*

He started to shut the door. And then his spider-sense
screamed.

Spidey spun around, saw a bunch of black-clad people
jumping at him, and knew perfectly well that there was
no point in waiting to see if they were going to be
friendly. He threw himself in a double-fisted punch at
the first one and decked him; rolled, bounced, shot webbing at one of the others, missed; bounced again, trying
to get a count.

*Six of them? Seven? There's no fighting room here.
Let's make the odds a little more even.* He bounced hurriedly back down the tunnel toward the cavern, made
the entrance, looked up, saw the stalactites.

It's worth a shot.

Gunfire sprayed behind him. *And me without my flak
jacket,* he thought. He looked up again, picked a stalactite, shot webbing at it, felt it anchor. Went up the webline, and swung, while bullets whined all around and
spat glowing fungus and rock dust off the surrounding
stony icicles.

Footsteps, echoing, as the guards ran into the cavern.
Spidey swung hard around the first stalactite, chose an-

other one, one of the biggest, shot webbing at it, anchored, pulled himself free of the first—

Suddenly, fire streaked past his ear and blew the other
stalactite to powder. Spidey swung hurriedly around the
other one, looking to see what the heck *that* had been.

A single man had come down the tunnel, the way the
others had. He was dressed in jeans and a dark jacket,
and he had an RPG launcher over his shoulder, or something that looked very much like it. He drew a bead on
Spidey, fired again.

Spidey launched himself out into the air—he had no
desire to be a guest at his own barbecue. The second
blast from the RPG ruined the biggest stalactite as Spidey caromed into another one, hung on for dear life, and
prepared to move on again in a hurry. *That one looks
nice,* he thought and shot webbing at it, felt it anchor.
Better go—

He swung from the web—and the stalactite detached
itself neatly from the ceiling.

For one bare moment Spider-Man understood, as if
from the inside, one of the principles of cartoon physics:
you must *know* you are about to fall before it can actually happen. He seemed to hover there for the split
second until he knew—and then, flailing, he went down.
Spidey had just enough time to glimpse the really large
stalagmite pointing toward where his back was about to
land. He twisted spasmodically, just missed it, and
crashed into two other smaller, blunt ones. One of them
grazed his head. He lolled back, unable to move for a
moment, literally seeing stars.

The black shapes, he could see, were picking their
way toward him—

—and then there was an appalling sound: a scream.
Not me, he thought fuzzily for a moment. *Too deep.*

He managed to lever himself up on one elbow, look
around. The black shapes, at least three of them, were
being waved around in the air by long black pseudopodia attached to the usually least welcome, but tem-

porarily most welcome shape in the world. Venom stood there, arms folded as if in amusement over something odd on his chest—Spidey squinted, abruptly recognizing the twin to his own sensor. With a quick, economical gesture, the pseudopodia chucked the three men hard at the cavern wall. They hit it hard and fell, none of them in good shape at all. Venom turned, reached out a very long set of tentacles and snatched the RPG from the man who held it, then snarled, "Niner!" and poured more tentacles at him.

"Niner" just smiled, let the RPG go, stepped hurriedly back from the extra pseudopodia, and put his hand in his pocket.

Another appalling scream. *Not me. Too high. No, it is me.* The sonic scream got inside his head and blasted the world and the inside of his skull white with sound and pain. He just barely saw it starting to rain stalactites, saw the pseudopodia writhing in agony, heard Venom's scream of sympathy and his own scream of agony. Then for a long time there was nothing left but the screaming, and the pain, and after a while that went away as well.

"—off them now and save yourself a lot of trouble, sir."

A voice, just a voice in the darkness. *Unfamiliar.*

"Oh, no, my faithful 'ninth arm,' you misunderstand my intent. I don't *want* to save myself trouble. After the Hundredth Day, things are going to be very quiet, except for certain indulgences I permit myself. Like these two. Almost too much to hope for, the second one. I don't intend to throw away such a piece of good luck. Indeed not."

Familiar voice. Too familiar. Can't move, can't do anything.

"You've had the guest suite ready all this while. Well, we've got an extra guest, it may get a little cramped in there—but we'll have plenty of time, all the time in the world in fact, to make more room for our extra lodger. Meantime, put them in there together.''

"Won't Venom—?"

"He might. Wouldn't that be interesting to watch? Still, I doubt he will for a good while yet. I don't intend to waste their entertainment value so quickly. Not for a long time, certainly—maybe never. We'll see. Anyway, we'll dose them at intervals with enough sonics to keep his alien pet in order. Go on, Niner, put them in the suite. We've got a few other things to do this afternoon before we can enjoy ourselves.''

Joy.

Make a note. No more stalactites.

No more . . . sta . . .

TEN

Spider-Man opened his eyes. It hurt. Everything hurt.

Very slowly and carefully, not wanting to find out too quickly about anything else that hurt, Spider-Man rolled over onto his face. His face hurt, but he had known about that already from the graze with the stalactite. His arms hurt, but not so badly that they didn't work.

A good thing, that, since he found himself staring straight at a flaccid, black, shining pseudopod between his face and the floor. It twitched.

He boosted himself up and away from it in a hurry— then groaned as many other parts of his body complained that *they* hurt, too, and what was he going to do about it? Spidey shook his head carefully, half afraid he would hear something rattle, and boosted himself into some kind of limp sitting position.

He looked around. They were in a three-walled room about twenty feet by twenty; it appeared to have been carved out of the same solid basalt as the hallway with the fissile storehouse in it. Floor, walls, and ceiling were all the same dull black. Off to one side was what looked like a black basalt toilet, no seat; in the corner of the room was a little triangular pool of water, like a tiny koi pond set into the floor.

The fourth wall fascinated Spidey. It shimmered—just a shimmering in the air, like heat haze, with no light, nor a glow—but he was sure he knew what it was anyway. *It's a force field,* he thought, *a genuine TV-science-fiction force field.* He suspected strongly that Doc Ock was out there somewhere, waiting for him to test it. Well, he could wait.

Beyond the force field was a larger room, barren, with various crates and boxes stacked up in it. Some of Doc Ock's people, some wearing the "goon uniform" that he first saw way back when Ock was going by the immodest sobriquet of "the Master Planner," others in more casual clothes. They flitted to and fro, bringing in more crates or taking them away. It looked leisurely; no one was in a rush. Some of the henchpeople threw interested glances in at Spidey, which he declined to return.

He turned his back on the outside world and examined the cell once more. It looked like it was intended for very hard wear and very extended use. *Charming,* Spider-Man thought, and looked across at his prone cell mate. Venom lay there sprawled, having been hurt a lot worse by the sonics than Spidey had: the symbiote lay strung out all around him in stricken rags and tatters.

He disliked the idea of going near the thing, but there didn't seem any point in letting Venom lie there and rest a perfectly good, if hostile, set of brains while they could be useful in getting them both out of there. Spidey hunkered himself over closer to Venom, shook his shoulder a little. "Venom. Come on, snap out of it, you big baby."

No response.

"I should think he'd be out of it for a good while," said the familiar, rasping, gloating voice from behind him. "You'll be wasting your time. But you'll have lots of it to waste, from now on."

Slowly, Spidey turned around. There stood Doctor Octopus, just outside the force field, looking at him through those bloody sunglasses of his, and smiling. He waved a hand at the field, as if through air. "Don't you want to try it?"

"Not in the slightest," Spider-Man said, "since it'd probably kill me. Or make me wish I was dead. I have this nasty feeling that killing me—us—is not on the menu."

"Oh, no, not at all. You two are a guilty pleasure," said the Doc. "Rather, *you* are: Venom was an unexpected dividend. But over the next couple of months I intend to spend a lot of time enjoying your reactions to what you see going on around you. Helplessness: the most delicious of emotions which leads to all others—

rage, grief, resignation. Though I doubt you'll come to that too soon.''

''I'll resign right now,'' Spider-Man said, ''if you'll let me out of here and give me a chance to pound you properly.''

''Certainly not.'' Doc Ock put his hands behind his back, a little primly, and smiled, while the god-awful metal tentacles wreathed and writhed around like square-dancing snakes. ''And I intend to watch with enjoyment your attempts to make me angry—what's the phrase?—'so that I'll make a mistake.' I have been practicing not making mistakes for a long time now.''

''You've been practicing something, all right,'' Spidey said, crossing his legs with a little hiss of pain, and making himself as comfortable as he could. ''High finance, mostly. I never thought of you as a banker.''

''You never *thought*,'' Ock corrected him. ''That was always your problem. React first, think things through later. Annoying, how your wretched half-baked thinking would sometimes serve you well enough to interfere with my plans. A long time now I've put up with that kind of thing from you. But no more. I intend to demonstrate to you, at leisure, what real thinking can do— and you'll have leisure to appreciate it.''

''Is this the part where you gloat over me?'' Spidey said.

''For years,'' said Ock, with a smile of pure pleasure. ''But, as an exercise for the student, I'm delighted to give you a chance to tell me what's been going on.''

''You're destroying the world?'' Spidey said.

Doctor Octopus chuckled. ''What silliness. When the building is burning, you don't pour on gasoline. You put the fire out.''

''Oh,'' Spider-Man said. ''And with terrorists and loonies all over the place trying to get their hands on nuclear material, *you're* processing it and shipping it all over the place, here and in Europe, and selling it to anyone who'll pay, and this is how you put the fire out? An interesting new definition of 'saving the world': I hadn't heard this one before.''

''I *am* saving the world,'' Doc Ock said calmly. ''From the irresponsible populations that are destroying it. When I'm finished, there will be a lot fewer of those populations. But more to the point, I'm gathering every useful technology together into the hands of the people who will use them wisely—''

''In other words, you.''

''Perspicacious boy.''

''Gee, you know big words, Doc.''

''And what to do with them, insect.'' Just for a moment, a glitter of pure hate showed in Doc's eyes. ''In the past twenty years, this world has changed tremendously in terms of scientific advancement. Machines that were unheard of as little as a decade ago are now household appliances—and being misused as often as used properly. The time is ripe for one person to command all the technology.''

''Nice goal,'' Spider-Man said. ''The question is, will all those other people let you?''

''There won't be that many of them to argue the point,'' said Doc Ock, ''in a very little while.''

The chill got into Spidey's bones at the sound of that.

''See what's happened in the world in those twenty years,'' Ock said. ''The age of the superpower should have come to an end with the collapse of the Soviet Union. There should have been an astonishing leap forward in terms of science and medicine and managing the world, with that shadow lifted. But still small nations squabble and kill each other's people over wars that were fought and lost five hundred years ago. All the technology is here to make this world a paradise, but the nations of the world just go on wasting their potential. They'll waste it until there's nothing left. The time's now ripe for one person to command the world's economy, one who'll use it to best advantage, in science's service. The greatest scientist ever to live.''

Spidey cocked his head just slightly sidewise, wondering whether Venom was conscious enough to get any of this. *Can't be. He'd be raving already.*

"All it takes is one man with a vision," Ock said, "and the world can be changed. *Is* being changed: the changes are already in progress. A hundred days or less, and no one will know this for the same planet."

A hundred days—Spidey thought of that phone call from Galya. "All this money-laundering," he said casually. "Whose economy are you messing with?"

"Everyone's," said Doc delightedly. "Why leave anyone out? And there are so many ways to do it. Destabilize local currencies by speculation in the local markets. Deflate a country's cash reserves."

"Counterfeiting," Spidey said, suddenly remembering a little barrel of ink that Venom had found along with other smuggled goods on a Florida beach: the "color-changing" ink used on the new European Community bank notes—called, simply, the Euro—impossible to duplicate, now the most stolen and most expensive substance in the West.

"Yes indeed. In about a month, the Euro will suffer a most devastating drop in its value when it's discovered how much of the currency is worthless, unbacked by the member banks. So will the dollar and the yen. The ruble, worth little enough as it is, will go into hyperinflation within minutes. The world's currencies will go into free fall."

"Whole economies will crash," Spider-Man said softly, horrified.

"Yes. It will start there. Many wasteful industries will die in that first shakeout—"

"First."

"Well," said Ock, the extra arms curling and wreathing gently about him, "I always did favor the belt-and-suspenders route. There are simply too many people on this planet. Resources are being wasted faster than they can be replaced. I had given some thought to smallpox and anthrax,'' he said, tilting his head a little, as if considering it again, ''but they are unreliable agents, and difficult to control. No, the sweet compliance of the atom suits me better. Plutonium doesn't breed without help, and won't mutate into some unpredictable new form without warning. I have acquired a fair amount of it, and over time I've distributed a great deal of it, here and there, where it'll do the most good.''

''All over the country, you mean!''

''Every major city. City-dwelling has not been good for our planet, by and large,'' Ock said judiciously. ''Now nearly half this world's swollen population lives in cities. A moment's surgery, in a hundred days, and,'' he made an airy gesture, ''the burden becomes much less. I don't have a quarrel with simple people who live on the land. I'll rule them in their best interests, and they'll provide food and the raw materials we'll need for the new sciences. At the same time, I don't want to ruin the cities totally. It's surgery—or rather, chemotherapy. Kill the cancer, save the body.'' He smiled again. ''They'll thank me for a thousand years after.''

Spidey sat very still. Then, slowly, he got up, and walked as close to that force field as he dared.

What gives you the right to do this?'' he cried.

Ock only blinked. ''I'm the one best qualified to bring this result about,'' he said simply, ''and the time is right. Wouldn't you say?''

Spider-Man stood there and just shook.

Doctor Octopus peered past him at Venom, and tsked a little. ''I hope I didn't give him too much,'' he said. ''Keep an eye on him. This has been very entertaining—I look forward to seeing how he reacts to it.''

And Otto Octavius walked away, actually whistling to himself.

Spidey sat down next to Venom, still trembling with rage and fear. For a long time he was silent.

Then, so softly it was barely a breath of sound,

Venom said, "And we thought we knew what madness was like."

Spidey, acutely aware that they were probably being watched, pretended to lie back down on his back, not too close to Venom but not too far away from him either, and moaned a little. The moan was genuine enough. After a few long breaths he whispered, "If you've got any thoughts on this, I wouldn't mind hearing them."

There was a very soft hiss: after a little while, Venom said, "We should consider our available assets. We ourselves are not entirely out of commission, though holding the symbiote in check is something of a strain at the moment."

"Yeah, I know," Spidey said morosely, "it wants to eat my spleen or something."

"It wants to eat *all* of you," Venom said, "but at the moment we have no intention of catering to its whims. Later, when we are free, will be another matter. We decline, however, to be entertainment for that crackpot."

Spidey paused a moment, thought about that. "Okay," he said. "Let's fight."

"Your sense of humor is as impaired as ever."

"No, I'm serious. Venom, listen to me! We didn't even have to make him angry—he's *already* made his mistake."

"In what regard?"

"How much of that did you hear?"

"To our intense regret, all of it."

"He said he built this place for me. *Not for you.* We've got so much history together, he knows my capabilities inside out—*but not yours.* There may be some weakness in this place that you can exploit that I can't."

There was a long pause. "It is well reasoned," Venom said softly. "We would suggest you wait an hour or so. The symbiote is indeed somewhat 'under the weather.'"

"You're on."

Another pause. "This is not to be taken as a waiver

243

of my statutory right," said Venom, "to eat your spleen at a later date."

Spidey snorted and disguised the sound more or less successfully as a sneeze. "As long as the world doesn't get blown up," he said softly, "that suits me fine."

Silence.

Spider-Man lay back and took the single most unsuccessful one-hour nap of his life.

Slowly, over the next half hour or so, Venom's pseudopodia began working again. He pulled himself together over the course of a few minutes: the symbiote knitted itself back into a costume, and then, over another ten minutes or so, began putting new pseudopodia out and making little grabs in Spider-Man's direction. Spidey let this continue for a little while, then "noticed" it, and withdrew to his own corner.

What Spidey desperately hoped had escaped the attention of whatever surveillance was turned on them, was that while the pseudopodia were snatching at him, one of them—fined down to a hair, and practically invisible—had been investigating the force field. He had no idea what the results were, but Venom showed no sign of any ill effects, except that the look he was giving Spidey was becoming more ferocious and hungry by the minute.

Finally he spoke. "This is an opportunity we had not thought to have for a few days yet," he said. "It seems a shame to waste it—especially as it will be good practice for dealing with that slide-rule pusher when he comes back."

Spidey glared at Venom, stood up slowly. "I wouldn't bet that it's going to go the way you want," he said. "It hasn't before."

"There's always a first time," Venom said. And he leapt.

Pseudopodia whirled out and wrapped around Spidey, and he grappled with it in a very mixed state of mind:

he did not want to hurt Venom because he was going to need his help later, but he also did not want to be any closer to the symbiote than he had to. They reeled back and forth, they bashed into the walls. At one point, Venom picked Spidey up bodily and dropped him head-first on the floor, then leapt on him again.

They grappled and rolled around the floor. Those god-awful fangs dripped slime on Spider-Man and the tongue was everywhere at once. Their faces were close together. The symbiote made a noisy wailing sound. Eddie Brock's proper human voice whispered in Spidey's ear, "The force field is permeable. We had to narrow down to less than an angstrom wide, but some got out. With time—the controls—"

"We'll see where he keeps them," Spidey gasped.

Venom punched him. Spidey, furious, punched him back, then scrambled to his feet, picked Venom up, and threw *him* at the wall.

Unfortunately, there was very little room to work in a space like this, and some disadvantages. At one point Venom held his head under water in the corner pool. He struggled for air, gasped and thrashed, and finally got free—only to have the symbiote grab him to do it again. *It's getting too enthusiastic,* Spidey thought desperately. *Does it even understand the concept that this is a put-on? And if it does, does it care?*

The pseudopodia shoved him under the water again. *Nope,* Spidey thought, and choked and gasped and came up coughing water, and grabbed Venom and attempted to throw him straight across the horizon. The room actually shook a little when he hit the wall.

And outside the other wall, Doc Ock was standing, looking pleased. "Goodness," he said, "I hadn't thought you'd have had it in you so soon."

He glanced over to one side at something. *The controls for the force field,* Spidey thought, desperately hoping that Venom had seen it, willing him to have seen it.

Venom staggered to his feet. "You utter madman,"

he growled, stalking toward the force field, "we'll see shortly if legend is true, that you gain intelligence by eating others' brains."

"Wouldn't recommend it," Spidey remarked from the other side of the room, getting ready to leap. "Mad Octopus Disease is incurable."

Venom jumped at him. They rolled and punched again—but Spidey noticed that Venom stayed near the force field. Pseudopodia blurred the air.

They rolled. Spidey screamed as Venom struck him in the bruised rib. But through the pain he felt the slightest flash of satisfaction. He had seen the one pseudopod that was thinned down to almost literally nothing. On the far side of the force field, he saw the same pseudopod, which had fed through the field, an angstrom thick. *Buy it time,* he thought. *Let it get thick enough to do some good.*

They fought. Venom banged Spidey's head against the floor. They rolled, but not too far. Punches rained down, bruised the faces under the masks unmercifully. Spidey dragged Venom to his feet again, reared back for one last enormous haymaker, the last blow he felt he would ever have in him.

A soft sound, like a sigh. Spider-Man looked over Venom's shoulder and saw the heat haze suddenly go away, and also saw Doc Ock's face abruptly go blank with sheer surprise.

There was no need to say anything; they both dived out the door as Ock dived for the control to slap it back on.

He hit it too late—and pseudopodia whipped out and wrapped around him like ribbons around a much-longed-for present.

There was a shout from behind Ock as he struggled. People streamed into the area as if they'd been called.

He had some kind of remote on him, probably, Spidey thought: *a panic button.* He had little time left to think about it, as the people in black unholstered weapons and started shooting at him.

He was running on autopilot at the moment. Spidey webbed guns out of hands, bounced across the room, kicked and punched, and generally was a bad target. Most of his attention, though, was on Venom and Ock, struggling and swaying together, tentacles against pseudopodia, the fangs and the dread against the tremendous strength. *This is not good,* Spidey thought. *After I deal with these guys, there's still going to be Ock. How many times have we fought? And let's say I do win: then what have I got? Venom—and a very keyed-up Venom, after the last couple of hours.*

He swallowed. *When did I last update my will?*

As he was bouncing away from one more felled guy in black, Spider-Man heard an odd, inhaling sound. His spider-sense stung him like a wasp, and he jumped straight up.

The output from the flamethrower went by right underneath him. Spidey clung briefly to the ceiling, gasping and choking with the rising gasoline fumes, as someone he remembered seeing before, a guy in a floppy black hat with grommets, chased him with the flames. He scuttled along the ceiling.

"Just a little fire for the bug," said the man cheerfully. "Not like the fire that's coming, though. That'll be worth seeing—and nothing can stop it now."

With a tremendous effort, Venom lifted Doc Ock right off the floor and flung him crashing off to one side. Then he turned, murder in his gaze. "Niner," he said, and stepped toward him.

Niner turned the flamethrower toward Venom, hitching his shoulders a little to settle the fuel pack comfortably. "Should be quite a sight," he said, "all the fire, up there where the view and the food's so superior— but I don't think you'll be around to see it. You're just trouble. Better get rid of you now."

"This is Ock's sidekick?" Spidey said.

"Niner," said Venom, circling around toward him. "Amusing to see plain old garden-variety jealousy operating. We had thought the style in sidekicks now was dogged devotion."

He leapt. Spidey, off to one side, could see Doc Ock scrambling to his feet again. "Oh dear," he said softly. "My turn in the barrel."

He jumped too—catching, as he did, just a glimpse of Niner as Venom snatched the flamethrower out of his hands, ripped it off at the hose, and then wrapped the pseudopodia around him in what looked like an indissoluble embrace. Niner was no longer a threat.

He had no more time to spend on that: suddenly there were metal tentacles wrapped around him, and he was dealing with another embrace of his own.

Ock was almost purple with rage: it was nearly worth choking to death to see. *Nearly.* Spider-Man struggled to get free, but as always, it was like struggling with angry adamantium pythons. Spider-strength sufficed him to get them off him. He bounced out of range for a moment, trying to get his wind, and didn't get it, as one of those pythons reached up to the ceiling and snatched him down again.

Not without cost. Ock was still flesh and blood elsewhere, and as he pulled Spidey in at full speed, he also caught, backed by his own strength, Spidey's fist right in his face. He reeled back. Spider-Man bounced away again. *Just for a breath . . .*

Then all four tentacles caught him, lifted him high. He shot webbing at them; they broke it, and smashed him to the floor.

The world went white. No question about the rib this time. No question about maybe three of them. The legs were refusing to work, too. Broken back? No, he wouldn't still be able to feel the legs then.

He struggled to at least get halfway up. Ock had turned his back on him, had stalked over to Venom and grabbed him the same way. They were struggling, but the contest couldn't be in that much doubt, not really. Neither of them was fresh.

The tentacles held Venom high. Pseudopodia wrapped around them, resisting. There was a moment's swaying back and forth as dark razory ribbons struck and sliced at Doc's head, but not with the usual energy, a little feebly.

"You want to hold on?" Ock said. "Fine." And then the tentacles simply bashed Venom against the wall. Once—and the wall really did shake this time. Twice. Again. Again, like you would hit a fly you really wanted to flatten. Again.

The pseudopodia lost their grip.

Doc smashed Venom down on the floor. He lay there, still. The pseudopodia didn't move.

Spidey looked at him, where Doc stood looking down at Venom, only breathing a little fast.

He barely broke a sweat, Spidey thought in thoroughgoing disgust. *Look what he did to Venom. Venom! I've never been able to do that. And now he's going to do it to me, again. And then he's going to blow up the world, and my wife, and everything!*

No! I won't let him win! I didn't let him beat me when he dropped a ton of machinery on my back, and I won't let him beat me now!

He threw himself at Doc Ock, webbing like crazy.

At least the fighting started with webbing. Where it went after that seemed oddly predetermined to Spidey, as if he were doing some dance whose rules had been established a long time ago.

You shoot webbing at him, he shreds it up.

You jump up on the ceiling and come at him from that direction with webbing and then with feet and fists. He knocks you back.

You come at him again, hitting him like a cannonball, because all you can see in your mind is the sight of mushroom clouds everywhere, and your wife getting blown up—over and over and over.

He hits you, but you always hit him back, because if you don't, everything is going to die.

Everything.

Everything.

You hit, you kick. You're so hurt, it feels like you're kicking yourself.

It doesn't matter. MJ wouldn't like it if you stopped. "This," she would say, "is what heroes do."

And when you stop, finally, it's because the other party has stopped making the next move, failed to keep up the dance. You find yourself looking at a collapsed figure on the ground, terribly bruised and battered, metal arms lying helpless for the moment. And you wonder, irrationally, what you did wrong. Now, and all the other times.

I did it.

How did I do that?

Spidey shook his head. Ock lay still. Off to one side there was a faint beeping noise. Venom lay not too far from it, groaning.

Webbing, Spidey thought, *and lots of it.* He webbed Ock's arms behind him, and his legs, and the metal arms too, with special attention to them so that they couldn't work free. Then he staggered over to Venom.

Venom was moaning softly. It was a kind of piteous sound, especially since Spidey would have liked to lie down and make it himself. "Come on," he said. "Come on, Venom."

Wait a moment. Why am I trying to wake him up? I need to get out of here.

Then he heard the little beeping noise again. He looked for the source, and his eye came to rest on a little silver thing, like a small cylinder. It had an LED display on the top, and a little button.

The LED display said *56:04.* Then, *56:03. 56:02. 56: 01.*

A chill settled in the pit of Spider-Man's stomach. He picked it up.

The way everyone came. As if called. He had this with him.

He let go of it.

Dead man's switch!

He went to Venom and actually lifted him, picked him up: he needed all the help he could get. "Come on, Venom. Wake up! He's going to blow one of these things!"

"Wha—?"

"Come on! We've got to find his computers."

Venom just sagged down to the floor. Spidey could only stand and stare at him for a moment.

Then he staggered off down the hall toward Ock's lair.

Nothing was hidden there, which was fortunate as he had no time to search. Laid out neatly off to one side, in a sort of main control room, he found the radiation sensors, and all the computers up and running. The control room was deserted. Spidey suspected that a lot of Ock's people had decided that not even the wages he paid were worth staying around for at this point, with an angry super-villain and an angry super hero on the premises.

He looked at all the computer screens he could find. There were a lot of them. One system, though, was running a program called INVENTORY. There was a list on it. It was a list of hundreds of bombs.

All of them said INACTIVE. Spidey grabbed the computer's mouse, scrolled down it. And scrolled. And scrolled—

ACTIVE, said one. It had a number. It had a location in latitude and longitude. Spidey double-clicked on the entry.

A map of the World Trade Center appeared.

Oh, no, not again!

But it was the perfect place for an airburst. The closest you could come to one, without dropping it from an airplane. Maximum coverage.

It's going to kill thousands of people. Maybe hundreds of thosands.

Spidey recovered his sensor, strapped it to himself again. "Got to warn them," he muttered. "Where's a phone?" He looked around desperately, couldn't see one. "Where's a phone? It's been raining phones for days, why can't I find one when I need one?"

He caught sight of one, finally, between computer consoles. He grabbed it and punched numbers into it so fast he almost sprained a finger, that being the only part of him that was *not* presently sprained.

"Not the voicemail, please not the voicemail. Thank God! Drew! Spider-Man!" he shouted. "Call the World Trade Center, tell them to evacuate, now, there's a bomb! *Yes,* another one! Don't ask, just hurry, hurry!" He glanced at the dead man's switch. "Fifty minutes! Just get them out, get everybody there as far away as you can!"

He looked for somewhere to slam the phone down, couldn't find anywhere, dropped it on the floor and ran out as best he could.

Ock's elevator took him up into one of the access tunnels below the Union Square subway station. He made his way up onto one of the platforms and took the stairs at a run, causing some very surprised looks among the commuters.

The sirens had already begun howling. Spidey took to his weblines and swung like a mad thing across the city. As he approached the twin towers, he could see people streaming away from them. That suited him. *And here I am, the only thing in the city except for the bomb squad, going toward them.*

It's all very strange.

The sensor wasn't giving him so much as a peep as he landed on the roof of the South Tower and headed for the stairs. "Come on, give me some help," he muttered. But Laurentz had warned him that the sensors were fairly short-range.

Airburst. Top ten stories, certainly. Of two towers. Wonderful . . .

He took the elevator down to ninety and started quartering the corridors of the floor, with the sensor turned up as high as it could go. Nothing. It took him five minutes.

He ran up the stairs, quartered the next floor. Nothing. Ninety-two. Nothing.

He had never been so aware of time as a liquid, like blood flowing, trickling away. Everything was going to trickle away. There was no time to even call MJ and tell her he loved her. No time.

Ninety-three. Ninety-four. Ninety-five. Nothing.

And on up to the roof.

What if he put it below ten floors down? What if I miss it?

He ran back up to the roof, shot a webline over to the North Tower, and swung over, took the elevator down ten stories, while outside the sirens howled, and did it again.

Ninety. Nothing.

Ninety-one. Nothing.

Ninety-two.

Damn them all, he found himself thinking as he raced down one more set of empty corridors, and the sensor didn't say a thing to him. *Ock, and his bloody Niner. They always have to gloat. Fire in the sky—he knew about it all right.*

Spidey stopped dead, panting.

He did know.

What was it he said?

"—up there where the view and the food's so superior—"

My God!

Spider-Man burst out laughing and ran up to the hundred-and-first floor.

Seven minutes left.

The place was empty. He ran down the corridor to where a beautiful wrought-iron grille stood, with a sign on it: WINDOWS ON THE WORLD.

He plunged on in. No one was there; wineglasses sat abandoned on the tables, some of the most expensive vintages in the world, he'd heard.

He stood very still, and turned the sensor up.

Zzzzt.

Not a very strong signal. He took a few steps toward one bank of windows.

ZZZzzzzzt.

No? The other way.

ZzzzZZZZZT.

Right up against the window, between two tables, he stood. *ZZZZZZZZzzzzzt.*

A fairly strong signal. But nothing here to be making it.

Six minutes.

He moved away from the window.

Zzzzzt.

Weaker. But it can't be outside.

Where the heck is it?

He went back to the spot between the windows.

ZZZZZZZZzzzzzt.

All right, where is it? Spider-Man looked around him frantically.

And suddenly saw, in the corner, not too far away, the spiral staircase, leading downward.

He leaped down it, and found himself faced with a locked iron grille, with a beautiful little sign that said, WINE CELLAR.

Spidey laughed again. "Sorry," he said to the grille, and ripped it courteously off its hinges, setting it to one side.

The wine cellar was immense. Racks and racks and racks of wine, names like Rothschild and Grand Cru and Zinfandel and God only knew what else.

He turned the sensor up, and began working his way up and down the racks. Three minutes left.

Zzzzzzzzzzzzzzz.

Zzzzzzzzzzzzzzz.

ZZZZZZZZZZZZZZZZZZZZ.

He paused. Moved a little to one side—

ZZZZZZZZZZZZZZZZZZZZZZZZZZZZZZZZZZZZZ!

Two minutes.

Spider-Man looked at the wine rack—and, down in the bottom, saw one of the bottles of Rothschild with an unusually thick neck.

Very carefully, he knelt down beside it and eased it out. "About the size of a mortar shell," Laurentz had said.

More like a champagne bottle, Spidey thought, *but never mind that now.*

There was a very straightforward-looking switch on one side, and a little LED that said 01:32.

He took a deep breath.

MJ, I do love you—

—and this is *what heroes do.*

Spidey threw the switch.

The LED went out.

Just to be sure, he sat there for much longer than a minute and thirty-two seconds. Nothing happened. Outside, the sun shone, and the wind blew.

Inside, Spider-Man breathed again. Carefully, carrying the "wine bottle" under his arm, he went off to call Sergeant Drew's office and MJ.

ELEVEN

Much later, Peter sat on the living room couch with MJ and said sadly, "So only two more weeks of this?"

"Yup," she said. "Not as many stations picked it up as they'd hoped, so they're limiting the series to twenty-two episodes. They've already got eighteen. I'll be able to tape the next four, but that's it."

"It's a shame." He hugged her. "But we're in pretty good shape at the moment."

The phone rang. MJ got up to get it. "Hello? Oh, hi, Doris. Sure, he's right here." She handed Peter the phone.

"Hi, Doris," he said.

"Two things," Doris said. "One good, one maybe. CellTech will not be charging you for that phone bill. I've got eighteen of those numbers involved in an investigation into, would you believe it, cigarette smuggling."

"That's great! Thank you, Doris."

"Anytime. My special service for famous people. The other thing—you were asking about location data on those calls? The Union Square subway station, apparently."

Peter chuckled. "I'll tell Spider-Man."

"Yes," she said, "and that's another thing. When do I get to meet *him?*"

"Uh. I'll work on it."

"You do that. Let me talk to MJ now. Bye!"

"Yes, Doris," MJ said, taking the phone back. "Yes. Yes. Lunch? Sure. Where? You're on. See you tomorrow." She hung up.

"You have a groupie," Peter said, amused, as she sat down again.

"I've had a groupie for a long time," MJ said and hugged him.

They sat looking idly at WNN, which was full of news about Doctor Octopus's arrest and the unfolding of the nuclear and economic strands of his conspiracy.

Spidey had had a chance to very thoroughly debrief on
the subject—having been lectured on it by the perpetra-
tor himself—and Ock was presently in the Vault, being
debriefed himself, a business that would probably take
some years. Various world banks were scrutinizing
every piece of their currency. The AEC was running all
over the American landscape, picking up and defusing
small tactical nuclear weapons and weapons-grade plutonium.

And in all this excitement, Venom had fallen right out
of the news.

"I wonder where he went," MJ said softly.

"He wasn't in the caves at Ock's place when I got
back there," Peter said, "but according to Ock's computer, *somebody* printed a list of all the sites Ock
shipped bomb material to. I suspect that he'll be busy
making sure the AEC takes care of it—and stepping in
if they don't. I'm still surprised he didn't stick around,
though."

"Maybe he was embarrassed at Octopus beating
him."

"Or maybe he just wasn't up for another fight. I kind
of suspect that he's not going to forgive CCRC or its
baby, Bothwell, either. He may come back to haunt
them."

"Better them than you." MJ pulled Peter close.
"What did Kate say about the pictures?"

"Oh, she loved them. So, a little more money for the
kitty, no Venom, the phone bill is off our case, and Doctor Octopus is locked up where he belongs." Peter
chuckled and leaned his head back on the sofa, repeating
a line of Doc Ock's. "Paradise on earth."

"It is, isn't it?" MJ said and kissed him.

Diane Duane is the author of a score of novels of science fiction and fantasy, among them the *New York Times* hardcover best-sellers *Spock's World* and *Dark Mirror*, as well as the very popular Wizard fantasy series, the Spider-Man novels *The Venom Factor* and *The Lizard Sanction*, and the X-Men hardcover novel *Empire's End*. *The Philadelphia Inquirer* has called Duane "a skilled master of the genre," and *Publishers Weekly* has raved, "Duane is tops in the high adventure business."

Duane lives with her husband, Peter Morwood—with whom she has written five novels, including the *New York Times* best-seller *The Romulan Way*—in a beautiful valley in rural Ireland.

Darick Robertson started working as a comics professional at the age of seventeen with his self-created and self-published comic *Space Beaver*. Since 1990, he has worked on *New Warriors, X-Factor, Cable, The Incredible Hulk,* and two *Spider-Man* miniseries (*The Power of Terror* and *The Final Adventure*) for Marvel, *Superman, Justice League of America*, and *Transmopolitan* for DC, and *Man of the Atom* for Acclaim. He also helped design and create Malibu's Ultraverse characters, including *The Nightman, The Strangers,* and his own *Ripfire,* and provided illustrations for Diane Duane's *Spider-Man: The Lizard Sanction.*